HOLY GHOST ROAD

HOLY GHOST ROAD

John Mantooth

Cemetery Dance Publications

Baltimore

✄ 2022 ✄

Cemetery Dance Publications
132B Industry Lane, Unit #7
Forest Hill, MD 21050
www.cemeterydance.com

Holy Ghost Road

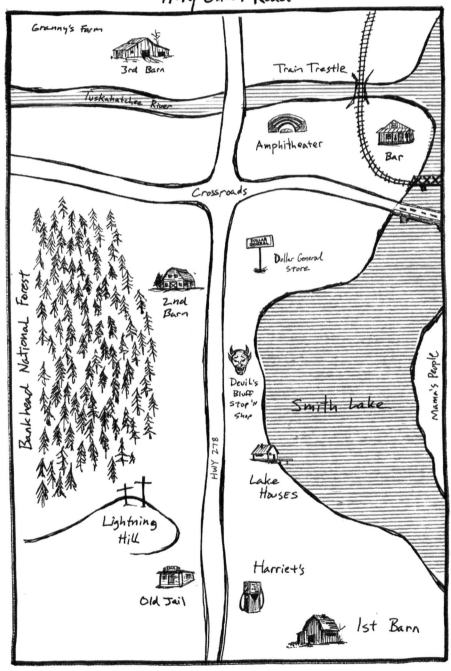

Granny's Farm
3rd Barn
Train Trestle
Tuskahatchee River
Amphitheater
Bar
Crossroads
Dollar General Store
2nd Barn
Bankhead National Forest
Devil's Bluff Stop 'n' Shop
Smith Lake
Mama's People
HWY 278
Lightning Hill
Lake Houses
Old Jail
Harriet's
1st Barn

The Barn

1

I COME TO Highway 278 in the dark teeth of the night, a nearly empty backpack slung across my shoulders, and the preacher we call Nesmith on my heels. Just moments earlier I witnessed him consorting with an evil entity that I believe to be the devil himself, and now he means to kill me, or something worse.

Or maybe it's Nesmith who's the devil, and that black-horned thing I saw waiting for his offering in the shadows of the barn was something else, not quite a devil, but a devil-maker. Nesmith's been living with us since he and Mama decided to get married, and I didn't need to see him in the barn with that thing to know he wasn't what he pretended to be but now he *knows* I know. Now, everything has changed.

278 is darker than the spaces between the stars, darker than emptiness. I feel the pain and dread of that nothing as I stand beside the silent road. The trees are empty as well, their leaves rattled away by scouring winds. Goddamn sky looks bare too, like some planet-eating monster

scraped a great claw across it, took out the stars and the treetops, knocked the moon asunder, spun the world crooked.

Left me down here, trying to find my balance.

Left me empty, with only the wind inside my own heart, hollowing me out with each gust.

On the outside, I'm just cold. Desolate. Tears make it worse. There ain't a word for how they feel drying on my face as I run.

A fire's burning out in the field, about a mile away. Smoke curls out of the leafless trees, a thin omen, but one I can't ignore. Once you've seen one omen, one sign, you can't stop seeing them. Like so many things in my life, I'm not sure if this is a blessing or a curse.

I've long suspected Nesmith wasn't what people in this town believe him to be, and now that I have proof, I wish like hell I'd been wrong. Proof makes the world look different. The road, the trees, the smoke, and its signature in the sky. All of it takes on a stark, ghost-like quality, like an illusion, but illusions can hurt just as much as anything else.

Forest, Nesmith said, drawling my name like he always does, so that it sounds lascivious. *You didn't see what you thought you saw, darling.*

He didn't even seem concerned. Surprised, sure, but a man like Nesmith doesn't really know concern. He just expects his words will straighten out whatever seam he encounters, that his tongue'll untie knots, that he'll slip free of any and all restraints. The rest of the world can be concerned, but not Nesmith. He's immune to all that.

But maybe not. Maybe, the concern will come later, once he realizes I'm not going to forget what I've seen, and he can't make me. He should know by now there's no making me do anything. Used to be a flaw, but lately, I've come to appreciate that people complain about my stubbornness.

I glance over at the smoke rising from the field again. Omen or not, I reckon the fire is someone else's problem. Got plenty of my own. Once, I would have believed it was my duty to do something about that fire, to call somebody, to help in some way. No more. Now, I'll just offer a prayer, because believing in prayer ain't a choice I have. Without that hope, I may as well just let Nesmith catch me and do with me what he will.

A car is coming. It's flying like everyone flies on 278, especially late like this when there's nobody around to see anything. I turn, hold my thumb up, bite my lip until I taste blood.

Please stop. Fifteen years and I ain't asked too much, just give me this. And Lord, let it be a woman.

Headlights cut into my skull, burn something in the back of my brain. I shut my eyes, steady my thumb. Keep on praying.

I need this, God. I need this, God. God, I need this.

The words tumble over my bloody lip.

The car doesn't even slow. Blows past me, maybe going ninety. I nearly lose my balance from the blast of hot air. It's okay, there'll be more. I got a head start, a good one. Despite what other powers Nesmith might possess, his physical body is weak, though he's been getting stronger. When he moved in with us six weeks ago, at the end of August, Mama rolled him into the house in a wheelchair. He looked so old then, I took solace in the fact that he was surely on death's door, but a few weeks after that, he perked up considerably. Started wheeling himself around the house. He looked younger, too. A miracle, he called it, and promised it wouldn't be the last. Swore it in front of the whole church. Then, last week, he popped up out of his chair mostly under his own power, his only help coming from the gnarled walking stick he poked the ground with as he began walking for the first time in twenty-something years. Despite all these improvements, he's still old and slow compared to me. I had enough time to smash out the headlights on his and mama's cars before heading out across the fields toward the highway.

After seeing what I saw in the barn, I'd sprinted to the house, hoping to grab Mama's keys. I meant to take her car straight down 278, across the Tuskahatchee and the county line. I wouldn't stop until I made it to Granny's farm. I thought of Granny as soon as I saw what evil Nesmith was up to. She'd warned me something bad might happen, but I reckon I'd been thinking "bad," as in something like him trying to grope me or get me alone in a room somewhere. That's the sort of thing I had plenty of practice dealing with. I'm only fifteen, but there's always men around who don't give a damn. I'm pretty sure Nesmith is one of those men, preacher or no preacher. But that hadn't been what she meant.

To be fair, I'm still not sure exactly what she did mean. I'm not even one hundred percent sure of what I saw. The black-horned goat thing, sure. But the memory of what it was doing, what Nesmith was doing… it's vague at best.

Whatever I saw put the need to get to Granny's in me strong. Granny's a special person. Not just a *good* person. She's that, sure. But she's also special in the true sense of the word. As in, there ain't others like her. Granny's got guts and isn't afraid of anything. She's also got what she calls sacred magic, which she'll be quick to tell you is all about seeing the world true. Seeing it for what it is. Once you can do that, she always tells me, there's nothing you can't handle.

Only problem is, I'm still trying to figure what's true and what ain't.

Anyway, I made it to the kitchen, determined to get those keys, but soon as I opened the backdoor, I heard the bitch. Not Mama. No, Nesmith's sister, Ruby Jewel. She was already there, standing by the stove, holding the keys to the Ford in one of those big, twisted hands of hers. She stood there just shaking them, letting them rattle gently like wind chimes, a smile on her face so smug, I wanted to slap it clean off. But I didn't dare.

Ruby Jewel is probably the only person who scares me more than Nesmith. She's blind, but sometimes it feels like she's not. She always knows right where a thing is. Like the keys. Not only that, but she always knows where a person is going to be and what they aim to do. Like, how she knew I was going to come into the house to find the keys.

She's old, maybe seventy or more, and tall, taller than Nesmith or Mama or just about anybody else I know. She's broad too, big as a man. Arms long and formless, but thick. Hips and legs the same, flat, solid wood. Tits like empty bags. Her face is the worst part. She's got this hawk-like face, all sharp lines and cruel angles. She wears heavy, dark make-up that almost looks like an earnest effort to be pretty, but one that has missed the mark and left her more of a cartoon than a woman. Like something come to life out of a fairy tale.

She's been living with us, sleeping in my brother's old bedroom. When folks let their guard down, which is rare around here, they'll comment on the unnatural relationship between Ruby Jewel and her brother. She's like his bodyguard or something. Been like that ever since he performed his very first miracle and brought her back after she'd drowned in Smith Lake when they were little kids. Nesmith still claims it was the first time he felt the power of God surge through him. Still seems weird to me they'd live together, but I couldn't get Mama to see it.

He's taking care of her, Forest. That's what a good man does.

Seems like the other way around to me. Folks say when they were in elementary school, Ruby Jewel failed a grade on purpose just to be in the same classes with her brother. She was always pushing him around in his wheelchair too, before he started walking again.

I didn't speak a word to her, just went straight to the baseball bat Mama keeps by the back door, headed out to the gravel drive, and started smashing the headlights on Nesmith's and Mama's cars. Thinking fast isn't always something I'm good at, but the weird part was that I didn't even think at all. I just acted, like there was something inside me that had been waiting on this moment all my life. Shattering those headlights felt damn good. I was just slamming the bat against the last one on Nesmith's Cadillac, when the barn door slammed shut and the shadow of the black-horned thing floated out. I slowed my swinging long enough to wonder again what it was, and what power it had gifted to Nesmith. Thinking I still had time with Nesmith being as slow as he was with his cane, I was about to try to smash the windshield too, when I felt a presence behind me. A hand fell on my shoulder and something dark and wild ran across my body like fingers, with minds of their own. I spun around and saw Ruby Jewel looming over me. I threw the bat at her. I didn't really expect to hit her, but I must have because she gasped. Then my feet were crunching gravel, and I had my eyes set on the big field. I didn't stop running until I saw 278.

Now, I need a ride in the worst way, and I need it fast. Nesmith will get a car or fix his headlights, no problem. I've got thirty miles to go before Granny's, and he's not gonna stop until he catches me. It's the one thing I feel more sure of than anything else. There's something vague, something just below the surface of my memory that explains why he wants me so badly, but I can't name it. Something in the barn I am forgetting.

The brake lights on the car that blew past me come on. He's got to be a mile up the road by now, but he's slowing down. The car makes a U-turn. It's coming back.

Thank you, God, thank you God, thank you.

It's a pick-up truck. No surprise. A double-cab, and it eases up to me. Window goes down and a deep voice says, "I almost didn't see you."

I don't move. That voice. It's like every other male voice. And that's the problem. Most of the men I've ever known can't be trusted. Hell, I can only think of one man I ever trusted, and that's my brother Ben. Ben's a rare breed. Like Granny, he's special, but he has always struggled with seeing the world straight. That's not his fault, though. You grow up with the world leaning one way, you tend to think that's the way it's supposed to be. Why wouldn't a person think that?

"You want a ride or what?"

"I need to get to the other side of the river, a farm a few miles east of there."

"I can take you to the county line. Come on."

I can't help but hesitate. Normally, I wouldn't ever even consider getting in a car with some random man, but these aren't normal times. "You ain't even gonna ask what I'm doing out here after midnight?"

"Ain't my business," the man says. I can't really see his face yet, but he doesn't seem too overeager, so probably that's a good thing—unless he's playing me. The real predators always try to play you. So, there's that. I glance back toward the field, toward the barn on the other side of the trees. I can't afford to be picky.

"All right," I say. "Let's keep it that way. We'll both stay out of each other's business." I get in.

He's handsome in an older man kind of way, but his eyes and face are hard to read. He clicks the radio off before I can even hear what kind of music he's listening to. Too bad. I don't like the silence.

He gets back on the road, pushes the double-cab to sixty and settles in. Trees and houses flash by, the occasional gas station or church. Most of those churches will be empty come Sunday morning. The whole county will be at Nesmith's church, the First Assembly of the Lord's Ordained Prophet. It meets six times a week out at the Looney's Tavern Amphitheater. The ones who don't make it will likely be listening on his radio station.

"What's your name?" the man asks.

"What's yours?" I shoot back.

He laughs. "Fair enough. I'm Jimmy. Folks call me Shooter." He gives me the side eye.

"I'm too young," I say. "Don't look at me like that." Shaming them works sometimes.

He lets go of the wheel, holding his hands up. "Take it easy. Just trying to be friendly."

I want to call bullshit, but I hold my tongue. I've been working on that. Holding my tongue. Sometimes—well, *a lot* of times—it gets me into trouble. Can't afford it now. Just keep quiet. Try not to say nothing that would let him guess I'm running, much less who I'm running from.

As if he couldn't already figure that out.

Just so he won't feel such a need to talk, I click on the radio. I don't ask, just do. A church song fills the truck. Something about blood and the pure white driven snow. It's pretty, and I let my mind drift a bit, listening.

"You a church goer?" he says as the song starts to fade.

"Pretty regular," I lie, hoping to make myself sound like anybody else.

He nods. "Yeah, me too." The song ends. A brief silence and then a familiar voice. "This is Brother Don Nesmith, and you're listening to the Lord's own WRBZ 990 AM. If you like what you hear, we'd love to have you in person this Sunday morning at the Looney's Tavern Amphitheater. Rain or shine, we'll gather in our outdoor sanctuary for sunrise service, followed by eleven o'clock church hour and the sunset services later that day. Please come, and let the Lord take care of you. God Bless, and thanks for tuning into WRBZ 990."

It's probably nothing, but I start to feel a little anxious. He's listening to the damned station. Could Nesmith have already put the word out on me? Maybe that explains why he blew past me and then stopped?

"Gotta pee," I say and squirm a bit, trying to sell it.

"Well, you can't hold it for a little?"

"No. It hits me like this sometimes. Gotta go. Can we stop at a gas station?"

"Hell, it's one in the morning. Ain't gonna be none open. You better do it on the side of the road."

"Harriet's," I say. "Less than a mile. She's open 24-7."

He frowns slightly. "Okay. I reckon we can do that."

Nesmith comes on the radio again. It's one of his, "God in a minute" bits.

"Seven years ago, the Holy Spirit came upon me and gave me a heart for our veterans, for our men and women who have been overseas and come back broken. God spoke to me through his Holy helper and said, 'Don, my people are hurting.' Let no man think for a minute that there is anyone our Lord is prouder of than our veterans. I felt that on my heart in a real and powerful way. Which is why I set up the Veterans Holy Shelter in Addison. We take broken veterans and show them the grace of God. He makes them whole again. It's not me." His voice goes quieter, slower, dipping into a register that is supposed to sound more sincere, but just sounds like the same bullshit drawn out to me.

"If you know me at all, you know that I'm a humble man who has been blessed to find the greatest power in the universe, and that power is in the embodiment of Jesus Christ. He'll change you, ladies and gentlemen. He's changed so many in this county, so many men. So many women. Mothers and daughters, fathers and sons. So many veterans. I hope you'll let him change you too. It can all start this Sunday. Come to church. We meet outside at the Looney's Amphitheater, rain or shine. The Lord says, 'Seek, and you shall find. Knock, and the door will be opened for you.' And recently, in my own life, brothers and sisters, I felt God's hand again. If it's been a few Sundays since you've been to church, come see with your own eyes, the truth of God's power. I'm walking again. That's right. The spinal injury that left me unable to walk for nearly twenty-six years has been cancelled. It's gone. God said, 'No more!' He can do the same for what afflicts you, no matter the—"

All the sudden, silence does seem better. I switch off the radio and hope it doesn't make Shooter too suspicious.

The silence is worse this time because of Nesmith's words. His bullshit always makes everything worse. Especially when he talks about veterans. Liar. Fuck him and fuck his miracles. I don't know how he did it, but him walking again isn't a miracle, at least not in the sacred way. Maybe he used the goat demon thing to help him. That actually makes sense.

Harriet's comes into view at last. It's a dinky little place, two gas pumps out front and just enough room inside for the essentials—cold drinks, cigarettes, this and that. No alcohol, though. Winston County is still dry, at least this part anyway. There's just a single car parked outside the store, most likely Harriet's. She works the late shifts, and her boys cover the regular hours. Jimmy pulls in and parks right by the door.

"Hey, you never told me your name," he says, and I swear to God it sounds like he's trying to flirt with me.

"I know." I get the door open and climb out. Once I feel the pavement under my feet, relief washes over me. I'm free again. I glance back at the truck. He's on his phone talking to somebody. He waves at me. *Go on in,* the gesture seems to say. *I'll wait.*

The door dings when I open it, and Harriet glances up from her coffee.

I go over to her, turn my back in case Shooter can read lips from his truck. "I'm in trouble," I say. "I think that man means to hurt me. Can you help me?"

Harriet says, "Sounds about right. I got an office. The door on the left. It locks. You can wait there. He comes in, I'll tell him you ran out the back door."

"Back door?"

Harriet points to a corridor that leads to the restroom. "Down that hall. Deliveries."

"Maybe I should just run?" I say, wondering why I'm posing it as a question.

Harriet shakes her head. "Backroom. Stay put. He's got a truck. He'll just find you. Want me to call the police?"

"No."

Harriet seems to understand. Police around here are tricky. Depends on what you want them for. One thing is clear-cut: they back Nesmith. The sheriff is one of Nesmith's deacons. Sits up front at the amphitheater grinning like a fool every Sunday, dressed in his suit and tie. When the tongues start, Sheriff likes to interpret them. It's obvious he's just making shit up. Then I think of the barn and the black-horned thing and shiver. Maybe I've been wrong about all of it. Maybe the tongues are real, maybe they're sent by the devil instead of God. Knowing Nesmith and the sheriff, there is a strange kind of logic to it.

"You'd better go."

I decide to trust her and go. It's not easy. Trust has never been easy for me, but it's especially difficult now that I feel like enemy number one.

The office door swings open, and I step inside the small room. The first thing I search for are windows. There aren't any. I close the door and lock it. I wait, trying to make myself believe I'm going to be okay.

2

BUT BELIEF ISN'T enough. I remember going to church with Granny once and on the ride home her laughing at the preacher's foolish notion that all you needed was to believe.

"Belief is only the beginning," she told me. "It's the vehicle. Still needs fuel."

I didn't ask what the fuel was because I knew she'd tell me in her own time. Granny ain't never been in a hurry a day in her life. Even still, she's never late, and never behind. Used to drive Mama crazy.

"The fuel," she said as we turned onto her long gravel driveway, the little fishing pond on our right, and her remaining cows on our left. "The fuel's the action. You gotta take a belief, and you gotta translate it into action."

That had registered with me like nothing else. I'd always been suspicious of church, especially the singing parts, but also the parts that make everything sound too easy. I'm only fifteen, but I'm pretty confident there ain't nothing easy about this world.

The bell rings out in the store as a customer comes in. Curious to see if it's Jimmy, I turn the bolt over, putting my whole hand over it to muffle the sound, and swing the door open just a hair. I poke my face into the opening and peer out into the store. I can only really see one aisle from here, but there's a man standing with his back turned talking to Harriet at the end of it. He's a big, mountain of a man, muscular and hard-bodied. His boots are made for getting shit done instead of style. He wears camouflage fatigues, and his neck is so sunburned it's almost purple.

Fuck. He doesn't even need to turn around. I already know who it is.

Some people call him Helmet, as in Helmet-Head. If he's got a real name, I ain't never heard it. But I have heard some other things, things that make my stomach drop out of me and the top of my head feel like it's going to blow. He does work for Nesmith, but not like painting his house or fixing his fence. Not that kind of work. No, Helmet is his bodyguard, or at least one of his bodyguards. I'll always say Ruby Jewel's got the main job, but Helmet's a good number three to have around. Hell, he's like a search and destroy button, and I pray to God he's not here for me.

Helmet was one of Nesmith's first veteran "success stories." A local newspaper even ran a story about how he turned Helmet's life around. "Saved," was the headline, and that's what most people around here believe. It's a good thing there wasn't a picture with the article. Nobody could peer into those empty eyes and think they're the eyes of a man who has been saved by God.

Or anything else.

Speaking of eyes, now that he's turned around, I understand my prayer will not be answered. He scans the store. Maybe it's because his eyes are so empty they can take everything in. He spots me immediately. I close the door and lock it.

Don't move. Don't breathe.

Footsteps. Unhurried. Slow, even. Each time his boot comes down on Harriet's dirty floor, it's like a gunshot. Again, I scan the tiny office, this time not for a means of escape, but for a weapon, for something I can use to defend myself.

By the time I grab the stapler, he's just outside the door. He's breathing loud, like a dog panting in the hot sun. Folks say his breath is like that on account of the shrapnel in his lungs. They say he nearly bled out over there, but held on, only to get back to the states and find his woman and his four-year-old dead. Mama overdosed. They reckon the child just cried itself to death.

But now he's saved. By Nesmith. Fuck that noise. People can't really believe such nonsense, can they?

Of course, they can. They do.

It's weird to fear and pity something at the same time, but that's exactly the way I feel about Helmet. A victim twice over. No —three times; first the war and then his family. Finally, Nesmith.

The door handle turns. He pushes hard enough to make the doorframe groan, but it holds.

"I need a key," he says to Harriet. His voice is heavy, like a tree stump half buried in the Mideast sand.

I open the stapler up, make sure it's loaded. The second I see his face, I'm going to slap him with it. I imagine it colliding with his jawbone, the staple piercing skin and then bone from the force of my swing.

Harriet says something I can't hear.

Helmet's silent for a moment.

Harriet says something else. I can't hear that either.

"She's got to come out some time," Helmet says. His voice doesn't sound like a regular voice. Something's missing, and that makes me think of my brother Ben. He was my best friend once. When I was eight and he was sixteen, we hung out all the time. It may seem like a big gap, but to me and Ben it was nothing. We might as well have been twins. But that was before he signed up for the Army and they shipped him overseas, somewhere I never could get him to talk about when he came back home.

He was twenty-one then. I was thirteen. Mama couldn't do nothing with him, and maybe that's how Nesmith wormed his way into our lives. He had his center for helping veterans, and convinced Mama he could fix Ben, except all he really did was make Ben worse.

That was when I first started suspecting Nesmith wasn't all he claimed to be. It wasn't just that he gave up. I saw up close and personal that he didn't even really care about Ben. He was just another soul to save, another veteran "recovery" for him to tout.

Whatever is missing from Helmet's voice is also missing from Ben's. I don't know what to call that thing, other than to say it's something you never notice until it's gone, and then you can't stop noticing.

The door handle turns again. The frame bends as he pushes his weight against the bolt. I remember the stapler in my hand and realize it's not going to do half as much as I imagine it will. I search the office again.

HOLY GHOST ROAD

The desk.

It's easy to move, not as heavy as it looks, but it's better than nothing. There has to be something else. That's when I notice the phone.

It's a portable phone lying on a chair in the corner of the office. I grab it and check for a dial tone. It's working. My fingers begin pressing numbers of their own accord.

It rings. Voices rise outside the office again. Helmet saying something, maybe warning Harriet in that cold, wooden voice that he's going to have to break her door down. I try not to think about it. Three rings.

It's late, well after one in the morning now, but she'll answer. She'll sense that I need her. She'll tell me what to do.

There's a loud crack outside the door. It sounds like Helmet has decided to just cut his way through with an axe. A second crack makes me jump. Wood splinters. Shit.

"Heller?"

The sound of Granny's voice lifts my spirits immediately. I can't help but smile. *Heller.* That's her *hello,* and it's about the most beautiful sound I can think of.

"I'm in trouble, Granny."

Silence. Measured. She's listening. Another swing of the axe. The damn blade pokes through the wooden door now. Another swing or two and he'll be in.

I'm all set to explain my situation when Granny speaks. "I already know. You finally woke up and saw what I feared." She pauses long enough for me to hear something creaking in the wind on her end of the line. "You don't remember much about it do you?"

"No ma'am."

"I reckon it'll take a little time before it comes back—but listen to me. Cause time's short. If that man gets his hands on you, you're done for. You hear? Don't let him touch you."

"Granny," I say, as the tears come down my face. "I don't understand what's happening."

As soon as I say it, I realize my mistake. Granny's always had a thing about understanding. She's going to tell me understanding is overrated.

"Pshaw, don't worry a bit about that. When it's time to understand, you'll get it just fine. Until then, don't worry none. People are always trying to rush understanding, and when they do that, they don't get the full story. Let it come. Be patient. You hearing me?"

"Yes ma'am," I say, It's a relief to hear the words.

"Good, now listen to me, and we'll get you out of there." Another blow from the axe. Wood flies into the office. I can see his damned sunburned face through the cracks.

"He's gonna swing again and when he does, you're gonna wait until the very moment he pulls the axe from the door. That's when you're gonna open it. Once you open the door, don't even hesitate for a heartbeat. Run."

"He'll grab me, Granny."

"Not if you're fast. Not if you do it like you mean it."

"Okay."

"Now, go. You got to make it happen, Forest. *You.*"

HOLY GHOST ROAD

"Thanks, Gran— I start to say, but the line goes dead.

Harriet is yelling at Helmet, which gives me enough time to move the desk out of the way. Once that's done, I stand back as far as I am able from the door and still clutch the doorknob in my right hand.

"...Brother Nesmith'll pay for the damages," Helmet says. He's not mad. He's not sorry. He's not anything. Just a voice coming out of a body.

I get ready as I hear him approaching the door again. I tense every muscle in my 95-pound body, try to feel the power in my legs, my shoulders, my core. Let it rev inside me, so when the moment comes, I can explode through the door, out into the store and—somehow—past Helmet. Once I get past him, I'll be all right. I'll slip across the road and into the Bankhead National Forest. From there I can make my way across the Tuskahatchee and over to Granny's.

A deep breath seems to suck the air out of the room. The axe is suspended in mid-flight through the splintered door. And then it connects. Hard. But not quite hard enough. The door stays intact save for the gap he's torn out in the middle. He pulls the axe out and as soon as it clears the splintered wood, I flip the bolt and fling the door open.

In less than a second, I see everything I need to see: Helmet is off balance. He's still recovering from the exertion of the swing and pulling the axe free. There's a space for me to get past him, a tiny window. I bolt into the store, screaming as I do. Helmet barely registers surprise, but that's okay. I know Helmet is surprised because he's stuck in his spot, on his heels, unable to swing the axe or even reach for me as I blast out of the office and bounce off his broad chest, using him to help me change directions.

John Mantooth

Once my body is turned around, I sprint down the small hallway and out the back exit. I nearly run straight into Jimmy, who I reckon is supposed to be watching for me. Except he ain't watching shit. He's smoking and scrolling through something on his phone. By the time he knows what's happened, I'm across 278, already eyeing a likely opening in the trees.

Behind me, it sounds like Jimmy's making excuses and Helmet's not having it.

I chance a look before ducking into the trees. Helmet's spotted me, and he's heading this way.

3

THERE'S A WHOLE world that a lot of people don't know about. I discovered it when I was a very young girl, playing in the woods behind our house with Ben. He not only taught me to climb trees, but to appreciate them. We'd spend hours in those woods, in those trees, daring each other to go higher and higher, dares that I almost always won. Being tiny helped with that. On the ground, being little has its disadvantages, but not in the trees.

What Ben and I did was more than just *climbing* trees. We escaped inside them. We *lived* there for hours, sometimes days at a time, and in doing so, we discovered that there was really a separate world right above the one we already knew.

We discovered how to see the world from different angles. We realized all the stuff we had missed down below, how we never really *saw* it before because we were too busy avoiding most of it. Either that or just using it.

In the Amazon, they call it the canopy level, and it's probably the only place outside of Granny's farm that I've ever found true peace. It's also the place where I best understand Granny's advice about seeing the world true, how once you do that, the sacred magic will come to you. It's when I'm in the trees, among the leaves and branches, birds, and squirrels that I come closest to seeing the world as it really is.

So, when I realize Helmet means to chase me into the woods, I start hunting.

The tree I choose is one of those out-of-place oaks, the kind that would be better out in a field where it could really spread its limbs, become the landscape, tangle sunsets in its branches, inspire awe from all who see it, but by some whim of nature, it's here, squeezed between an asphalt highway and the beginning of a great forest.

The first limb is the toughest because it's thick and too high for me to reach without jumping. A running start gets me there, and as I wrap my arms around the huge limb, I feel the lifeblood of it. I know that this is not the night for me to be caught. Once I swing my body around and get my legs under me, I scramble quickly toward the top, feeling the rhythm of the branches, intuiting their evolution, their growth. Each place along the massive trunk where there should be a limb, there is a limb.

I only stop when I can see the full moon through a gap in the canopy. Only then do I peer down and see the world anew.

Helmet—from here—is lost. It's in the way the moonlight hits him, the way he absorbs some of it and casts the rest to the ground. It's in the way he walks. From the ground level, his matter-of-fact, mechanical movement signals a mind that doesn't know doubt. But from up here, his body appears machine-like and clumsy. Like a child's remote-controlled car, always hitting dead-ends and waiting on something to redirect it, to keep it from moving in one direction endlessly. I realize, like me, like everyone, he's also struggling to see the world true.

I force my eyes back to the moon. There's a danger in humanizing him. I can't forget that he's here on behalf of Nesmith. It's Nesmith who is holding the remote control. And this is his world.

Eventually, Helmet wanders off, but I don't relax. I don't reckon he'll go too far on foot, which means he's likely to hear me if I make any sound at all.

A long while passes. The moon moves, or the earth moves, or maybe it's the clawed-out sky moving. Whatever the case, there's only black above me now, and the black space makes me think about what I saw earlier in the barn. It's only now that I truly begin to process what was happening when I saw it.

I'd been dreamwalking.

Not *sleep*walking. That's how I used to think of it, but there's a difference. Seeing something while dreamwalking doesn't make it less true. No, in fact, it's the opposite.

But what did I see, exactly? It's still blurry, incomplete.

What did Granny say on the phone? It would take a little time before it came back. It's hard because I want to know now.

Patience, I hear her say. *It'll come when it comes.*

So, instead of trying to figure it out, I focus on the ground below me. I clear my head of the dreamwalking, the barn, of everything except what I can see around me. Time for all of that later.

That's when I hear the car out on the highway.

4

THE CAR'S ENGINE revs and downshifts and finally idles as it comes to a stop. From my spot in the oak tree, I'm just able to see the headlights.

I spot Ruby Jewel first. From this vantage point, where the truth is easier to discern, my optimism fades. She's blind, but she moves as one who sees more than others. The moonlight doesn't bounce off her. She absorbs it, is powered by it.

For the first time since being in the tree, I feel threatened. I feel exposed. Ruby Jewel doesn't need to see me. She can sense me.

People say it was the drowning accident that did it, that she was actually dead for a brief time, that she (or maybe her brother) bargained her way back. She lost her eyes, but gained her life.

And something else.

I glance around, suddenly sure there are eyes on me. A bat skitters across the opening in the trees, a wild, frantic shape against the sky. I push myself into the tree trunk, trying to will my body to become a part of it.

Ruby Jewel stands for a long time before Nesmith joins her. From here, I see a shadow trailing behind him. It's the black-horned thing from the barn. It's just a specter now, almost shapeless, but I know its true form.

Nesmith studies his sister expectantly. She vibrates slowly and rocks back on her heels. From the underbrush close to the base of the oak, I hear an animal shriek. Its cry is one of surprise and violation.

The rumors are true.

Besides the rumor of her death and resurrection, people also say she can see through the eyes of animals.

The fox emerges from the undergrowth, his eyes shining in the moonlight, his fur dark and slick. He darts off into the deeper woods, to hunt for me.

I breathe a sigh of relief. She won't find me with a fox. I'm safe as long as neither of them look up. As long as I'm quiet.

But then something happens. Something awful. The shadow that follows Nesmith begins to move of its own accord. It twists and swirls and straightens, taking on a thousand shapes, yet no shape at all. Nesmith doesn't even seem to notice. He's as still as Ruby Jewel – and she's a statue. Her mind is off somewhere inside the fox as it roams around the forest, afraid of the foreign presence that's clawed itself inside its mind.

The goat shadow sees me. I'm sure of it, but strangely enough, it doesn't alert Nesmith. Instead, it just watches me for a moment, and even though it has no face or eyes, I'm sure that's what it's doing. Then, slowly, as if satisfied with what it sees, the shadow begins to dissipate. It drops to the ground with the others, and merges into a gloom too deep for the moonlight to touch. I let myself breathe again.

"Maybe she doubled back to the road," Helmet says.

Nesmith looks at Ruby, and even though there is no logical way she could feel his stare she does. She shakes her head and says, "Nothing. Not even tracks."

"She can't just vanish," Nesmith says.

They're all silent as they contemplate my ability to disappear.

"Where will she go?" Ruby Jewel says, at last.

"Her father's mother," Nesmith says. "She's a problem."

"So, we eliminate her." Ruby Jewel's nonchalance is chilling.

"It's not that simple. Did you not hear what I said? She's a problem. Means I'm going to have to think this through. She's got what the girl's got, but ten times more. Her power is undiluted."

Ruby Jewel nods, as if this makes perfect sense. Meanwhile, I'm more confused than ever. What does he mean that Granny's power is undiluted? And what the hell do I have? The dreamwalking? That question seems to dislodge something inside my memory. Not an answer, exactly, but something else: an image. Granny was there. Granny had been inside the barn with me. Her presence had been brief but undeniable.

"We should get some sleep. She ain't making it to her grandmother's tonight," Ruby Jewel says at last.

"Unless she catches a ride." It's Helmet, and I'm surprised he's got thoughts of his own.

"I ain't worried about that," Nesmith says. "She catches a ride, I'll catch her."

"What happened out there?" Ruby Jewel asks. "In the barn?"

Nesmith glances at Helmet and then back at Ruby Jewel.

"She woke up. She had help."

Ruby Jewel nods and clears her throat, spitting what comes up onto the ground. "Was it working, though? Before she woke up?"

Nesmith nods. "Yeah, it's close now. Very, very close."

This makes Ruby Jewel cackle with joy. "She ain't fighting back?"

"No. She's been very open to it," Nesmith says. "Practically begging for more. "

It takes everything I've got not shout at him, not to scream *liar* down on top of them like a goddamn storm. I haven't begging for shit. Have I? If only my memory wasn't so cloudy. But I hold my tongue regardless, gripping the tree like it's a lifeline.

"Just like her mama," Ruby Jewel says.

Nesmith giggles. "Both of them are sluts all the way through," Nesmith says, and there's something almost magnificent at the ease in which he lies. Is it a symptom of too much power? The ability to weave lies through truth as if you are the only one whose perspective even matters? It feels as if this is the strongest magic of all, and the most twisted. The power of a lie, believed.

"Whatever happens," Nesmith says, as they move back out toward the road, their voices fading, "she's to be kept alive. You both understand this?"

HOLY GHOST ROAD

Still seething over his lie, I almost miss the significance of what he's said. *He wants to keep me alive?* This should be good news, but I'm not sure it is. Living under his power is worse than dying. That's the truth.

There's two kinds of magic, Granny told me once. *There's the kind that calls for rituals and exacting standards, measurements, ingredients, bargains with entities. That's the profane kind. It can be used for good, sure, but the price is steep. Most of the people I know who traffic in such use it for selfish reasons. I recommend staying away from it. But the other kind of magic, is the magic of sacred recognition. Recognizing that the magic is already there, out in the world. A person—with the help of the Holy Ghost—can access this kind and use it for good. But even though this kind of magic requires no exacting ingredients or formal rituals, it requires something even more difficult. The ability to see through the bullshit, to see the thing as it really is, to see there is a ghost hanging over this world, and that ghost is as holy as a newborn baby.*

I fall asleep, remembering Granny's words, even talking with her some. Her voice is in my head so clearly, it's like a second version of myself. I always know what she'll say, how she'll explain things.

But hell if I know how or why she was in the barn with me.

5

I WAKE IN the darkness sometime later. The fox has returned, its eyes hollow sockets reflecting shards of the yellow moon. It sits and regards me solemnly. Ruby Jewel is either too far away to inhabit it, or maybe she's just gone somewhere else. Some hellscape where her broken spirit can fly among the dead, inside the winged skeleton of a hawk or bat.

Down the tree I go, determined to keep moving, to not waste the darkness.

Thirty miles along 278 gets you to Granny's. I've already made it three, I reckon. Twenty-seven is a long ways yet.

I had grabbed a backpack before running out of the kitchen. Like the bat I used to smash those headlights, the thought of grabbing the pack just came to me. It's what I used to carry my books in for school, but since Nesmith moved in with us, he'd convinced Mama to homeschool me. That's when I started to hate him.

It was clear to me from the beginning that he wanted me homeschooled because he understood what taking me from my friends would do to me. But there was another reason too. The high school is on the eastern edge of the county, only about seven miles from Granny's farm. There was a teacher named Ms. Doris who lived not too far from Granny, and on the weekends, she'd take me to Granny's farm so I could spend a couple days. On Monday mornings, she'd bring me back to the school. Mama hadn't had a problem with this arrangement because the more I was out of her hair, the more she could hit the bottle and visit the juke joints without feeling guilty about bringing home a man or getting too drunk. I remember when her behavior used to concern me. I'd give anything now to have the old Mama back. This new one is an imposter and a liar. Her new drug is Nesmith and the power being engaged to him brings her. At least with alcohol she'd still tell me she loved me. At least with alcohol, there was the hangover guilt.

Anyway, I had grabbed the empty bag almost on instinct. Now it's time to see if it really is empty.

I find an opening in the trees where the moonlight is strongest and kneel to unzip it. There's a notebook that says *Pre-Algebra* on the front, a couple of unsharpened pencils, a civics textbook, an unopened water bottle, and a smashed candy bar. I decide to save the candy bar for later. Ideally, I'll be at Granny's before long, but it's probably best to parcel it out just in case.

I go ahead and drink half of the water now. It's warm but tastes good.

The next hour is bad. The woods are tricky, the terrain rough. Without a flashlight, I need to depend on the light of the moon to see anything, and it is often completely blocked out by the trees. The night seems endless. I keep expecting the sun to poke through the trees at any minute, but the darkness remains unbroken. Most of the time, I have my hands out, moving at a snail's pace to avoid falling and twisting an ankle.

As I move like a blind woman, I think of Ruby Jewel and how capable she seems. How different she is than the blind man who'd come to Granny's house once, seeking healing. That was a long time ago. Ben and I had both been visiting, so I couldn't have been more than eight or nine. Granny gave him her usual bit about how she wasn't a healer, but she'd see what she could do to help. Most of the time, she just listened when people came in with physical ailments. She told me once there wasn't magic in listening, but art. Everybody could manage it a little, but most lacked the gift of getting it just so. This gentleman—I remember his long white beard and hands that wouldn't stop clenching into fists—wanted something more.

"I heard you can walk through dreams," he said.

I'll never forget the way Granny reacted to this. She wasn't angry. Not exactly. Granny barely ever got angry about anything. She seemed a little sad. Resigned to it, but sad, nonetheless.

"Take your sister in my room, Ben, and shut that door. Don't come out until I tell you. It might be a minute."

We knew better than to question or argue with her. Ben took my hand, and we went to her room and shut the door.

I spent the better part of the next hour with my ear pressed against that door, trying to hear something. All I ever made out was some muffled words and a few gasps of pain that sounded like they were coming from Granny. Later, she'd explain to us both how much walking inside another person's dreams took out of her, how sometimes it hurt her so much, she didn't think she'd ever be able to do it again.

"We should check on her," I said.

"She's fine," Ben said. "She can take care of herself." He held up a book that he'd found beside her bed. Granny loved Westerns. It was a Louis L'amour. "Lay down. I'll read to you."

It gets blurry from there. At some point, Granny called for us to come out of the room. The man was gone. I asked if she'd been able to help him.

She shook her head, "No, but I tried." She looked tired, pale and weak. Possibly even in pain.

"Granny?"

She waved me off. "Go outside and play. Sun's already going down. If you hurry, you can catch a ghost."

Ben and I did as she said. Just as Granny hadn't healed the man, we hadn't managed to catch a ghost either. But that was the thing about being at Granny's. The possibilities always seemed just within reach, and failure was never a permanent state.

6

AT LAST, THE woods clear and I can see a small wooden structure framed against the starry sky. The moon is at full power here, and there's a glow to the meadow that seems like something from a fairy tale. As I move across the moonlit meadow, a pair of headlights on my right helps me get my bearings. I'm just a few hundred yards from the highway.

Good. I need to keep it close to make sure I stay pointed in the right direction.

The small wooden structure isn't a house, which I'd assumed it might be at first. In fact, as I draw closer, I realize I've been here before. It's the old jail. As soon as I recognize it, a feeling of hopelessness washes over me. This is only a few miles from our house, maybe five at the most. I've made very little progress, and I'm already exhausted.

Without a second thought, I slip inside the jail. It's a county historical site and they keep it open to the public. I guess somebody could vandalize it, but nobody around here pays it much mind. It's just an empty wooden shell, the kind of thing you see every day of your life, but never really *see*. It'll do fine for a place to sleep.

John Mantooth

There's a high window at the back of the building, and it frames the moon like a painting. I take the candy bar from the backpack and put it on the ground beside me, then lay down using my backpack as a pillow. It takes some moving and sliding around, but eventually I get so that I can see the moon through the window. I watch it, counting the clouds drifting by, listening for cars out on 278. It's the most peaceful I've felt in months, and I can't help but wish I didn't have to sleep, that I could lay here on the very cusp of fading away forever. But there's no such thing as forever, and even if there was, I'm not sure I'd want to go there without Granny and Ben.

Lightning Hill

1

SLEEP IS TOO brief. The sound of a big-rig rumbling past on the highway rouses me, and my eyes go to the window. The moon's pale fire is gone, replaced by purples and pinks, the colors of dawn.

Sliding the water bottle into my backpack, I rise and head outside to find a place to pee. The light is strange now, like the earth itself is glowing, lit up by something internal rather than external. Granny used to tell me she never missed a dawn or a dusk.

Two most important times of the day. This is where the world is most susceptible to magic, when the Holy Ghost can come closest.

After I'm finished, I take in the area now that the light is better. The meadow goes on for a bit, but there's trees on the other side of it. Sucking in a deep breath, I try to sense the Holy Ghost. Try to ask her to guide me today, to keep me safe. I don't know what I feel, but I feel something. A wonder, maybe. It's around me in the sky, across the field, in the trees that move in a slow dance. Not only that, but it's also inside me, an expanding peace, a hope. I hold my breath to keep it in place as I jog across the meadow.

I'm almost to the tree line when the car approaches. It's not like the other cars that fly past. This one is slowing. This one is stopping.

Don't look back. Just don't.

The line of the woods is just in front of me. As I step in, a voice calls my name.

"Forest!"

The voice is familiar. Without thinking, I turn to see who it is.

Standing at the edge of the meadow near her car is my mother's friend, Ms. Abby. "Forest? Are you okay, girl? Do you need a ride?"

For a long second, I just stand there, staring at her. I *really* want to say yes. I really want to get into the car with her and ask her to drive me to Granny's. Ms. Abby has always seemed like a nice woman. She's always been kind to me. I'm close to doing just that when a memory announces itself with a sudden fury inside my mind:

Last spring. Communion at the amphitheater. Nesmith has just finished one of his more impassioned sermons. He holds out the cup and Ruby Jewel holds the bread. The church lines up. It's a long line. I remember wondering why there is only one line, but I guess I know why. Nesmith doesn't like to share. He wants to be the only one giving out the wine. It's stupid, sure, but that's Nesmith. Anyway, in the memory I can see Ms. Abby's face as she kneels before Nesmith in his wheelchair, and he lifts the cup to her mouth. There's something wanton, something sexual there, her desire for him, to please him, is clear to me all the way from the back of the line, as I stand near the top row of the amphitheater.

Something else too. He seems so much older in this memory. It's as if the same dark magic that healed his lameness has also turned back his internal clock, made him into a younger man. I can't help but think this has everything to do with the black-horned goat from the barn.

"I'm okay," I call out and then turn and begin to run.

Once I'm in the trees and out of sight, I circle back and peer at her from the cover of the woods. She's on her phone. Shit. I've got to move. Stay ahead of whoever is coming.

I run, thankful for the growing light, thankful for the day.

2

I MAKE THE base of Lightning Hill when I see them. Ruby Jewel and Nesmith again. He pokes forward with his cane while she holds his arm.

Lightning Hill is the stuff of legend in Winston County. Four years ago, Nesmith made his name in this county when he prophesied a great storm. He said the storm would wipe out a dozen homes and lightning would lay the entire hillside bare. He said it would be God's message to his people to repent, to turn back to Him.

Sure enough, just two weeks after the sermon, the storm came. This hill had been called Farm Hill and was once dotted with trailers among the trees. The storm blew the trailers off the hill and then the lightning came. Some folks claim that one great stroke of lightning forked a thousand times and each fork hit an individual tree. Others say it was only a single bolt that caught one tree on fire, and then the fire itself did the rest of the work. Didn't matter much either way. Nesmith had been right. People flocked to his church. Farm Hill was renamed Lightning Hill, and people came from far and wide to visit. Hell, some of them even built monuments—a house of crosses, a rock cairn topped with a marker said to have been struck by lightning, and all manner of smaller memorials that now covered the hill like the trees used to.

Nesmith referred to Lightning Hill often in his sermons, calling it a place of power, a place where God had touched Winston County and made his presence known. I even believed him for a while. But after he moved in with us, and I got to know him better, I began to suspect his God wasn't a God I wanted anything to do with. Still, he hadn't lied about Lightning Hill. It's a place of power for sure, and I'm pretty sure it's not a coincidence that this is where he's caught up to me.

Even from this distance, I can see the way he walks, his cane stabbing the ground with each faltering step. It's my one advantage, even here, and I can't afford to waste it. I strike out running up the side of Lightning Hill, dodging the cairns and memorials, keeping the house of crosses on my right, wishing I had more time to slow down and really take in the dark wonder of this place, but time isn't anything I can spare. I crest the top of the hill and keep on going.

Flying downhill, my hair lifts from around my head and I swear it could be wings. Near the bottom, where the trees are still whole, a cottonmouth has darted into my path. I put on the brakes and veer to the right, but as I veer, it does too. There's a quick second when I know this is how it will end, that I'll lie dying at the bottom of this cursed hill as the poison spreads through my body. But of course, I'll live long enough for Nesmith and his blind bitch to poke their way over the hill and laugh at me while I'm in the throes of the sickness, while the cottonmouth's bitter poison hollows me out.

HOLY GHOST ROAD

My only option is to jump. I've slowed down as much as I can. I can't cut and keep my balance, so I make the leap.

It's not a good jump. To make matters worse, I push off against a rock. Half of my foot is on the rock and half of it is on the ground. My ankle turns, but I'm committed to the jump now, already in the air. Catapulting forward, I clear the cottonmouth, but my body lurches at a bad angle, and I come down hard on the same foot I've already twisted. The rest of me crashes against the roots of a nearby tree. I sit up quickly and scooch my ass away from the snake.

I stand, putting all my weight on my right foot and hop over to another nearby tree. A slithering sound follows me, and I am dismayed to realize this isn't a climbing tree. It's honey locust, one of my favorites, but not one I can climb in a hurry – at least not without getting hurt. Honey locust trees have these thorns in clusters all over the trunk and lower branches. Even if I do make it to the top to take refuge, I'll likely leave a bloody trail that will lead them right to me no matter how high I'm able to climb.

I keep moving, hopping as fast as I can manage. I focus on another tree, a solid oak, like the one I hid in last night. Nearly there, I glance back, and see the damned snake is following me, weaving through the grass like a curved arrow, gaining on me, nearly within striking distance. I fall again, twisting my ankle again as I tumble over. I ignore the pain surging up my leg and turn over onto my ass, using my hands to push myself along the grass until my back is against the base of the oak.

Now, I see the hill in all its glory.

John Mantooth

From down here I can really appreciate how the trees have been sheared apart as if from a great scythe swung by God himself, but I can also see that serpent easing right up to me like they always say Satan likes to do. I wish I could take a picture, but I don't have a phone, much less a camera, so I take a picture in my mind of the snake raising his head, tongue a-flicker, sunrise peeking over the hill and spreading out through those half-trees like egg yolk across a charred griddle. And at the very top of the hill, I see her standing there.

Ruby Jewel, her white housecoat flapping in the morning breeze.

My journey to find the only person in the world who can help me is over before it has even begun.

I close my eyes and do the only kind of prayer I've ever been any good at. I just say *God, God, God, God, please, God.*

3

I OPEN MY eyes when the snake is near enough to strike. Its mouth is opened wide, and I see past its needle-sharp fangs and into the thick cotton of its throat. It's winding up, taking its time, and that's when it dawns on me this isn't any ordinary snake.

It's like the fox from last night, its own spirit, soul, consciousness, whatever, has been pushed aside so Ruby Jewel can come in.

At the top of the hill, Ruby Jewel still has not moved. She's enjoying my fear, soaking it in through the snake's eyes. Maybe she's even feeding off it somehow –or maybe she wants to keep me here until her brother can climb his slow self over the hill to watch me die.

I slide both my hands across the ground, feeling for something I can use as a weapon, something hard, a rock or stick. My fingers graze a slick stone. Very slowly, I wrap my hand around it, digging my nails into the dirt a little to dislodge it from the earth.

The snake is still poised to strike, but if Ruby Jewel is indeed in control, I can use that to my advantage. Nesmith told her just last night I should be kept alive.

John Mantooth

I raise my empty hand slowly, until I'm sure the snake is watching it and not the hand holding the rock. Then as fast as I am able, I bring the rock up and back down in a smooth arc clobbering the serpent's head and driving it into the ground. I press the rock as hard as I can against the ground until I hear a squishing sound. The snake is dead, its head smashed.

At the top of the hill, Ruby Jewel holds her head, screaming out in pain. Good. She can use animals, but she can hurt like them too.

I've got to move while I can, but my options are limited.

Running is out. My ankle is busted. Climbing a tree seems foolish with Nesmith right there, at the top of the hill, watching me.

I try to think, or pray, or just be still for a minute. Clearing my mind. That's how I think of it. I learned it from Ben, who'd learned it from his friend Jimmy who'd been all over the world and said there were more religions than you could shake a stick at. Of course, round the world don't matter much here in North Alabama. In this world there's only two Gods and telling them apart is half of the battle. There's Satan and there's God, and sometimes a person might say they're for one, but be held under the thrall of the other, and vice versa. Sometimes a person might claim neither but *be* claimed by one. And then there are people like me, still trying to sort everything out, trying to make sense of this crazy world and do what's right in the face of it all.

But the mind clearing thing always works.

Whenever I do it, my life feels like a blank slate, with no past and no future, except what I choose to write. Even now, with Ruby Jewel on the ridge above me, I feel the peace and hope wash through me.

HOLY GHOST ROAD

My mind goes to the place that lives inside me. I think of it as the true me, the me before all the bullshit, the me I hope is still there.

I see Ben. We're climbing trees, out behind the house, and it's peaceful and easy. He never minded spending time with me. Never minded hanging out, offering advice. The advice I remember now is from a long time ago. I must have been five, maybe six, and he was telling me if I was ever in the woods behind our house and something was chasing me, a tree was good place to hide.

I shake my head, frustrated, breaking the blankness, breaking the moment. I already know this. Hiding ain't really going to work with Ruby Jewel and Nesmith watching which tree I climb.

Still, maybe it's my best option. My *only* option considering what I've done to my ankles. I open my eyes.

Ruby Jewel isn't acting like she's in pain anymore. She's standing there, hands extended, beckoning Nesmith to finish the last little bit to the top of the hill. If I hurry, I can get up this tree before Nesmith crests the hill and Ruby Jewel turns her attention to me again.

I force myself to stand on my injured ankle. The pain is the terrible kind that makes my whole body hurt and my jaw ache. The lowest branch of the oak is in easy jumping reach, but jumping is out of the question with this ankle. I'll have to shimmy.

Shimmying's a technique I taught myself when Ben used to pick out trees near our trailer and challenge me to climb them. I couldn't stand to let a challenge go unmet, even if it meant tearing the skin off my hands, wrists, and arms.

Wrapping my arms around the tree first, I pull myself up until my feet are off the ground. Then I use my legs to grip the tree too. I'm wearing a pair of blue jeans and a tank top, so my arms take the worst of it. Sticking myself onto the trunk like a piece of gum, I start shimmying. The bark breaks against my skin, and my skin tears against the bark. But for the moment, the pain in my ankle is gone.

A little bit more...

Movement in the woods. Someone or something coming this way.

Squeezing my legs around the trunk, I reach for the limb, grabbing it in my raw and now bleeding hands. I hoist myself up to it, and then to the next one. Now, the going is easy. Limb after limb takes me higher into the canopy of the tree. I'm a monkey, flying along. I don't need feet or ankles, only arms and thighs and a stomach that can stretch and bend with each new challenge. As I climb, I seek out a sturdy limb large enough for me to rest on *and* stay hidden.

Only when I'm high enough to feel safe do I chance a look at what is moving in the woods. It's a man, and he's stumbling along between the trees quickly, warily, as if he is being chased.

I pause on a strong limb, my back against the trunk. Peering down, I get a good look at him as he breaks through the trees and out into the meadow.

Hopelessly awkward, thin, bony, all legs and arms, he wears glasses and is going bald on the top of his head. Maybe he's even older than I'd first suspected.

"Hey," I hiss.

HOLY GHOST ROAD

He stops, his whole body stiffening. He glances around slowly, tentatively, as if he doesn't really want to find out where the voice is coming from.

"Up here," I say, and glance at the hill. Ruby Jewel is helping Nesmith now as they make their way to the bottom. I don't have long. "Above you."

"Oh God," he says. "Oh God." And just like that, he starts to run. I can't let him get away. He's quite literally my only chance.

"Stop, or I'll shoot," I say, trying to supercharge my voice, rev it up to a level that will make me sound scary. It must have worked because he stops dead in his tracks and holds his hands up.

"Please don't shoot," he says.

"Look up here." I keep my voice as deep and serious as I can.

Slowly, he turns his body and raises his head. When he sees me, he says, "You don't have a gun."

"No shit, I don't have a gun. I just said that because you weren't going to stop. I need your help."

He holds a hand to his brow and squints up at me. He shakes his head. "I need help too."

"Let me guess. You're lost?"

"My car... My keys..." He shakes his head. "If I could just find them." He sticks his hands in his pockets. "Or my phone."

"Oh, you are truly lost," I lie. "The nearest road is a long way from here." I want to berate him a little for being so dumb to help sell the lie, but I don't have time. Ruby Jewel and Nesmith are almost to the bottom of the hill now. She has her arm out and her brother grasps it for support. The blind leading the crippled. Better get to it.

"I can help you find it, though. First, you have to help me."

He nods. I'm pretty sure something very bad has happened to him. He seems out of sorts in almost every conceivable way. The more I stare at him, the more I see it. He's not wearing shoes. What little hair he has left is unkempt, wavy, and standing up along the bald spot. Even his glasses are bent and crooked on his face. Each detail seems to lend support to the thesis I'm forming. Something has sent him running.

Like me.

Difference is I know where I'm heading. He seems genuinely confused.

"How did you get up there?"

"Climbed," I say, "but I don't have time for twenty questions. Now, listen and listen good…"

He shakes his head and turns to Lightning Hill. "What happened to the trees?"

"Act of God," I say, "but forget that. You see those two people moving slow down the side of the hill?"

He nods.

"They don't look like much, but that man is hunting me. If he finds me, I reckon he means to…"

"What?"

I shake my head. He won't understand.

"Kill you?"

"Worse than that."

"Worse than killing you?"

"There's always worse."

He seems as if he wants to argue but stops himself, thank God. "What do you want me to do?"

"Lie," I say. "You can do that, can't you? Way I see it, everybody can do that."

He doesn't seem convinced.

"Hey," I say. "I'm going to help you find your car."

That seems to trigger something in him. "Okay. Deal. What do you want me to say?"

4

IT FEELS WEIRD being up here and looking down on this man I don't know as he attempts to save my life.

He's not great at lying, but Ruby Jewel and Nesmith seem none the wiser. They listen intently as he tells them he saw me tear into those woods.

"Nearly knocked me over," he adds, and then does the single stupidest thing he can do. He looks right up at me in the tree. I glare at him, and he turns back real quick. Luckily, Ruby Jewel is blind, and her brother is focused on the woods. I let myself breathe just a little. My lungs ache from holding my breath for so long.

Ruby Jewel takes Nesmith's arm, and they start toward the woods. I'm thinking we got away with it when all at once, Nesmith stops, resisting his sister's pull.

"And might I ask you what you're doing out in these woods on this fine day?"

I stop breathing again. The man just stands there. Nesmith waits expectantly for his answer. *Just tell the truth,* I mouth.

Ruby Jewel turns her blind face around toward the man. It's obvious she thinks this is a good question too.

Say something. I try to push the words from my mind to his, but he doesn't hear them.

"Is there something wrong?" Nesmith asks in his preacher voice, the one that sounds like he's concerned about you, like he's waiting to be a Goddamn vessel between you and heaven if you'd but tell him what he wants to hear.

He still doesn't say anything. I've got to act, got to do something. Slowly, I unzip my backpack and pull out the old civics textbook. Holding it like a frisbee, I sling it as far out into the woods as I can. Damn thing flies like it's got wings. It burrows a path through the canopy of the woods and falls through branch after branch making a clatter that might as well have been an airplane crashing through the trees.

Ruby Jewel is the first to react. She grabs Nesmith's arm again and yanks him toward the sound.

"Stay here," Nesmith says to the man in that voice he has that makes people want to follow his orders.

The man nods dumbly, as Ruby Jewel helps her brother toward the sound. I wait until they've disappeared into the woods and hopefully out of earshot before I hiss at him again.

"Go," I say.

"What about our deal?"

"Ain't gonna be no deal if you can't use your fucking words."

"I froze."

"Exactly. Go on. Get somewhere and hide. Come back in an hour if you can manage it without getting lost." I'm being mean, too mean maybe, but I'm pissed. He almost blew it.

"Hurry," I say.

He's genuinely confused, now. Pitiful, really. Damn it. I don't want to feel sorry for him, but it's happening anyway.

Finally, he gets moving, walking toward some trees on the other side of the meadow.

He disappears over the horizon, leaving me alone again.

5

NESMITH AND RUBY Jewel emerge from the trees about a half
an hour later. Ruby Jewel's carrying my civics textbook in one hand and
letting Nesmith lead her around by the other. I hold my breath as they
make their way toward my tree.

When they get just underneath, Ruby stops and cocks her head to
one side.

"I smell her."

"Where?"

Ruby Jewel lets go of Nesmith's hand and touches the book she's
holding, running her fingers across the cover, and then putting them to
her nose.

"Damn wind," she says. "Makes it hard to pinpoint. I think she's
moved on."

"It's okay," Nesmith says again, and that's when I notice the shadow.
It's on the ground, stretched out behind him, its length unnatural, its
shape goat-like, but also human. It sees me, just like it saw me before. For
the first time an odd thought hits me. A question, really. Does Nesmith

even realize the shadow thing has attached itself to him? The more I watch the thing, twisting behind him, the more likely it seems he doesn't. Perhaps it's only me that can see it.

The shadow writhes around Nesmith and then separates and twists upward along the tree trunk until its misshapen head is just beneath my feet. I hold my breath, determined not to scream, gasp, or even move. Horns form from its shadowed head and then a goat mouth with large goat teeth. Empty eye sockets open in the darkness and the mouth draws back until its teeth are bared in a terrible smile. It's as if it wants me to know I might avoid Nesmith, but it'll still be there no matter what.

The thought of jumping from the tree comes to me suddenly. It's more of an urge, really. It seems like the only way to escape the gaze of this thing. I feel my body trying to lunge forward, out into the open space beyond the tree and the demon goat's shadow, but my hands have a mind of their own, and hang onto to the branches. I stay in the tree.

The shadow curls away from me, seemingly willing to wait for another opportunity.

Nesmith —still unaware of me or the shadow— looks a little nervous, like he knows something is amiss but can't say what. It's not the first time I've seen him look this way. He tries to hide it, but there are things he's afraid of.

I saw the fear in his face the first time he realized who my grandmother was. It was at one of the church picnics before he and mama ever started dating. At that time, he was still relatively unknown in the county. He had his church, sure, but he didn't have his radio station or his charities, and most importantly, he didn't have his influence. Ruby Jewel wheeled him up to our table and he introduced himself, his eyes lingering on Mama before turning to me. He looked at me like he knew me already, and I hated that feeling. Mama introduced me and then told him my grandmother had been a preacher.

"Is that so?" Nesmith said. "A female preacher. That's rather unheard of, not to mention it seems a little shaky, biblically speaking."

"Oh, her Granny was more than a little shaky, biblically speaking. She was tossed out of the church for heresy."

"Heresy?" Nesmith said, appearing really interested.

"Sure," Mama said. "You never heard of Sister Redwine?"

"Sister Redwine?" he asked, his voice normal, but I could tell it was taking him some effort to keep it that way.

I knew he was pretending not to recognize the name. Everybody in Winston County knew who Sister Redwine was. She was the woman who'd broken away from the First Assemblies church that used to be the most popular one in the whole county to pastor her own flock at the Church of the Heavenly Mother, and when she did, all hell broke loose. Half of the First Assemblies people followed her, while the other half lost their minds because she was a woman, didn't have a seminary degree, and (most blasphemous of all) started turning their traditional doctrine right over on its ass. She was labeled a heretic and blasphemer, and eventually she closed the Church of the Heavenly Mother, saying she could better serve God by withdrawing to her farm. It was an unprecedented move. Preachers around here don't ever quit, especially when their church is growing. I've got a feeling this part scared Nesmith as much—or more—than anything else. He's a man who would be lost without his title, without the power that came with it, without the adulation of the thousands who gathered every Sunday at his outdoor church. All of them, to a one, proclaiming their love for God, leaving in me an unspoken question: who was their God? From my seat in the back row of the amphitheater, it looked a lot like Nesmith himself.

I'd known right away Nesmith was going to be a problem, but how was I to predict *this*? Even with Granny's warnings, how was anyone to know he'd take over the county, and brainwash a large percentage of the population into thinking he was more than just a preacher? That he'd move right into the bedroom below mine and bring his weird-ass sister with him? And most of all, how was I to know he'd do anything for power, including clandestine meetings with black-horned entities in our barn?

And perhaps, most concerning of all, why does the previous night's encounter with the thing seem so shrouded in a dull fog now? It's as if only small pieces of the full memory are available to me.

Nesmith and Ruby Jewel head back up the hill. The shadow of the demon goat is gone too, so I say a brief prayer of thanks. The wind touches my face, and I decide it's a ghost, the Holy Ghost, the one Granny says everybody misunderstands that has protected me. It's a wind, a spirit, a movement in the trees. It's a secret, a glorious and beautiful secret.

6

TWO HOURS PASS. I try to elevate my ankle, though some ice would be better. It's swollen and blue and green around my calf. No way I'm going anywhere on this ankle. I really hope the man comes back. I can help him find his car, and he can help me hop there. He's as safe a person as I'm likely to meet in this county simply because he's not from here. He's an outsider, and not yet under Nesmith's influence. That's not to say everyone in the county is, though it seems like there are more every day. It's still a risk, though. Being an outsider also makes him someone who doesn't understand the way in which this world—my world—tilts.

The hours creep by. Noon comes and goes. The wind shakes leaves out of trees. They collect on the ground in scattered piles. Clouds drift over Lightning Hill, at first just sliding past, but later gathering and blocking out the sun for minutes at a time. Time slips. I slip. From waking to dreaming and then to the barn again, finally reclaiming the memory, redreaming it.

The moment I rise from the bed, I feel the weirdness of the dreamwalk, the sense of seeing where the one world bleeds into the next, the place where boundaries become elastic. Despite knowing I'm in this state, I want to see where it takes me, as the world of dreamwalks for me is a world of true things, the one where I see most clearly the strangeness of reality.

Yet, it's been a long time since I've been here. Why?

There's no answer to my question.

Downstairs, I make my way past Ruby Jewel's room. Her door is cracked slightly, and there are shadows gathered within, shadows that have formed a kind of breathing wall. I hear them as I float past.

I try to stop at Mama's room. Her door is shut, but I want to open it and see what she is doing (what Nesmith is doing), but I'm being pulled along almost as if I have no will of my own.

I keep moving. I feel like a searchlight, like I should know just what I am trying to find. Except I don't know. Not really. I just have to keep moving. My legs will take me where they want me to go.

Out the back door, shadows move under a high moon. They're coming from near the barn or inside the barn. In this dreamwalk, the barn is more of a church, its arched roof forming a spire, a steeple lancing the hazy firmament. There is something terrible there, and now that I understand it's my destination, I want to wake up, go back to my bed, back to regular sleep, to the regular world, where all the terror is hidden inside of a room whose door is mostly—mercifully—shut.

There's more. I've been here before. Many nights. But why? For what purpose would I make the trip out here?

Granny's voice comes, a whisper on the wind. *Dreamwalks take us to the in-between places, cellars, attics, pastures, barns. Outposts and waystations. It's where you can grow. It's also easier to have a dreamwalk in these kinds of spaces. Dreamwalks in the in-between places are powerful and dangerous things.*

It's taking me there now, pulling me. After a certain point, I can't go back, I can't escape.

The big door to the barn is crooked, even though I swear Nesmith fixed it the week before. Doesn't matter. Crooked is what it is, and no amount of hammers or nails can straighten some things out.

"Hello?" a voice calls. It's inside my dream. But it's not supposed to be here. An intrusion.

I float in a different direction toward the sound, the moment, the reality I'm supposed to be in.

But I'm still moving in the other place too, inside the dreamwalk. I open the door to the barn and see Nesmith is inside. He seems impatient. He's standing near an altar made from hay bales and tree branches. He waves me over. I don't want to go, but my body moves anyway.

"Watch it!" the voice from outside my dream calls. I freeze, my body tensing as something shakes me out of the dreamwalk.

As always, I experience coming back like a long fall through blank space. The tree limb under my feet looms larger than it is and then the world snaps back into place with an elasticity of a thick rubber band.

I'm standing on the limb, balanced on my uninjured foot, the ground thirty or forty feet below me. My body wavers, and I feel weightless, as if I could just flutter down like a leaf.

"Careful," the voice says. I see him now. The bald-headed man. He's come back, and that makes me smile. Nobody's ever come back for me. Well, nobody except Granny.

"I'm fine," I say, but as soon as the words come out, I feel myself losing my balance, spilling forward. I reach madly with my hands for something to grab. I clutch a branch with my right hand and manage to break my fall.

"Are you okay?"

"Fine. Fine. I just..." I remember the strange way I was compelled toward the barn, and the way Nesmith had been waiting there for me. Going there last night had been no accident.

"You just what?"

"Oh, sorry. I dreamwalk. Always have. Which is why I probably shouldn't nap in trees."

He fixes me with a strange look. I get those a lot. I climb down and he helps brace me onto the ground.

"Dreamwalk?"

"It's what I call it. Or what my grandmother taught me to call it. It's a little like sleepwalking, but..." I trail off. I almost said *better,* but that doesn't really seem accurate anymore. Once, dreamwalking had been a lot of fun, something I even looked forward to, and then Nesmith talked Mama into putting me on the medicine and the episodes seemed to stop.

"But what?"

"But... different. That's all. My grandmother was able to help people by actually walking inside their dreams. At least until she got too old, and the whole process started to be bad for her health."

He just stares at me as if I'm some kind of alien.

I smile. "Sorry. Sometimes I ramble."

He nods, seemingly all too ready to dismiss what I just said.

"But you're sure you're okay?" he asks as he braces me. He's stronger than he looks. Not strong like Helmet, but not a weakling either. From down here, I can see his face better. It's—how can I describe it—a fragile face. His chin is slight, almost completely collapsed into his bird neck, and his jaw is thin, his features too fine, almost feminine. But it's his skin I find most striking. He doesn't look white, but he doesn't look black either. Hispanic? Not quite.

"What?" he asks me.

I shake my head, embarrassed at my rudeness. I typically don't mind being rude to people. Most of the time that's about all they deserve, but I ain't racist, and I don't want anybody to think I am either. I just… I don't know. I'm used to seeing somebody and putting them into a category, I guess. White, black, Hispanic. I don't quite know what to do with this man. Maybe that's a good thing though. I feel like Granny would say it was.

"You're like the men at the gas station."

"Who?"

"They kept looking at me. Like I was some new breed of animal."

"I don't think that."

He stares at me. He doesn't seem convinced.

"Let's get you to your car," I say.

He nods. "Yeah. My car."

"What took you so long? I said wait an hour. It's almost dark."

He shakes his head. "I wanted to be sure they were gone."

"Scared you, huh?"

"What? Oh. I guess. It's the woman. She's blind, right?"

I nod.

"She doesn't move like she's blind. I think she's a fraud."

"She lives with me. She's no fraud."

"Wait, that's not your mother and father, is it?"

He sees right away how angry that makes me.

"Sorry. I guess they're too old anyway."

"It's okay. It's just my father is dead."

"Sorry."

"This way," I say and point through the trees, ready to move on from this particular topic. "It'll take us out to 278. You'll be able to find your car from there, won't you?"

"I think so."

I glance at his feet. "You lost your shoes too?"

He nods and helps me forward, toward the trees. We make slow time, me hopping and leaning on him, his bare feet causing him to take care, but at least we're moving.

I don't know how long we've hopped along before the gnawing starts in my stomach. "Hold it. I gotta have a snack."

He nods. "Good. I need a rest."

I sit down on the leafy forest floor and dig into my pack. First, I drink some water and then tear off half the candy bar. I must be eating it fast or something because he stares at me.

"What?" I ask. "You don't like it, look the other way."

"How long has it been since you ate?"

"I'm fine."

"You say that a lot. Even when you're about to fall from a tree."

"It's true. I am fine. I *was* fine. I didn't fall."

"Okay. Fair enough. You got a name?"

"Of course I got a name. Who ain't got a name?"

He nods, smiling a little, which is surprising. Most people don't smile around me unless they're men who want something. Then it's more a leer than a smile anyway. This isn't like that. His smile is genuine. I sit for a minute, staring at the half of the candy bar I haven't eaten. I hold it out to him.

"I'm Forest, one *r.*"

"Nice to meet you, Forest. I'm Elijah."

"Like the prophet?"

He shakes his head. Not in answer to my question, but in response to the offer of the candy bar.

"My mother was a believer."

"You ain't?"

Another quick shake of his head. "No." He watches me eat. "What about you?"

I unscrew the top of my water bottle while I chew the candy bar. It tastes better than anything I've eaten. That's hunger for you. And that's how I view religion, though I ain't about to get into it with this man. People want faith, spirituality—call it what you want—so much, they'll take any old thing and devour it. Most of it's like a candy bar. It'll feed you, but it's not real nourishment. But then there's whatever Nesmith is offering. That's a candy bar too, but one that's addictive, and laced with some kind of drug that makes folks lose their minds.

"I believe," I say. "But that ain't saying much. It's *what* you believe in that matters."

"And what do you believe in? Dreamwalking?"

I put down my water. Stare at him. "For starters, yeah."

"Anything else?"

"Stuff."

"That sounds… vague."

"Yep."

"That's it?"

"Sure is. You want more? Forget it. I don't know you yet." He looks a little hurt, so I decide to soften the blow a little. After all, I want him to give me a ride. "I'm just cautious."

"I see. Because of the people who are chasing you?"

I put my water back into my backpack and zip it up. "Ready?"

He looks around. "How far is it from here?"

"That depends. You ain't told me where you left the car yet."

"The Ramey Place. Heard of it? Well, near there. That's the problem. I had to park about a mile away because the road leading to the farm was too muddy to drive on."

"Well, of course I've heard of it. What were you doing at the Ramey Place?"

HOLY GHOST ROAD

"Now you want to ask *me* questions?"

"Fair enough. Forget it then."

"No, it's okay. I'm an open book." He helps me to my feet. "I work—or *did* work considering I might not have a job anymore—for the Southeastern Skeptics Association. SSA for short."

"You're kidding, right?"

"No," he says without a trace of irony.

I lean on him and begin to hop. He's quiet. Probably not sure how to take me. That's the way I like it. When people don't know how to take you, it keeps them on edge. When people are on edge, they ain't so likely to try to take advantage of you. "You do know what a skeptic is, don't you?"

"Of course. I'm not stupid." I glare at him. "I don't like when people assume I'm stupid. Of course, I know what a goddamn skeptic is. But I didn't know there was a whole society of them."

He shrugs. "I hooked up with them a year or two ago. Got involved in field work. Mostly in Alabama, but sometimes I venture to Tennessee and Georgia as the job demands."

Venture. As the job demands. He's smart, or at least thinks he is, but you can't always tell by how somebody talks. Folks think I'm dumb sometimes, but I haven't made anything less than an A on a report card since I was in the seventh grade and missed nearly the whole year because Mama wouldn't get me up when Ben was overseas. Also, most people you think are smart, only know how to look smart. Knowing how to look smart might take a certain kind of talent or even intelligence, but it's not a very valuable kind. The valuable kind—at least to me—is the kind that knows the difference between shit and shinola, between truth and lies. That's a very rare kind indeed.

"So, your job is to disprove things other people believe in?" I ask.

"Well, I guess you could say that."

"How's that going for you?"

He looks over at me, a little hurt. "I'm not sure I understand your meaning."

"Well, it just seems to me that people have got to work that out for themselves."

"You'd be surprised," he says, but I can tell he's not as confident as he'd like to be.

"And what did you come to be skeptical of here in the Free State of Winston?" That's an old joke. Apparently, once upon a time some of the people in this damned county had some sense and actually tried to rebel against the state of Alabama when *it* rebelled against the Union and seceded.

"The old Ramey Place. I already told you."

"That's the one where the sun don't shine on part of the field, and there's a two-headed cow or something?"

"That's the one, but those things were easily debunked. We were concerned about the barn."

"Oh shit. The barn. Yeah… that is spooky. That whole family killed."

We're moving at a good pace now. The trees are thinning, the ground is nice and level. I've got my hops timed with his steps. We're in rhythm, which when you think about it is a little weird. He's a man, a young man,

I guess, but an adult. I'm just fifteen, and we couldn't be any more different. Don't worry, I ain't one of *those* girls. I don't get crushes on men. Hell, I don't really get them on boys either, though I sometimes like to imagine if the right one came around…

"So, what does the Southern Society of Skeptics say about the Ramey Place?"

"South*eastern*."

"Whatever. What did you find? I mean, something must have spooked you."

I feel him tense a little as we walk. "What happened to me is easily explainable. I just need to get to my car and phone…"

"Your phone is going to help you explain what happened to you?"

He doesn't answer. Maybe he's done talking. I guess I don't blame him. I'm doing my thing again. Pushing him away. Except, here's somebody I need close. Just for a time, though. Just until he can get me to Granny's.

"What I mean," he says as we start up a steep hill that should be the last one before we'll see 278, "is I just need to take a hot shower, get some food in me, and spend some time breaking down what happened out there."

"In the barn?"

He nods.

"So, tell me. What happened out there?"

"Okay, but keep in mind, these types of situations almost always have explanations. Experience has taught me that. Some people don't want to find the explanations, so they stop looking. But if you look long and hard enough, you'll find the truth."

"'Less it finds you first," I say. It just sort of comes out. It's something Granny used to say a lot. *People are always looking for the truth, but most of the time it's truth itself that does the looking.* I never understood that, at least not on any level I could explain, but it resonated with me anyway.

"Well, unfortunately, truth doesn't find people," Elijah says.

"Maybe you just gotta be open to it."

"Maybe. Anyway, to your question. What happened at the Ramey Place is easily explainable."

I nod but think this probably isn't the case. Hell, if it was so easy to explain he'd quit saying it was easy to explain and actually explain it.

"I had a bad dream. I was sleeping in the barn, because that's supposed to be the center of most of the activity. When I woke from the dream, I just freaked myself out a little. I got scared. It was irrational—I see that now—but I ran. I just kind of freaked out for a minute. It was dark and I got turned around."

"A barn? Wow."

"What's that supposed to mean?"

I shake my head. There's no way I'm telling about *my* own experience in a different barn. "Never mind. The Ramey Place is a good ways from here. You came a long way."

"I did?"

"Seems like you'd know that."

He falls silent again. "I got confused. I… I… left my phone too. My wallet. Everything."

HOLY GHOST ROAD

"You got your keys?"

He stops. "Oh shit."

My heart sinks. "Don't tell me you left your keys too."

He pats his pockets and shakes his head. He may be about to cry. "This is so fucked up. So so so so so fucked up. In 2022? How can this even be happening? I don't have a phone; I don't have a car. I'm lost in the woods in Alabama. It feels like I'm still dreaming."

I'm quiet for a while, trying to give him some space. I guess I get it. I've seen the way Mama gets with her phone, the constant checking, scrolling, holding. And maybe I shouldn't judge since I've been lucky enough to never know what having one of those things is like. The being lost part has got to be rough too. Not that I've ever had to deal with that myself. Maybe it's just Granny's house, but I got a damn map in my head straight from anywhere to there.

"Well," I say, hating that I have to say it, "change of plans. We find the Ramey Place, get your keys and phone, and then find the car."

He nods, but the nod quickly devolves into a shudder. He's definitely losing it now. He lets go of me, and I hop over to lean against a tree. My ankle is just numb now, but I don't dare put it on the ground for fear of the pain coming back.

Elijah sits down and looks up at the canopy of trees. "I'm dreaming. This is a dream. What do you call it? I'm dreamwalking. Yeah, that's why nothing is working out. That's why I'm an hour and a half from home but feel like I'm on a different continent." His hands go to his face, and he just sits there for a long time.

I take solace in our hiding place within the trees. None of the animals are looking at me funny, and the day has turned nice and warm. The air smells like rain, and while that might be a problem at some point, right now it's only a sweet smell. I close my eyes and think of making it to Granny's door. I'll go in through the utility room like I always do, so I can open the freezer and see if she's got popsicles. She buys the cheap kind, a box for like a dollar, but she always gets banana, and that's something we agree on—there's nothing better than a banana popsicle. I'll grab one—no, two, because she'll want one as well—and soak in the smell of shelled beans and whatever she's cooking in the kitchen, fried bologna probably. Up the single step I'll go, swinging the door open. I'll see her there by the stove. She's a long, tall woman, maybe as tall as Ruby Jewel, and like Nesmith's sister, she's got a hardness about her, but it's a different kind of hardness. Where Ruby Jewel's is... well... garish and cruel, Granny's hardness is like an old tree, solemn and wise, its bark stripped and battered so much it leans into the weather, gives as good as it gets, because a tree is a force of nature too, like the weather, the storm, and so is a woman. I want to be that kind of woman.

"I'm ready." The voice is small, nearly defeated, but it's a voice, nonetheless.

"So, we get to the highway and follow it east until we come to the Ramey Place," I say, "then we'll get your phone. And your keys."

"Okay."

"See, we have a plan. This is just a little bump in the road."

HOLY GHOST ROAD

He nods and then looks at me strangely, as if he's just come to some conclusion. I don't like that look and want to ask him what in the hell he's deciding about me, but I let it go. He's moving again. Don't want to jinx that.

Shoulder to shoulder we go, me hopping and holding onto Elijah as he drags us both through the woods.

Half an hour later, we come out of the trees and look down a gently sloping hill onto highway 278. That's when it begins to rain.

7

I FALL AT least three times as we try to get down the hill. Elijah falls once. The rain is so sudden, so violent, it sweeps the hillside out from under us. Turns it to mud. By the time we make it to the highway, we're soaked, and Elijah is having problems breathing.

Standing on one foot, I turn to look both ways down the highway, momentarily confused. The rain has made it difficult to see very far. There's steam coming off the road. Lightning flashes around us, stabbing the road, the trees, the lake on the other side of 278.

"I've got an idea," I say and grab Elijah's arm. I start to yank him across the road when he pulls me back. A pick-up truck blows past us, nearly hitting us.

"Now," he says, and together we cross the road, which is already covered in what feels like a couple inches of water.

On the other side, I point toward the lake.

"That's not the way to the barn," he says.

"We need to get dry. The barn can wait."

He shakes his head as if he's not sure he can handle the thought of delaying his phone, wallet, and keys.

"We'll be struck by lightning," I say as another shard lights up the road just a few yards from where we stand. This is followed by an ear-splitting blast of thunder, and it's that sound that seems to wake Elijah up.

"Okay. But where?"

"Down by the lake there's cabins. Most of them will probably be empty because it's October and the middle of the week. We'll find one and break in."

"What? No."

Another fork of lightning strikes a tree on the top of the hill, near where we were standing just moments ago. I grab his hand and yank him down a slight incline and hop toward a dirt road branching off from 278. It's a mud road now, but one side is on higher ground than the other, and all the water and mud cascades along the low side. We stay on the high side and follow it through the storm. I keep thinking the rain will let up, but it doesn't. It pummels the road and the trees and the lake in the distance. There's a so much rain, it's hard to see. My eyelids are dripping, and I keep wiping them with wet hands.

"There," Elijah says. The cabins—a cluster of them, each with its own dock—are about a quarter of a mile away.

It takes us what seems like thirty minutes to make that last little bit. We dodge mudslides and deep pools of water, and even a snake that thankfully pays us little mind as it too scurries for cover.

Finally, we stand on a gravel drive in front of the first cabin. The whole development has been built up on a ridge, safe—at least for the moment—from the rising water.

"You've done this before?" Elijah asks.

HOLY GHOST ROAD

"Once," I say. "It's easy." These cabins are all the same. No garages, which means it's easy to tell if someone is staying in them. All but one seems deserted. I point at the one with the truck in the driveway. "That's the one to stay away from, so let's go to the far end."

We make our way along the gravel road that connects all the driveways of the cabins. As we walk, I try to peer between each cabin to see their boat docks. A boat could mean someone is home too. I only see one and that's at the same house with the truck out front.

The rain has let up some by the time we reach the last cabin, but at this point, I couldn't care less. I'm done. Soaked to the bone, tired, and ravenous, all I want is to change clothes, to take a hot shower, and sleep in a bed. Oh, and eat something. God, I hope there's something to eat in this place.

"Hold it," I say when he starts toward the door. I head around the side of the cabin for a better view of the dock. Empty. No sign anybody is home.

"Most of these places have lockboxes," I say. "For the keys."

"Oh. Well, where would that be?"

The rain has slacked up some more. It doesn't quite feel like we're inside of a war zone anymore, just close to one. On the steps there are two potted plants. I hop up and stand in between them. There, stuck to the underside of the wooden porch railing. The box slides free. It's a combination lock. Looks sturdy too. The place I broke into last summer with Josh Rawlings had a flimsy one he broke open by smashing with one of his boots.

"Is there a shed around?" I ask. "Like a toolshed or something?"

"Hang on. I'll go look."

While I'm waiting, I try a few combinations, silly stuff like my birthday and then Granny's birthday which makes me realize she'll be eighty soon. That's old, but not for Granny. She's a force of nature, the kind of woman who will make it to a hundred easy. I can imagine her on one of those Good Morning shows when she's 115, being honored as the oldest living woman. I'd be there too, of course, taking care of her. But something tells me, she'll still be taking care of me too.

How does family go wrong? Granny's the best person I know, yet her son—who I never really did know—managed to fall for my mother, who might not be the actual *worst* person I know (that honor goes to Nesmith), but she's pretty close. She's pretty. That's what everybody says, and sure for forty, I can tell she looks really good. And I imagine that's why Nesmith singled her out over the rest of the women in this county. She's the catch. At least on the outside. On the inside… she's just weak. And it hurts me that she could fall for my father *and* Nesmith. It's this kind of stuff that makes the world a shitty place.

Of course, Granny would tell me the world doesn't owe me an explanation, but that's one of the places where I'd have to disagree with her. I say it does. I haven't had it half as bad as some folks, but my life's definitely had its moments. First my father, then Ben doing his shit, and then the Nesmith and Ruby Jewel stuff, which is why I'm here, trying to break into somebody's cabin.

Elijah comes back around the corner, holding a sledgehammer. "Well, ain't that a sight for sore eyes," I say and put the lock box down on the concrete porch.

He comes up, lifts the sledgehammer high and brings it down, smashing that little box to a thousand pieces.

8

AFTER FIGURING OUT where to turn the hot water on and rummaging through drawers in the two bedrooms to find clean clothes, we both take showers. When I'm done, I pull on a pair of almost new looking panties that are a little too big for me, but not so big they won't stay up. I find some blue jeans that are too long, but I roll up the legs. I'm out of luck with bras. Whoever's stuff I'm going through has bigger boobs than me, so I put on two t-shirts, and hang my bra across the shower rack to dry.

When I exit the bedroom, I find Elijah wearing an oversized t-shirt and short pants he's pulled tight with a drawstring. He's standing in the kitchen, staring into a mostly empty pantry.

"There's coffee, three slices of almost moldy bread, a half a jar of peanut butter, and a can of tuna fish."

"How about pain medicine? Tylenol? Advil?"

He shakes his head. "I couldn't find any. Not even any alcohol."

"Anything good in the fridge?"

He steps over to open it. "Soda. Some butter."

"Freezer?"

He pulls the door open wide so I can see inside. "Ice cream. Pistachio."

"I want that."

He gives me a look.

"For starters."

We sit at a big table beside a big window and watch the rain hit the lake. It isn't until I take the first bite of ice cream that I realize just how extreme my hunger is. Elijah is eating the peanut butter on a piece of bread and drinking a coke.

"No phone," he says between bites.

"Yeah, folks don't bother with them these days. They just bring their cell phones."

He shakes his head and spoons more peanut butter onto the bread.

"I was thinking," he says, "that we should probably head down to the cabin with the truck and ask for help."

"No."

"But why? Look, I get that you're on the run, and maybe you have some trust issues, and that's…" He shakes his head. "That's fine, but not everybody is out to get you. Whoever is staying there will probably have a phone. We can call for a ride. We can call the police about your… uh, situation. Tell me why that's a bad idea."

I glare at him. "It just is, okay. It's a bad fucking idea. Like the worst."

He grimaces as he chews his sandwich and chases it with the coke. "So, what's your plan?"

"Get some sleep. Wake up before light and head to the barn where you left your stuff. Then we'll get your car."

HOLY GHOST ROAD

"And then what?"

"I just need you to take me across the river, into Cullman County."

"River?"

I nod. "The Tuskahatchee. It forms the border between the two counties."

"And what's in the other county? Why will you be safe there?"

"Never mind that. The important thing is that's where we can part ways. I help you. You help me."

He's quiet for a moment, and I can almost see the wheels turning in his head.

"You trust me enough to travel with you, but not enough to tell me what you're running from or where you're running to. You're an interesting human, Forest."

"It's not about trust."

"Then what?"

"My business is my own. Besides, you wouldn't believe it anyway."

"Perhaps I could help you not believe it, too."

Damn, that's tempting. I don't want to believe I saw what I saw, but I also can't make sense of the world through the lens of what I want.

"I'm going to get some sleep," I say. "We need an alarm or something."

"I'll wake you. I usually only sleep for a few hours at a time."

"Okay. It should take us a while to get from here to the Ramey Place, so maybe wake me at nine?"

He looks at his watch, caressing it with his right hand. "Got it."

"Which room do you want?"

He shakes his head. "Either."

"Okay. I'm going to the master."

"Hold it." He goes to the pantry and rummages around for a plastic bag. He finds two and double bags them. Then he opens the freezer and gets out an ice tray. He breaks the ice out of the tray and into the bag over the sink and ties the bag off. "Sleep with this on your ankle. At least as long as you can take it. And find some pillows to elevate it. In the meantime, I'll see if I can find something around here to use as a crutch."

"Great." I hobble toward the master bedroom, but pause before going in. "Thanks, Elijah."

"You're welcome."

I linger. For some reason I want to tell him the truth about Nesmith. The desire is sudden, and I realize there could be relief in telling someone else, that holding in the weirdness, the evil, isn't healthy. We're meant to talk about the things that scare us, the things that chase us, at least it seems to me.

"What?" he says.

"The man and the woman who are coming after me, he's a preacher named Nesmith. He's... he's sleeping with my mother. He's got her fooled, and I caught him... in the barn doing something he shouldn't have been doing. And he knows it. So, he wants to get to me before I get to where I'm going."

"Cullman, right?"

"Yeah. My grandmother's farm."

"You'll be safe there?"

HOLY GHOST ROAD

I nod.

"Well, I'll do my best to help you get there safely."

"And we'll get your car and your phone."

"Yeah." He smiles and shakes his head, looking a little ashamed. "I guess I'm sorta lost without them."

We wish each other good night, and I fall into the big king bed, asleep even before my head hits the pillow.

9

IT'S THE DOOR closing that bring my eyes open wide, makes me gasp and sit up in the bed. Something's happening, something right under my nose.

Footsteps out in the main room. I rise and slide across the hardwood floor in socked feet. I unlock the bedroom door and open it enough to see that the lights are still on out in the den. Stupid. Good way to attract unwanted attention. I swing the door open and see Elijah standing in the kitchen with a cup of coffee. "Hey."

"Where have you been?"

"Oh, well, I was about to wake you. We're going to be okay. Help is on the way."

"What did you do?"

He steps back from me, and I remember once how Ben told me I could be really scary when I got mad. *For a little girl, you don't play.*

I'm not playing now. I lean in. He backs up some more. I speak through gritted teeth. "What in the *fuck* did you do?"

"Take it easy. I know you've got trust issues, but they're misplaced. I just walked down to the other cabin and borrowed the gentleman's cell phone. He was very friendly."

I feel all the blood rush to my face, my forehead. I feel like the pressure of my anger and dismay is going to blow the top of my head right off. Deep breaths. One, and then another. They don't help. "Who did you call?"

"Don't worry. I called the police. Sheriff said he'll send somebody right out."

For what seems like a full minute, I don't say anything. I'm so angry, I might say something I'll regret. Or worse, I might haul off and hit him. So, I just stare, bite my lip until I can taste the blood. That's a comfort for some reason. It steadies me.

"I ain't going with the police."

"That's just foolish."

"Maybe for you it's foolish, but for me it's staying alive. Nesmith runs this county. I mean *all* of it. The damned sheriff is a deacon in his church. They're like fucking best friends. You think he's not going to take me right to Nesmith?"

"I think you might be a little paranoid. Even if that were the case, I'll be with you. I'll demand you stay with me. We'll get the officer to take us to the barn and then to my car."

"And then what? Even if this 'officer' were the most honest damn man in the world, he wouldn't leave me, a fifteen-year-old girl, with you, a full-grown man. It don't work like that."

HOLY GHOST ROAD

"And why do you think your grandmother is going to be able to help you when nobody else can?"

"Because she's special. You wouldn't understand."

"Try me."

I laugh. "Okay. She's got power. Sacred magic. She knows how to find the Holy Ghost. People don't mess with her."

He stares at me. "You're kidding right?"

"Fuck you," I say. "I'm outta here."

I grab my bag and go to the pantry. I throw what's left of the peanut butter and the can of tuna fish inside. Then I head to the fridge and grab the four remaining cokes. "If anybody asks, you didn't see me. Can you at least handle that?"

"Wait a damned minute."

"I don't have a minute, damned or otherwise." I head out the door, stepping over the smashed lock box. My ankle is killing me, but that's probably because I'm trying to walk normally. I'll need to hop, which is going to be tough. It's that, or deal with the pain. I choose pain.

I head down to the lake and follow the shoreline in the direction of Cullman. When I glance back at the cabins, I see the blue lights of a police car, and that spurs me to move faster. The pain in my ankle responds immediately, ramping itself up to extreme levels. I ignore it and keep moving.

Leaving Elijah is harder than I would have expected. He was nice. Never tried nothing funny, or even looked at me like so many men do who should know better. Most of all, I found him fascinating. And maybe there's a part of me that wanted to help him a little. He didn't believe in nothing except logic, and I feel like I know a little something about belief.

Not to mention I lost my damn ride.

I glance back again. Someone is running along the shoreline behind me. For a moment, I'm sure it's the police, but then I moonlight shining off his bald head and I know Elijah's had a change of heart.

10

"**WHAT ARE YOU** doing?" I say as he braces me so I can take the pressure off my foot.

"I decided to trust you," he says. "Set a good example. And… if I'm being honest, I had a flash of…" He shakes his head.

"Of what?"

"Never mind."

"Intuition. That's what you were going to say."

"No. I just decided you needed me more than I needed my car."

I'm grateful, but don't know how to tell him. It's not a way I'm used to feeling.

"Hill coming," Elijah says. "You ready?"

"Yeah." I hold on to him and hop. We're climbing Devil's Bluff now. It earned its name when years ago some good Christian folk claimed there were devil worshipers using it to make sacrifices. This is the kind of shit Elijah won't believe, but I'm not making it up. It was back in the seventies, I think. There are rocks all along the top of the bluff that let you look out over the lake. Stories go that these Satanists made sacrifices on the rocks with knives or axes or whatnot and then tied weights to the bodies and dumped them over right into the lake.

Do I believe the stories? That's a good question. I suppose I neither believe nor disbelieve them. Granny's taught me the danger of thinking about things too literally. For a while that was a tough one for me, but eventually I came to understand. Some things ain't true in a literal sense but might be true in another one. Granny said there were planes of thought and planes of reality. And if a person could learn to navigate them properly, that person could do just about anything.

So, if I'm to take that line of thinking and apply it to Devil's Bluff, I reckon there was indeed some kind of sacrifice that went on there. Maybe it involved rolling bodies into the lake and maybe it didn't. Maybe those that were doing the sacrifices were doing them for Satan, but most likely they were doing them for themselves. And maybe what I saw in the barn was the literal and figurative getting mixed up in my head, in the moments between dreaming and being awake. I don't know.

But I'm not sure it matters. Not for my purposes. For my purposes, I'm sure Nesmith is messing with things he shouldn't be. Magic, but not the sacred kind. It's all about purpose. You can reach into the darkness and pull something literal out of the figurative, screwing up the fabric of reality, but the real question ain't so much what you're reaching for, but why you want it. Are you trying to make the world a better place for everyone, or just for you at the *expense* of everyone?

One way or another, magic always seems to be tied up with sacrifice. Either the kind you make yourself or the kind you force upon someone else.

HOLY GHOST ROAD

I stop walking. We're halfway up the hill. The highway is in sight. There's also a gas station that sells bait and tackle and snacks called Devil's Bluff Shop and Stop.

"What?" Elijah says.

"Just thinking," I say. What I don't say is that I feel like I've put a lot of what Granny taught me into words, and I don't want to forget it. It's the part about what you're using the power for. Something clicks into place, and for a second this crooked world seems a little straighter. Or no. Maybe I just see it straight, maybe I am finally realizing just because the world is crooked doesn't mean there still isn't a straight path we can take.

But right now, my path is taking me up this bluff, and I realize if I'm going to make it much further, I'm going to need some pain meds.

"You ain't got no money?" I ask Elijah as we skirt the parking lot of the Devil's Bluff Shop and Stop.

"It was in my wallet."

"Shit. I need some Tylenol or something."

He takes a deep breath. "Right. I get that."

"Can you get me some?"

"What? Me? Why do I have to get it?"

"People don't know you. Nesmith's probably got the whole county looking for me."

"I've never stolen anything in my life."

I grimace. Partly so he'll know how much I need the pain meds, and partly because I just need to grimace. "Don't think of it as stealing. Think of it as helping."

He shrugs. "I wouldn't know how to even do that."

"It's easy. Go in. Go in with a purpose, okay? Like, don't wander. That's suspicious. You gotta move like you're going somewhere. Sell it. The bathroom. That's how you do it. Walk in like you need to use the bathroom. On the way there, don't break your stride and just grab the pills. Keep them in your hand, your palm until you make it to the toilet. Then put them in your pocket. When you come back out, don't hesitate. Just straight out the door."

He studies the store, maybe trying to envision how it will happen.

"Sometimes they keep that stuff behind the counter. What if it's there?"

"Then it's there. But you ain't gonna know until you go in."

"Where will you be?"

I look around. I've been here before. There're two doors. One on the gas pump side and one on the lake side. "I'll wait at the other door. The one on the lake side. Come around when you're finished. We can keep to the bluff."

"Okay." He takes another deep breath.

"Hey," I say. "This ain't a big deal. You already trusted your intuition once tonight."

"That's not what happened."

"Bullshit it ain't."

He lets his expression break. Just a bit. Enough to let me know maybe I'm right.

"All that logic ain't always so logical," I say, and then start around to the rear of the store. I don't look back. Like I said before, it's weird, but I trust Elijah.

11

THERE'S A WHOLE set-up back here. A couple of picnic tables and some steps leading down to something a sign calls, *The Devil's Rock.* Only in Winston County could a gas station double as a tourist attraction. But none of that's as interesting as the other thing I spot back here.

A payphone.

I don't even give it a second thought. I dial 1-800-COLLECT, using the method Granny taught me if I ever needed to get in touch with her. Usually, I'd walk to the little bait shop by my house and call her. Mama says I don't need a phone until I'm sixteen, but I don't think it's actually about her making a decision she thinks is in my best interest, as much as it is she just doesn't want the expense.

Granny accepts the call and asks me where I am.

"That Devil's Gas Station."

"You ain't making good time."

"I hurt my ankle."

"How bad?"

"Pretty bad."

"And that man who was about to grab you? You ran right past him, didn't you?"

I smile, remembering how she'd told me on our last call I'd make it. "Yeah, I did, Granny."

"Yeah, you sure did. And now, you're going to meet this next challenge too because that's what you do, Forest. You meet challenges. You ain't one of those people who pulls away and says something's too hard. You dig in. You hear me? You dig in."

"Yes ma'am."

"Good. Now, what else? I can tell something else is on your mind."

She's right, of course, but I don't know how to say it.

"Go on. This call ain't cheap."

I smile again. Granny's always been a cheapskate.

"I'm starting to remember things."

"What kind of things?"

"My dreams. I mean dream*walks*. The other night... in the barn... what I saw in there..."

"I know exactly what you saw, girl. Know it better than you."

"How?"

"Don't worry about that. When it comes to you, it'll come. It's one of those things, the more you think on it, the more it slips away. Gotta wait on it, like a ghost you see out of the corner of your eye."

I want to ask her more. I want to beg her to explain, but I know Granny too well. Once she'd made her mind up about a thing, there's no use in arguing. She's got the willpower of a mountain.

"There's something else bothering you. Go on. Let it out."

She was right. Again. "I'm worried that I'm bringing trouble to your door, Granny. The preacher, Nesmith, is after me. He's going to follow me until he catches me or..."

"Or what?"

"I was hoping, if you can't tell me how it started, you could at least tell me how it's going to end."

"Forest, you know I can't do that. Even if I was capable, I wouldn't do it because life's got to be lived. Just remember what I told you. Keep digging."

"Okay, Granny."

"Now, there's something that's been bothering me."

This is new. Nothing ever bothers Granny. "Ma'am?"

"It ain't enough for you just to come here."

I wait, utterly confused as to what she's talking about.

"I'm gonna need you to bring me something."

"Okay..."

"Remember the dreamstone I made you when you was just a girl?"

"I remember."

"Where is it?"

"It's beside my bed where you told me—" I stop. Actually, I realize it's not there. It hasn't been there for some time. Days. Maybe weeks.

"Go on," Granny says.

"I don't know where it is."

"Exactly. I gave it to you for a reason. You need it. *I* need it."

"Well, where can I find it?"

"I reckon you'll figure that part out. But Nesmith is tougher than you think. We can take him down, but not without that."

"Okay," I say. "I'll bring it." I have no idea how I will fulfill this promise. I start to ask her for more details, for something that will help me locate it, but she cuts me off.

"You better go. The lake ain't as cold…" The line crackles and I lose her for a second.

"What?"

"The lake ain't as cold as you think this time of year."

The line goes dead. Granny's been cryptic before. It's sort of who she is, I guess, but this takes it to a new level. *The lake ain't as cold as you think this time of year.* What the hell does that even mean?

Should I be worried it's taking Elijah so long? He's nowhere to be seen, which just means he's in the bathroom. Probably actually taking a piss. There's a grinding sound from out in front of the store. Headlights sweep through the front windows and out the back, going over me where I stand.

A big truck parks, its engine still idling. A man hops out and I tense; even though I can't see his face because it's covered by the snack specials hanging in the front windows of the store, I can see his shoulders and midsection as he walks to the door. I know that walk. That build. I've got to hide.

The steps lead down to the Devil's Rock. I take them two at a time until I'm on the rock, pressed against the iron rails, looking out over the drop. *This is the place they rolled the bodies off,* I think. *Once they were sacrificed for whatever it is people get sacrificed for.*

HOLY GHOST ROAD

It's at least fifty feet down, maybe more. Moonlight reveals rocks down below, more than one or two. There's a ding as the back door to the store opens. I realize I probably made a mistake coming down here. Only one way to run, and that's back up the steps. Something tells me Helmet isn't going to let me make it past him twice.

But there's another way, right? I turn to the lake below. *The lake ain't as cold as you think this time of year.*

No. *Hell* no. That's a death sentence.

Granny had to mean something else.

Footsteps on the concrete above me. I crouch down next to the railing, try to make myself small.

Helmet inhales deeply, breathing in the night. The air is warm for October. It's a beautiful night, now that the rain has passed, and for a moment it's easy to let myself believe he's just come out to look at the moon, to admire the lake, to take a moment. But then I remember who it is, and how he doesn't seem like the type to enjoy anything.

No, he smells me. I don't know how, but he does.

He's coming down the steps now, and I've got a decision to make.

I stand up and evaluate the drop again.

Fuck.

I can't do it. I just can't. Maybe if Granny were here to push me, to tell me it's going to be okay, that it's just what's in my head that I'm scared of and not the reality of the thing, I might be able to do it. But as it stands, I'm going to have to fight.

His expression is grim in the moonlight, like a man for whom words are a waste. The sounds they make are meaningless, just more noise that can't come close to competing with a world of raw physicality, a material world of blood and bone.

There's something else there this time. In his eyes. Recognition. He sees me differently now. He may have underestimated me before. I was a girl, just a little thing. Now he knows I have grit, and that makes me feel good.

"You don't have to do this," I say. "I don't know what that asshole is holding over you, but you don't have to be this way. You were a good man once. I heard you were a hero over there. It's not fair to come back and find your life has been swept out from under you."

Uh-oh. I realize too late I've said the wrong thing. He picks up his speed, skipping the last few steps altogether and lands on the rock with a silence I find more unnerving than him being close. What is he, some kind of ghost? A large man like this should make a sound. He reaches for me, and I try to kick him in the balls. I miss, my foot glancing harmlessly off one of his hard thighs. My bad foot isn't ready to stabilize such a kick and I collapse right there on the rock. My face hangs out over the drop, and as I feel his big hands grab me, I tell myself I should have jumped when I had the chance.

He's so fucking strong, I'm like a toy in his hands. He flips me over even as I pound and beat on his chest and face and slings me across his shoulders. He carries me like a man might carry a fallen tree, my face toward the moon, my fists continuing to pound his back, but I don't think he feels the blows at all.

It's only when he turns to head to the stairs that I realize he can be hurt.

HOLY GHOST ROAD

He gasps, and then staggers back. Elijah stands a few steps up from us, holding a lead pipe. I don't know where he got it or how he managed to hit Helmet, but he did, and now he's lining up another swing.

This next swing catches Helmet's knee and there's a crack. It's enough to knock Helmet off balance. He stumbles down the concrete steps and drops me. For a horrifying, lurching second, I'm positive I'm going over the side, to make the long fall into the lake. Instead, my chest lands on the top rail, knocking the wind out of me.

For a time, me and Helmet are both laying there, face to face, eye to eye. He doesn't look surprised. He just looks sad. I scramble to my feet as my breath comes rattling back. I cough and sputter and try to kick him in the face, but he catches my foot and holds on to it. He uses it to push me toward the lake, flipping me like I'm a lever, until my head hangs out over the dark water upside down.

"Put her down," a voice calls from near the top of the steps.

I don't even need to look to know who it is.

A hand scoops me upright and sets me down on my feet. My bad ankle protests, but I just let it. No way I'm not going to stand straight up and face these assholes.

Elijah takes the last few steps in a single leap. When Helmet reaches for him, he swings the pipe, keeping him at bay. He works his way next to me in this way, until both of our backs are to the long drop.

Helmet reaches for him with a big hand, and I swear he means to engulf Elijah's head and pop it like a zit, but Nesmith whistles sharply.

"Leave them to me."

It's like Helmet is a guard dog or something. He just stops, retreats up the steps and stands beside Nesmith on his left. On Nesmith's right is Ruby Jewel. Of course.

Nesmith grins.

"You have been quite the rebellious young lady, Forest. Perhaps it's the Redwine in your blood. They never were much for submitting to God's will."

I'm about to snap back at him, but he shakes his head quickly, and it's like my breath is gone and I don't have enough air to say the words.

"And now look at you. Running away. Foolish actions from a foolish girl. I'll take you home now. Your mother is worried." This is how he speaks. *I'll take you home now.* As if it's a foregone conclusion I'll go with him, as if there's no reasonable way I can resist. And he's right. At least as far as lot of folks are concerned. But not me. Granny told me right away what he does to people is a kind of glamour, a spell even, and that by practicing telling him no on the small things, the bigger ones would be easier. I kept it simple and told him no nearly every time he spoke to me, which caused a lot of strife at home, but makes it easy for me to just ignore him now. Though, I can tell his spell is messing with Elijah, at least a little. It's in his body language. All the confidence he'd found when he attacked Helmet moments earlier has transformed into a trembling uncertainty.

Granny's words come back to me now with the power of a bullet right to my brain.

The lake ain't as cold as you think this time of year.

I nudge Elijah.

"What," he says out of the side of his mouth.

HOLY GHOST ROAD

Meanwhile, Nesmith is talking about how worried my mother is, how she's only ever wanted the best for me, and how that's all he wants too. Casting that spell.

"Going over," I say. "You should do it too."

"What?"

Nesmith stops his speech.

"No, child, you do not want to do that."

Hearing him say those words, hearing him tell me what *I* fucking want to do with such absolute confidence, only makes me want to jump more.

I climb up on the rail.

"Are you sure about this?" Elijah says. He looks like he wants to come with me. There's something in his eyes. I can tell he wants to take a chance, but he's also drawn to the calm reason Nesmith emits. I hold out my hand.

"Fuck," Elijah says, and grabs my hand. We stand up on the rail together, balancing.

"Stop them!" Nesmith says, and that gets Helmet moving like he's been shot out of gun.

"On the count of three," I say, but Elijah has other ideas. He squeezes my hand and says, "Jump far. Avoid the rocks." And then he lets go of my hand and leaps.

There's a splash far below. Over my shoulder, I see Helmet reaching for me. It's now or never. I decide now is best and jump.

Mama's People

1

FALLING IS LIKE a dreamwalk.

Everything that was once familiar turns strange. The air bends around me, and it's impossible to tell if I'm falling into the sky or out of it. The wind stops my ears, makes every sound vanish. Trees flash by. And lights. So many lights, none of which I can make sense of. They just streak my field of vision like messages I can't decode. And just when I acclimate to this new world of motion and silence, the water beneath my feet explodes, and I'm awake again.

Cold and awake.

And alive.

Takes a minute for me to be sure, but it's true. Only my ankle hurts, and there's a ton of water up my nose, but other than that I'm fine. I'm okay.

I come up for air, and as soon as I pull in some, I call out for Elijah.

He doesn't answer.

It's so dark, I'll never find him if he doesn't answer, so I just keep calling out.

Some time later (it seems like minutes, but is probably only seconds), there's a splash to my left and then a deep gasp followed by coughing.

I swim over. He's alive but can't talk. There's a lot of sputtering and splashing, so I just reach for him and try to wrap him up in my arms. Eventually, his breathing evens out and he stops flailing.

"I'm okay. I'm okay. I'm..." He leans his head up and looks back toward the rock at the top of the bluff. "We need to go."

He's right. I'm surprised Nesmith hasn't already sent Helmet after us. Maybe he thinks we're dead.

"We need to go," Elijah repeats, but he seems incapable of moving.

"Swim," I say. "That way."

He looks across the lake. Or tries to. There's nothing to see but water forever.

The other side of the lake is a long way off. The other side of the lake is the kind of swim that can kill a person. I know people who've done it, but I never have.

Another idea hits me, though almost as soon as it does, I second-guess myself.

"We need to move," he says, peering back toward the bluff. "Somewhere."

I nod. "Okay. I think I can find it."

"Find what?"

"The island."

HOLY GHOST ROAD

"How far?"

"We can make it," I say, and I feel pretty sure it's the truth. What I'm not as sure about is if I can find it, but I figure we've got a decent chance if we swim straight. I remember visiting once and sitting out on the little dock while everybody got drunk and high. I could just see Devil's Bluff across the lake.

"Follow me," I say.

I realize I'm still holding onto him. Other than climbing, swimming is probably what I'm best at. Growing up near Smith Lake, swimming was something you just learned.

I let go of him. "You can swim underwater, right?'

He nods.

"Good. It's only until we get a little further out into the lake, so they won't see us."

And just as I say that a flashlight beam canvasses the silken surface. It's weak, especially from this distance, but we still need to get under the water and stay there for as long as possible.

I pull him down and start to swim away from the 278 side of the lake and toward an island I thought I'd never visit again.

2

DIGGING THROUGH THE water feels good. It's a place where my injured foot barely slows me at all. I pull the water around me with long strokes and keep gliding just beneath the surface until my lungs begin to burn, and only then do I come up, sucking in a great gasp of the night.

I pause long enough to sense Elijah moving through the water a few yards behind me. A quick glance back to the rock and the moving light and I go under again, digging, pulling, unsure how I even got here.

Two nights ago, I was in my own bed, my life was... is *normal* the word I want to use? No. My life was ordinary, but there was still something beneath the surface, something unsettling. For one thing, I'd stopped remembering my dreamwalks. It was the medicine that did it. Klonopin. That's the stuff Nesmith brought home. Said it would help my anxiety. Except I didn't feel anxious until I started taking the damned stuff. And I really did take it too. At least for a while.

Seems strange to me now I'd ever take those pills, but I guess I must have once believed there was something wrong with me, that it was me and not the world that was wrong. So, I tried them. For a while. At some point, I couldn't tolerate them anymore. I don't know if it was the way they made me feel or just some newfound confidence that helped me understand I wasn't wrong. After that, I just started flushing them.

Maybe that has something to do with why the memory from the barn is fragmented. The dreams seemed to stop when I was on the meds. But did they really? Maybe they continued all along, but had been hidden from me, lost under a heavy veil of medication. Maybe the other night was the first time my head had cleared enough to remember a dreamwalk, even if it had only been bits and pieces of one.

It makes sense. I almost wish it didn't, because it means I've likely been to the barn before. That I've probably knelt before the goat demon, beneath its black horns.

The water suddenly feels colder than before. I come up for air and try to get my bearings. Nothing but darkness in all directions. Off to my left, Elijah glides soundlessly through the water.

My mind turns back to the phone call with Granny, her admonition to find the dreamstone. She'd given me that years ago, when I'd first started dreamwalking. She claimed she'd made it for me, carved its shape out of a larger rock and smoothed its edges with the labor of her own hands.

I put a little bit of my own essence in it, she'd told me. *Some blood from my veins so that when we're apart, I can still look out for you.* As long as I slept near it, the stone would keep me safe. It least that was what it was supposed to do, according to Granny.

I'd placed it on my nightstand without too much thought, and then slept beside it for several years. Then, one day it was gone. I'd noticed, of course, but it was the kind of thing I forgot almost as soon as I noticed.

Now, I realize the stone went missing shortly after Nesmith moved in.

Other than that, I can't say how long it's been gone. Why haven't I thought to look for it before now? So many questions. Very few answers.

And what possible good can the stone do me now?

I sigh with frustration. Sometimes Granny's requests just don't make sense. And how am I supposed to get it back, assuming he even has it? I swim some more, trying to not think about it too much. Let it come, like Granny always preaches.

Seems like hours we're slogging through the water, its silken coolness becoming a part of us, just like the stars and the moon. I find a place of peace, where the black-horned thing can't touch me. It's like Granny's place will be, a kind of heaven without dying. That's the only kind I could ever make sense of anyway. If the dreamwalks are seeing the world like it really is, dying is not seeing anything at all. Blank darkness, thicker than this lake.

An outboard motor vibrates the water, fills up my ears. Could it be Nesmith already? For a horrible instant, I see both Elijah and me cut up by the propellers, the dark water going darker. Me and Ben used to hear cautionary tales of the kids who swam too close to idling boats and ended up getting chopped up like meat in a grinder when the driver decided to engage the outboard motor.

Nesmith could say it was an accident. Every damn person in this county would believe him. That's the frustrating part, at least to me.

Why people are so willing to suspend their disbelief over that asshole. Must be they want a piece of what he has, or maybe it's just the demon working like demons do.

I feel Elijah's hand on my shoulder. He pulls me back, so we're nowhere near to the boat as it blows past.

The driver is a young man, holding a cigarette. His hair is long and blows in the dark wind, shines in the moon glow. Beside him are two girls, probably my age, huddled together because it's too cold to be out on the lake unless you've got a really good reason. Like a party. There's always a party down at Rocky Face Point. It's a jumping rock where the teenagers like to go and act stupid, get drunk, and have sex.

I've been once or twice. Okay, exactly twice. It was after Ben vanished, after Nesmith moved in with Mama, and I was pretty damned low. Look, I ain't judging it. For a bunch of kids, that's their thing. It's fun. It's what they want.

Thing is, I didn't want it, and I guess that's why I went. Because I just wanted to feel bad. It's a weird thing when you think about it, to feel so bad that all you can do is try to feel worse. Doesn't make a lot of sense, but in my fifteen years in this county, I ain't seen very much that does.

Except for Granny. And once upon a time, Ben made sense too.

We're swimming normal now, above the water, the bluff seemingly miles behind us, but I know it's probably only half that or less. Still, we're free out here.

Half an hour later, we're both tired of swimming, so we float for a bit. I lay on my back, trying to be as still as possible. The stars go on forever, and endless spiral in the sky.

"I can't believe I did that," Elijah says.

"Me either. You must have believed in something."

He's quiet. The water laps around my ears. God, I could stay here forever. The sky and the lake and the moon and the stars almost seem like one entity, no up or down, south or north, right or left. Soon enough, time'll be gone too, and that'll be heaven, I think.

"I never said I don't believe in anything. I just don't believe in the things you can't prove."

"Like God and magic and werewolves, right?"

"Well, I'd argue none of those things can be proven, so I suppose you are correct."

"So, if you don't believe in none of that, what do you believe in?"

"Facts. Logic. Science."

"Don't forget your phone."

He's quiet, quiet enough to make me wish I'd kept that last bit to myself.

"Maybe you're right. Maybe I do believe in my phone. It keeps me connected. It keeps me centered."

"That's how all the other stuff is for me."

"Other stuff?"

I turn over and begin to swim again. Slowly. I wait until I hear him following behind me before answering.

"Werewolves, magic, God."

"You're serious?"

"Maybe. Yeah."

"I don't understand."

"Maybe when you meet Granny, you will."

"You really think she can protect you from Nesmith?"

I let the question linger a bit. Maybe because it's a question that's been on my mind a lot lately. What if I'm just bringing trouble to her door? What if even Granny can't overcome the power Nesmith found in the barn? And what about the dreamstone? If I'm being totally honest, her request that I bring the dreamstone doesn't exactly square with the idea she can handle anything. I mean, why would *she* need a dreamstone? The more I think about this question, the more it bothers me.

But if I say any of this to Elijah, it'll make it seem more real. Better to fake it until you make it. That's something Granny used to say too. I usually applied it to faking happiness at social events, and it really *did* seem to make a difference.

"Granny's got a different kind of power."

"And what kind is that?"

"Sacred power."

"Like from God?"

"Yeah."

"So, that surprises me. Seems like you'd be against what Nesmith is for. Isn't he some kind of preacher?"

"Yeah, some kind."

"So, why is he chasing you?"

"I saw something I shouldn't have seen."

"What, did you catch him having sex or something?"

"I think he's been using me."

"Using you? Are we talking about sex or not?"

"I don't think so. It's something else."

"What?"

"You won't believe me." I mean that, but it's also a cop-out. The truth is, I don't know how to explain he was using me. I'm not even sure how I know. It just sort of came to me.

The greatest secrets are the ones we keep from ourselves, Granny said once.

Jesus, I swear sometimes I could write a book with all her sayings. *"The Book of Granny and the Holy Ghost."* And it would be my own personal scripture.

"Okay," Elijah says, stuck on what I'm not telling him. "But I'm still curious. I understand why you didn't tell me before, but I think I've sort of earned your trust now."

"Like I said before, it ain't about trust."

"It's always about trust. You're afraid that if you tell me, I'll think you're crazy and then I won't help you anymore. Well, you don't have to worry about that. I already think you're crazy. Besides, you're helping me too. Remember? I've got..."

"You've got what?" I ask as I stop swimming. I feel like he's gonna say something important.

"I was just going to say, I've got a good feeling about you."

"Feeling, huh? That don't seem too logical."

"I suppose it's not. Let me try to rephrase. You're tough. You've got mental toughness. Fortitude. That's rare these days, and I respect that."

I start to swim again, and the next time I come up for air, there it is. Land. It has to be the island. Well, it doesn't *have* to be, but it *should* be. The other side of the lake should still be miles away.

I swim faster, feeling a burst of sudden energy now that I've made it.

When we reach the beach, the cold hits us hard. I start shaking and so does Elijah.

"We need to find some new clothes."

"Where we gonna do that?"

"Aren't there some lake houses we can break into?"

"Nope, it's just trailers and broken-down docks on this island."

"Well, people in trailers have clothes."

"I ain't stealing from people in trailers."

"Fair. I get that. Maybe somebody would just help us out then."

I don't like where this is going. He's right. These clothes are going to cause us both to freeze if we don't get some dry ones soon. The worst part is I know right where we could get some, but it will mean confronting something I don't want to confront. It'll mean making this already impossibly twisty journey even more twisted.

"What are you doing?"

"Taking off my shirt. We've got to dry off."

"Shit. Keep it on." I point up the beach a little. "That way. If we move fast, we'll be there in no time."

"Where's there?"

"I got kin on this island."

"What? Someone you can trust?"

HOLY GHOST ROAD

I think about how to answer. It's a hell of a question.

"No, but at least they ain't under Nesmith's spell."

"What's that supposed to mean?"

"I need help. You gonna help me or are you gonna ask questions all night?"

He comes over and I brace myself against him. We start moving, and quickly fall into a familiar rhythm. I decide to ask Granny about him the next time I talk to her. At first, I didn't think too much about Elijah. Just happenstance, right? But what if he was sent to help me out. And me to help him. It's sort of like we need each other, and a few days ago I would have said that's a bad way to be. Now… well, now I ain't so sure what I think.

3

MAMA'S WHAT'S CALLED a Gazaway around here, which in this county might as well be redneck for wild and crazy with a tendency to steal and do drugs. They're petty thieves by trade, though there's been a few exceptions to the family curse. Mama for one. She never held with the stealing, and actually went to school. That's where she met my father, in history class, the way the story goes. But Mama has her own issues, as we all do. She's always liked fancy things, and to be in charge. She's always wanted to be up above others, be better than, and to me that's worse than stealing. But either way, she escaped, found herself a better life across the lake.

There's Moatee too. She's Mama's cousin, who made it all the way to New York. She writes poetry and lives in an apartment overlooking the city. She sends pictures every Christmas along with some of her poems.

But that's the only two people I know of who ever got out. The rest of them found their lives to be easiest in squalor, more tolerable with drugs.

I have never liked coming to see Mama's people. She has six brothers in all, and one of them, Monty, is only about a year older than me. He doesn't seem bothered by the fact that he's my uncle. He tried to kiss me when I was nine and grabbed my ass on a visit when I was thirteen. Then, the last time I was here about a year ago, he accosted me down by the creek, and if I hadn't been smart enough to bring a knife along with me, there's no telling how that might have ended.

But Monty's only half the problem. There's also Trudy, Mama's only sister. Trudy's as beautiful as any creature you'll ever see, and as wicked too. I've seen her seduce boys and men of all ages just to laugh at them. She doesn't like me any, either. Mama says it's because she's jealous, but I can't believe that. I'm not nearly as pretty as her, I tell Mama.

You're prettier than you think, but even if you weren't she'd be jealous. You're young. She senses her star fading. You know how old she is?

I guess twenty-nine, and Mama laughs.

Try forty-one. She's only a couple of years younger than me.

It's more than a little weird to me a forty-one-year old woman would be jealous of me, and honestly it just makes me feel gross each time I'm around her. I barely have tits for god's sake. And sure, I've noticed boys checking me out me some, and there's always the perverts, but she's a damned goddess. A dark goddess, but certainly not one that should feel any threat from a child like me.

We make good time to what I think of as the compound. There are five trailers in all, housing Lord knows how many Gazaways. I can't keep up.

There's a little slough running between the trailers with a rickety old dock built onto it. Two small boats with outboard motors are tied to it, and I'm hoping they might let me borrow one of those. It's a long shot but we're family after all. I've got to play my cards just so, appeal to the right person, and maybe, just maybe, I can at least talk whoever owns those boats into giving us a ride across the Tuskahatchee and the county line.

There are old boats, parts, and all kinds of outboard motors piled in a big heap on one side of the creek. Something is crawling over one of the outboards with shiny, moon-haunted eyes. A raccoon, I guess, or a bobcat. There's a big mound of trash down by the creek, stacked nearly as high as the second level of the dock. It's in dire need of burning, but as usual, trash is the least of anybody's concern here. The two trailers closest to the creek sit on an incline and appear to be slowly sliding toward the water.

Other than the barking of several dogs as we approach, the place is basically dead. All but one of the trailers are dark.

"What is this place?" Elijah says.

"Welcome to Gazaway World," I say. It's one of the few things I remember about my father. Him calling it that. He died when I was six, so there's not much there. Gazaway World, though, that's something I'll never forget. Always made Mom laugh. Ben too.

It's hard to believe we were a happy family once.

"Where to?"

I think it over. The trailer with the lights on is where Monty lives with a couple of his brothers. I don't want to go there, but I also don't want to wake anyone up. Seems like a bad way to get someone to help you.

"Temperature is dropping," Elijah says. "If these people are family, they'll help."

"Okay," I say. "Follow me."

I hop over to one of the better-maintained trailers and knock loudly on the door. Nothing.

"Knock again," Elijah says.

I knock a second time, loud enough to wake the dead. A light comes on. "Go the fuck to sleep!"

I try the door. It's unlocked, so I push it open.

"Grandpa?"

"Who's there? Allison? Get your ass back to bed."

"It's Forest. Abby's daughter."

"Well, hell. Turn the light on, Missy."

Missy is my Grandpa's fourth or fifth wife. She's been with him for the last few years, and she's probably the best thing that's ever happened to him.

The light comes on, and we can see right into their bedroom. Grandpa's sitting up, a mound of pillows built up behind him for support. Missy is out of bed already. She's a skinny thing, and I glimpse her naked body as she quickly pulls on an oversized t-shirt.

"Lord, close your eyes," she says, but it's too late, we've already seen everything and now she's got the shirt on.

"You in some kind of trouble?" Grandpa says. There is no surprise in his voice, and that hurts me some. It's as if he's always expected this moment to come.

"Yeah," I say. "This is Elijah. He's been helping me, but we need some dry clothes and a ride back across the lake."

Missy steps past us. "You'll fit into Trudy's clothes perfect," she says, touching my arm. I wince, thinking how Trudy will feel about me wearing her clothes, but I don't say nothing. Beggars and choosers and all that.

Missy sizes up Elijah. "Billy. He's not one to share, but he'll be too laid up to know." She pats Elijah's shoulder, and I find myself grateful for Missy. Before she came along, Grandpa might have said something about Elijah's darker complexion, but Missy straightened him out on that front a while back.

Once she's gone, Grandpa opens the drawer beside his bed and lights a joint. He takes a deep toke and holds it out.

I shake my head. Elijah smiles but politely declines.

"Fine," Grandpa says. "But if you want a drink, the liquor's in the kitchen. You'll have to fix it yourself."

Grandpa's lived a hard life, and his face and body show it. His skin is blotchy and thick like cowhide, and his eyes—ever since I can remember they've been like this—are bloodshot and wet. I used to think he was just emotional, until Mama explained how sometimes alcoholics can't stop their tears, and then it made sense because in nearly all of memories of Grandpa, he's holding a glass of something brown. Either that or a whole bottle.

The pot is new, though, probably a healthier alternative Missy introduced him to.

We both decline the liquor, though I'm a little surprised when Elijah seems to genuinely consider it, at least briefly.

"Ain't he a little old for you, girl?" Grandpa says.

"We ain't together."

"You're standing together."

"Right, but he's just a friend."

"Keep it that way, okay? Every damn daughter of mine has got herself wrapped up with an older man. Older men are shit." He takes another toke, holds it in, and then lets it go, coughing a little cough that soon turns into a laugh. "What am I saying, younger men are shit too. This world is a fucking toilet, and we're all turds trying to survive the flush." He smiles at Elijah. "How's that for some philosophy?"

Elijah just nods. He seems a little stunned by this world, but I'm beginning to think he's just perpetually stunned, so what's new?

Missy comes back with the clothes. We thank her and I go into the bathroom and change first. Trudy's clothes are different than what I'd normally wear. The jeans are tight in the ass and low slung, the kind meant to be worn with a halter top. Even the t-shirt is a V-neck that dips way too far toward my boobs. The panties—thank God—are just panties, none of that G-string, thong shit some girls wear.

It feels good to be dry, and all at once I'm sleepy as hell.

"Your turn," I tell Elijah, and drop down onto the couch, knowing I'm going to go to sleep there unless somebody stops me.

And nobody does. I drift away into a dream world. There's water there and I'm swimming through it. Helmet is swimming beside me. Ahead of us is a waterfall, but we don't stop, and I realize sometimes your body does things without your mind. We tumble over the waterfall. Helmet's body bangs against the rocks. I float in the open air, and I realize the sky and the lake are the same thing, have always been the same thing if you believe they are. It's just a dream, no walking tonight.

4

THE BABY IS screaming. Not crying. These are absolute wails from the bottom of an agonized soul.

My eyes flutter open and there's a stain on the ceiling. Brown and big as the couch, it's there and then gone when I see an angry face leaning over me.

"What is she doing here? And why is she wearing my jeans?"

It's Trudy, and I want to go back to sleep so much. The dreams were confusing, but at least they were peaceful.

"Take it easy," a voice says over the screaming baby. It sounds like Missy. "What's wrong with Edie?"

"She just cries all the time. I'm praying about it."

"Let me hold her, okay?"

"Don't you dare." Trudy's voice sounds otherworldly, the way I imagine a demon would sound, so full of rage, it's scary and sad. Maybe the way the black-horned goat demon would sound if it had a voice.

I sit up, feeling sore. My foot is throbbing, but it's less blue than it was before.

"Maybe she's just hungry," Elijah says.

"Who are you?" Trudy's face is blotched with red, and she got veins that throb in her forehead. Her eyes are weary, like she can't imagine dealing with one more damn problem.

"I'm Elijah. I'm with Forest."

"And what's Forest doing here?" Trudy says.

Before I or anyone else can answer her, Grandpa comes out of his room. He's got a coffee cup in one hand and a bottle of Wild Turkey in the other. The bottle is empty.

"Don't worry none about that," he says. "She needed our help. Lord knows you've needed our help before."

"Don't start with me, Daddy."

"Get the boys to bring me some liquor. I'm out. And take that screaming baby out of here. If you don't want nobody else touching her, then keep her the hell at your trailer."

There's something different about Trudy, but I can't say exactly what. There's desperation on her face, and anger, of course, but beyond that— there's something else. A deep kind of sadness, maybe? Or confusion. I can definitely relate to that one.

"Fine," she says, and scoops up the screaming child. She cradles it in her arms and regards it with something that's half hate and half love. The love wins because her face melts a little. "We were just gonna borrow the rocking chair, wasn't we, Edie? Well, if they're going to act like this, we'll just leave." She turns and glares right at me. "You would end up with somebody like that." She continues to glare at me as if waiting on a response, but I've never been one of those people who can let a comeback out. Always seems like the thing I'm about to say is already in the air and saying it would just be restating the obvious.

"That's what I thought," she says, and storms out, slamming the door behind her.

"You shouldn't let her talk at you like that," Grandpa says.

I stare at him openmouthed and remember all at once what's wrong with this family ain't confined to a few nutjobs like Trudy or Marty. No, it runs fucking deep here. All of it.

"What's happening?" Elijah says.

Missy pats his arm. "I liked her better when she was on the pain pills. She's under a different kind of drug now."

"Don't make excuses for her," Grandpa says. "She's made her bed, and now, by God, she's gonna lay in it."

Missy must see the confusion on our faces because she goes in the bedroom and comes out with a bong. She pats the couch beside me, letting Elijah know he should sit. He sits beside me, and she lights a bong and takes a deep huff before passing to Grandpa who sits at the table with a little laptop and opens it up. He goes to some betting site to check his winnings, or more likely, his losings.

"Trudy's oldest, Wanda, got herself pregnant. That's her baby, little Edie." Missy says all of this calmly, matter-of-factly, like she's reading the weather. "About a month or two ago, Wanda takes up with another man. His name is Earnest, and he lives in Cullman, which is all fine and good except that she goes to live with Earnest in Cullman, and Earnest doesn't want the baby, so Wanda just leaves the baby here with us. Well, all of that's bad enough, but then you got the shit with Billy."

"Billy?" I say, interested in this drama despite myself.

"Billy's the father," Grandpa says. "And he's a real turd." After he says it, he glances at the door and then out the window over at Trudy's place. I glance over at Elijah. He's got a pained expression on his face, and I can tell he's thinking the same as me: poor, poor Edie.

"So, Billy decides he wants to know how his little girl is doing. He's the kind of man that once he takes a notion into his head, it's better to not stand in his way, because the more folks stand in his way, the more stubborn he gets. So, he shows up about two weeks ago, demands to know where his child is. Says he won't abide any child of his being raised by heathens."

Missy pauses, takes a deep breath, and fixes me with a look. "You know that preacher everybody's talking about?"

Fear forks through me like lightning. I sit up straight, my body clenching all at once. I nod slowly.

"Brother Nesmith," Grandpa says.

I realize all at once it's been a very long time since me or Mama have been in touch with anyone on the island. Long enough that they don't even know Nesmith is living with us.

Missy takes the bong back from Grandpa and studies it. "That's the one. Anyway, Billy shows up and he finds Edie alone inside of Trudy's trailer, Trudy having stepped out for a minute. So, he just lets himself in.

HOLY GHOST ROAD

Once he finds the child, he holes up inside Trudy's house with it. Won't let nobody in. Except for when the baby starts crying a few hours later. He comes to the door and starts yelling for Trudy. Well, as you can imagine, Trudy is pissed, it being her trailer and all. I try to talk her down, explain Billy don't seem right in the head. That he's gotten mixed up with that preacher. But that just makes Trudy more upset. She means to kick his ass, I think. She busts in there, and there's some yelling and then things get real quiet."

Grandpa laughs. "I called it."

"Called what?" I ask.

"I thought there was going to be trouble," Missy says. "But your granddaddy said they'd be fucking before too long. 'Two peas in a pod,' he said."

"And I was right. Cause if there's one thing the men in that Nesmith cult like, it's women," Grandpa says, turning back to his laptop as if the interesting part of this conversation has ended for him now.

"So now, Trudy is taking care of Wanda's baby and the father of Wanda's baby. And as such, Billy has very strict rules. Can't nobody else touch the baby except for him and Trudy or he goes nuts. He already nearly knocked out Wyatt the other day."

"Why don't you call the police?" Elijah says.

Grandpa smiles. "I reckon you ain't heard of Nesmith, have you?"

Elijah shrugs. "A little."

"Well, he's got the police fooled into thinking if they cross him, they're crossing the Almighty Himself."

I guess I wear my thoughts about that on my face- because Grandpa clears his throat. "We, uh, won't tell him you're here, but I gotta ask… what are you running from?"

"It's complicated," I say, "but we really got to get going. Can you help us?"

Grandpa nods. "My boat won't start. Leaves Billy's and the boys' boat." He shrugs. "I ain't gonna be able to make them. You'll have to ask and hope for the best."

"If they say no?" I'm feeling almost as if this was where Nesmith wanted us to come all along. Is he that powerful? Surely not. Besides, we aren't trapped yet. Billy doesn't know we're here, which means Nesmith doesn't either.

"If they say no, I reckon I got a phone you can use. Or you can swim." He chuckles. "You already did that once."

The thought of swimming across the lake again makes me feel sick. There's no way I could do it today. My body aches from the exertion of the previous night's swim. Maybe tomorrow, but that means hiding out here, and how long before Nesmith figures out where we are and decides to come calling?

No, it's got to be the boat. If we can get the boat, we can make it all the way to the Tuskahatchee in a matter of minutes.

"Who should I talk to?" I ask. "For the boat?"

"Well, it's technically Ralph's boat, but Ralph don't leave the trailer much. The twins stay on the island and hunt and fish, so that leaves

Monty. Monty has sort of become Ralph's go to. He runs errands for him in the boat. I'm thinking he'll have the key."

Missy puts her hand over her heart. "Oh Lord, can you talk to him, honey?"

Grandpa shakes his head. "Boy won't listen to a word I say. You know that."

Missy nods, her eyes getting wet with tears. "Maybe you two better call somebody."

5

WE DECIDE TO have Elijah call one of his friends in Birmingham. Even though his friend doesn't have a boat, he thinks he'll be able to find someone who does. I'm feeling optimistic for the first time in a while. Elijah says if the first friend can't help, there are others he can call.

I'd say what happens next was the unthinkable, but in all honesty, it's about what I've come to expect. Say what you want about Nesmith, but he's got powers. Whether from the goat demon or from Ruby Jewel or maybe just from his own evil heart, it doesn't matter. He's got them.

There's no signal. Not even the first bar on Missy or Grandpa's phones.

"Happens a few times a month," Missy says. "Usually down for a day or two," but I know better. It's Nesmith. Even here, it's him.

I'm so angry, I go to into the bathroom, shut the door and scream into my hand. Once that's out, I look at my face in the mirror and try to find something in my eyes, the set of my jaw, the curve of my lips, something resembling hope or, absent that, something that could be taken for resilience.

And I'm not sure why, but something in my face reminds me of Granny. People say we favor, but I'm not talking about that. No, this is more than just surface appearance. There's anger there, but also determination. That's what reminds me of her. I see the expression on my face, and I see it on hers. I close my eyes and let my mind roll back, images and thoughts flashing like a carousel projector going at high speed, until I see the exact look on her face—and I go there.

Hot summer morning. The sun still angled so that it seems to shine right in our eyes. We're in the garden, been there since daybreak pulling tomatoes from the vine when something rattles close by. I know immediately what it is and I run to Granny, clutch her dress. She's so calm. I remember that best. She isn't the least bit fazed. She just asks me where it is, but I don't want to tell her because I'm afraid. I don't remember if I'm afraid she'll be bitten or if I'm just afraid. She tells me to stay put and goes off hunting for it.

She's carrying a garden hoe, and I'm pretty sure she means to kill it. I'm conflicted about that. I want to be safe, but I don't want the creature to die. I'm relieved when she spots the snake and puts the hoe down. What she does next shocks me. She drops to her knees and faces it at eye level, a grim determination etched across her face.

"Granny," I hiss. "Don't."

She waves me off. A flick of the wrist. The snake watches her with something like bland curiosity. Granny keeps her eyes fixed and moves closer. Closer. She slides her knees through the tilled dirt of the garden ever so slowly, never breaking eye contact. Later, she explains as long as you keep your eyes on the snake's, it isn't as likely to strike. But, the second you look away, it'll kill you sure as anything.

HOLY GHOST ROAD

I watch in utter amazement as she gets near enough to touch the snake, and then does just that. Her hand grips the serpent just behind its head and she lifts it, flickering tongue and all, into the air. She maintains eye contact the whole while, as she holds her arm out and walks to the edge of the garden. She and that rattler staring at each other the whole time. I swear even after she flings it out across the fence line, it's still staring at her as it sails into the woods.

"Did it get scared?" I asked her when she came back.

"The snake?" She chuckled. "No, I don't reckon it did."

"Then..." I shake my head, not even sure how to ask the question that's making me feel anxious.

"Then how did I keep it from striking?"

"Yes ma'am."

"I asked it not to."

My face must make it clear I don't believe her.

"Listen," she says. "If you're about to hit me and I asked you not to, wouldn't that work?"

I shrug. "Maybe."

"Right. If I asked it the right way, you'd listen, right?"

"But that's different."

"How?"

"You didn't say anything to it. Even if you did... I don't think snakes can understand English."

"There's more ways to talk than with your mouth."

This sticks with me the rest of the weekend, and I keep coming back to it, asking her again and again to explain it to me.

It's late on Saturday night when she finally puts it in a way that makes sense, a way I haven't forgotten.

"Look at that stool," she says, pointing at a broken wooden stool sitting in front of her fireplace. "That's what we call material."

"Material?"

"Stuff. You can touch it. Make sense?"

"Okay."

"Me and you and that snake. We're material too."

I nod. That all makes sense too.

"But there's more to me and you and that snake than there is to that stool, right?"

I feel like it's a trick question, so I take a minute to think it over. In the end, I decide there has to be more to us than the stool.

"What's the more?" she asks me. "What's been added to me and you and that snake that isn't in that stool?"

I struggle with this one for a while. First, I say *blood*, but then she points out we can pour blood onto the stool, and it will still just be a stool. Then I say the ability to breathe, and she nods and says, "If that stool could breathe wouldn't it still be a lot different than me and you?"

I tell her I suspect it would.

"Well, what else you got?"

I'm done. She seems done too. Problem is, I still don't understand.

"Granny, what's this got to do with talking to a snake?"

"All I'm saying is that there's more to me and you and that snake than just what you can touch, see, and smell. There's invisible stuff, intangible stuff, and those that can tap into it, can shake the world, girl."

I didn't totally understand even after that, and I still don't now, but I do know hearing her say it made me feel powerful, made me feel strong. And most of all, I don't have to understand it all to believe in it.

So I tell myself while still staring in the mirror inside the trailer's tiny bathroom, that if Granny can deal with the rattler, I imagine she'll be able to deal with Nesmith too. It'll happen in similar fashion. What would cause an ordinary person to wilt beneath the pressure won't even touch her. She'll just do what needs to be done and banish Nesmith and his minions right off her property.

Granny has a saying that strikes me now as appropriate: *I know that I know that I know.* I feel that way about Granny's abilities, her power. I just don't feel it about my own.

6

WITH THE PHONES out and Grandpa's boat dead, I'm stuck with trying to round up Monty for the key.

I'm dreading it so much, I put it off until after we've eaten the eggs Missy cooks for us. And even then, I have to tell Elijah to stay put. The brothers will eat him alive. I don't tell him that, but maybe he gets a sense of it. He's frowning a little as I leave him sitting on Grandpa's couch to limp across the creek to the most derelict looking trailer I've ever seen.

"Hold it," Missy says.

I turn, not sure what I'm expecting to see, but it's definitely not her holding out a pair of crutches.

"These might help," she says.

I nod and thank her. They do help. A lot, actually. I make my way over to the trailer where all the boys live.

The front door is gone, but at least somebody's managed to nail some hooks on the frame and hang a big tarp across it. But there's nothing to knock on, so I stand there for a minute, trying to figure out how to do this.

My mother has six brothers—or *had* six brothers. There's Monty, of course. He's the youngest and the one I fear the most, because it genuinely seems like there's something wrong with his head. But there's also two that died overseas in the Middle East. Their names were Russ and Angel. That leaves the twins, Brett and Shep (who are drug dealers and typically don't pay me much mind), and the oldest, Ralph. I don't really know Ralph. He lives in this trailer, but he's got the big bedroom in the back to himself, and like Grandpa said, he doesn't come out much. Never did. Even before the pain pills. People say he's the closest thing to a crime lord you're going to find in Winston County, but Mama always said he was sweet to her.

I don't know if that matters much though, considering Mama's judgment.

There's not a single sound inside other than snoring. I don't want to wake them up, but I also don't want to hang out here all day, wasting time. Eventually, Nesmith will think to look here, and when he does, he'll just come take me. Some of Mama's brother's might be badasses, but Nesmith has got Ruby Jewel, Helmet, and—I guess—the devil himself on his side.

Not to mention this Billy character, who mercifully still has not returned from wherever he is.

I work my way up the steps and push the tarp out of the way.

The place is a disaster. Clothes, food, wrappers, tools—you name it, spread out across the floor. One of the brothers—I'm not sure which one—is asleep on the couch. I duck into the kitchen, hoping I might find the boat keys there.

The kitchen is somehow even messier than the den. Dishes are stacked up in both sides of the sink. Roaches crawl across them, feasting on dried up food. Dozens of beer cans line the countertops. Some of them are turned over, stuck to the counter in small puddles of dried beer. A terrible smell wafts up from the sink and I step back to get away from it.

That's when I spot Monty through the kitchen window. He's coming toward the trailer with a hunting rifle. He's dragging the carcass of something dead behind him. He's wearing flip flops, short pants, and is bare-chested.

On instinct, I reach into the sink and grab the cleanest and sharpest knife I see. I unzip my backpack and head out the door, hoping he won't realize I was in the trailer at all.

It works. He doesn't see me for some time as I stand beside the trailer, watching him approach. When he sees me, he whistles low and slow.

"You a sight for sore eyes, girl. I like them blue jeans."

"I need a ride," I say, coming right to it. It never pays to fuck around with a boy like Monty. He'll take any small talk the wrong way.

"A ride, huh? We can follow this creek a little deeper in the woods, and you can ride all you want, Forest."

"I ain't talking about that kind of a ride, and you know it. A boat ride, back across the lake."

"Well, I'll be. A damsel in distress. What kind of trouble have you got yourself in? Besides that hurt foot?"

"Is that a dog?" I realize now what he's dragging ain't a deer or a bobcat. It's too furry for a deer and too big for a bobcat.

"Name was Alfie. Belonged to some faggots down by the water tower. Wouldn't stop barking, and Ralph said he'd give me a hundred bucks to make it stop. Boom! Done. That's the kind of man I am. I get shit done."

"You shouldn't have killed that dog."

He smiles at me, proud of himself. "And why not?"

"It's a dog. It was somebody's pet."

"Did you not hear me? They was faggots. Queers."

"That don't make any difference."

"And I say it does. Ain't natural. Ain't right."

"You ain't right."

His expression changes, and I remember he's got quite a temper.

"You need a ride, huh?" he asks. "Where you going to?"

"Across the lake."

"What's across the lake?"

"Home."

He drops the dog and leans his rifle against the dock. He sits down, letting his feet dangle in the water. From within the pockets of his shorts, he pulls out a small red apple and takes a bite. With his mouth full, he says, "Why you here anyway?"

"That's my business."

"I'll bet you run away from home with some boy, and he's done left you and now you want to go back home."

"None of that's true."

"You ain't on the run?"

I say nothing. It's enough, though. Monty knows my silence means he's caught me.

"I'll tell you what, I'll take you to the other side first thing in the morning."

"No. It needs to be today."

"Well, I got plans today."

"Fine, I'll ask one of your brothers or Trudy."

He takes another bite of his apple and laughs. "They're just gonna tell me to take you. You ain't been around in a while, but the only people in this whole little trailer park that ain't hooked on pain pills are me, Missy, and Trudy. Missy can't drive a damn boat, and Trudy... well, shit, she's hooked on something even worse than pills."

"I'll pay you," I say.

"Well, now we're talking."

"I'll give you fifty dollars once we make it to the other side of the lake."

"You ain't got fifty dollars."

"You ain't even got a boat," I say, hoping to goad him.

"Well, I got the keys to Ralph's boat, and Ralph don't get out much these days. Prefers the comfortable haze of taking pills in his own damn bed."

I suck in a deep breath and realize he's too wily to be tricked or played so easily. I'm going to have to come up with something else, something he'll never see coming.

"How about a date then?"

"A date?"

"Me and you."

"Now, I like the way you're thinking. Finally getting over the uncle shit, huh?"

I nod.

"Say it."

"Say what?"

"Say, 'I don't think it matters that me and Monty is related.'"

"I don't think it matters that me and… you are related."

"'Cause it don't," he says, almost to himself. "I mean, we ain't even got the same mom. My momma ain't even related to you at all. To me, people ain't related unless they come out of the same pussy."

I hold my tongue and nod.

He swallows, and I want to vomit. I can tell this is turning him on. Just stay the course, I hear Granny say. Trust yourself.

"Well, what time do you want to do this date, and where should we go, Niece?"

The lake is clear as far as the eye can see, but something tells me it won't be that way for long. Billy'll be coming home, and when he does, he'll find a way to contact Nesmith. Either that or take me to him directly.

"Let's do it this afternoon," I say, trying not to sound too eager.

He grins, and I think how stupid boys can be when they're horny. He's wily, sure, but like most men, all his good sense goes out the door when he thinks his dick might get some attention. It never crosses his mind to question what's making me act so different. He just goes with it, riding the high of anticipation.

He tosses the apple core into the creek and picks up the rope he's tied around the dead dog and begins to pull it on up to the trailer.

"I'll come by and get you at Daddy's, girl. Be ready, all right?"

7

AROUND NOON, THE trailer park starts to wake up. Grandpa and Missy come out of the bedroom. Languid music drifts up from the dock. Through the open windows I smell meat over a fire. It mixes with the dank smell of marijuana smoke. The day is warm and the sun cuts through the orange and red leaves like long swords of pure light. It's the kind of afternoon that makes even a terrible place seem good. A peace pervades, passes over the little park, and even the hours I spend waiting on Monty to show up doesn't seem so bad.

When Monty finally shows, I'm sitting on the dock with Missy and Grandpa, and most of the afternoon has slipped away. He's wearing a pair of dark blue jeans and a clean shirt he's gone to the trouble of tucking in. If it weren't so gross, it would be pitiful.

H waits for me on the bank, and I pick my way off the dock on crutches, praying that Grandpa and Missy don't judge me too much, thankful that Elija has taken my advice and stayed inside. It's embarrassing to be doing this. Even if he wasn't my uncle, I'd be sick to think of going on a date with Monty.

I just pray he's got the key on him. I glance at the boats as I walk past. Two of them tied up in the wide and deep part of the canal. Which one belongs to Ralph? I'll have to guess once I get the key.

Monty catches up with me and reaches for my hand. I bat him away.

"Playing hard to get?"

"We ain't holding hands," I say. But then remember the idea is to excite him enough that he'll let his guard down. "Not yet anyway. Let's at least get into the woods."

He nods, eagerly. "I brought two condoms."

"Two?"

"I can always go twice in a row."

I've got bile in my mouth just hearing that. My one experience with sex was with a guy I liked, but it was awkward and painful, at least at first. I can't even make myself try to imagine what it would be like with Monty.

"Take me someplace nice, Monty," I say.

He doesn't answer me. He's distracted by something behind us. I follow his gaze and see a boat pulling up to the dock. "Billy's home," he says.

"Let's hurry," I say.

"Well damn, girl. We'll get there. No need to rush."

8

WE END UP near a little waterfall. I don't think Billy saw me, but I'm worried he might see Elijah, or somebody might mention to him that we're here.

I've got to put that out of my mind. One thing at a time. First, Monty.

The waterfall is actually pretty nice, a place that under different circumstances I would enjoy. It's got soul, a certain something that makes it more than a stool. More than material. I make a mental note to ask Granny if places can be like people in that way.

Monty's staring at it, holding my hand in his, and I'm trying to ignore how sweaty and warm his hand is. Feels like holding onto a turd.

He turns and takes my other hand. "I don't see nothing the matter with two people doing what they want to do. I'm your uncle, but that ain't really the same as being close family. As your uncle, I feel like I can help you out, teach you things. You ain't never given me the chance, really."

I nod, playing along as best I can. I've got my backpack on and the knife's inside it, so—worse comes to worse—I'll kick him in the balls or claw his face to give me a minute to get it out. But the longer I play him, the better chance I've got of finding the key.

"Let's play a game," I say.

"What kind of game?"

"Truth or dare."

He grins. "I like that. I'll go first."

"Okay, I'll take truth."

"Wait, I thought I was going first?"

"You are. You're first so you get to Truth or Dare me. I choose Truth."

He nods, a little uncertain, but my confidence goads him into continuing. "Okay... let me think. Here's one. You ever had sex before?"

"No. I'm a virgin." Lying seems like the safest bet here.

He nods his head quickly, excitedly. "I figured. That's good too. Means no other boy's done spoiled you."

"Right, but it also means we gotta go slow."

He lets go of one of my hands and reaches for my boob. I sidestep the reach like a pro. It's a move I've been doing since seventh grade. Plenty of assholes in the world to make sure I get my practice in.

"Remember, slow. We're still playing Truth or Dare."

He grins. "Right. Sorry. You're just so fucking hot."

"What do you want, Truth or Dare?" I ask him.

"Dare for sure."

I don't smile, but I want to. He's falling right into my trap.

"Okay, now we're getting somewhere."

HOLY GHOST ROAD

He smiles and touches himself almost absentmindedly. I force myself to not make a face. "Take your clothes off."

"I was hoping you'd say that," he says, ripping off his shirt and tossing it on the ground. He kicks off his boots and then peels his dark blue jeans down right along with his underwear. He's left, standing before me in only his sock feet.

"Your turn," he says grinning.

"Not yet. Your turn isn't quite over."

He grins. "Oh. Well…"

I keep my eyes on his, not watching what's happening down below. I'm pretty sure he's touching himself.

"Toss me your clothes."

He throws the shirt first and then the jeans.

"Don't forget your boots."

When I ask for the boots, he pauses for the first time, suddenly catching on that I might be playing him. "Why do you need my clothes?"

"You'll see." I decide I don't need the boots after all. I pick up his blue jeans and go through the pockets. Nothing but a twenty-dollar bill and the two condoms.

"We ain't even gotta use that," he says. "Feels better without it."

"Is that right?" I say.

"What now?"

"Stand in the creek."

"Why?"

"Because I said so."

"Oh, okay. I like this. You telling me what to do and all."

He steps back into the creek. The waterfall is behind him, and if the spray against his back makes him cold, he gives no indication.

I take off my backpack and unzip it.

"What are doing?" Monty says.

"You didn't bring the damn key," I say.

"What?"

I withdraw the knife.

When he sees the knife, it all hits him at once. He seems to understand in a flash of insight I was never planning on having sex with him. Not only that, but he recognizes I disdain everything about him. He comes flying out of the water in a pure rage I can't quite account for.

I get the knife up, but I never imagined actually having to cut him, so when the time comes to cut or be knocked down by a naked Monty, I get knocked flat. He lands on top of me and grabs my wrist, turning it with such force I don't have any choice but to drop the knife.

What follows is the beginning of a nightmare. He's going to rape me. That's the first realization. It's followed by others. They fly at me like whispers coming from the blades of grass right next to my ears.

He's so much stronger than me

He smells like cheap spray-on deodorant and day-old sweat

My body feels numb and small and useless

There's more, but they're all flying at me so fast, and I can't keep thinking them because thinking them means I'm not doing anything. Thinking them is the same as letting them happen.

HOLY GHOST ROAD

I try a prayer instead, but I can't figure out who to pray to. Should I ask Granny or God or just the waterfall?

I turn my head, trying to focus on how I can escape, trying to find anything, a rock, a stick, a sign. That's when I see it.

It's a sign and a weapon. It's salvation if I can make it happen.

A snake lays in a bed of dead leaves not too far from where Monty and I are.

"Snake," I say.

He's unbuttoning my pants and the next time I say *snake*, I knee him in the groin. He grunts and grimaces, and then bears down.

"There's a goddamn snake," I shout.

Finally, he pauses. Looks around. His eyes calculate and search at once. He fears another trick almost as much as he fears a snake.

Then he sees it.

"Oh shit."

He slides off me, and I don't hesitate. Hell, this is an answered prayer if there ever has been one, and I'm not going to waste it.

Something comes over me. It's like a cool veil that makes the day look different, makes the snake and the leaves look different. Most of all, it makes me feel different, like I'm powerful, like I'm more than just material. There's an energy in me, about me, all around me that boosts me, give me hope.

"What the fuck are you doing?" Monty says, but he's far away now, in a different realm than the one that exists between the snake and me. It's not a timber rattler like the one Granny picked up, or a cottonmouth like the one Ruby Jewel tried to strike me with. This is a diamondback rattler, the kind that can kill man with one strike. Sometimes surviving a bite can be even worse. Granny had a neighbor who lived through a bite only to have his leg fall off, but the infection hung on, turning his whole groin and midsection to a rotting, stinking mess of zombie flesh. As he died, he was begging for somebody to please shoot him.

I just need the damned thing to look at me. It's curled up in the leaves, facing the other direction. I give it a wide berth as I go around to the other side. This means I've got to step into the creek, but I hardly notice the cold water as it rushes over my shoes. My ankle is numb. It doesn't hurt. Nothing hurts or will ever hurt again.

Gazing into the snake's eyes is a little bit like gazing into Helmet's. They're both cold, nearly lifeless, all languid potential, the weight of the venom they carry pooling in their gaze. My hand goes out, and for just a second, I feel my gaze wavering, my courage faltering. I want to blink. I want to turn away, but I feel Granny watching me. I sense when I see her next, she'll know of what I've done, and she'll be proud of me.

I remember what she told me about talking to it, so inside my head I speak my inner voice, the one that prays and reads books and tells myself stories. The one that makes sense of this world when nothing else can.

I'm gonna touch you. I'm going to hold you, the voice says. *Don't strike. Don't strike. Don't strike. I won't hurt you. I won't hurt you.*

As I move closer to the snake, there's something in its eyes that scares me. Before all I saw was potential, a kind of indifferent waiting. Now, it recognizes me, and it bristles slightly at my words. There's something like haughtiness in its expression now, but I can't be afraid. This is my weapon. This is my sign.

When I touch the thing's skin, I understand that though a snake might be like me and Granny in some ways, there's other ways it's alien from us too. And there's a realness in that, a truth. Here is what Granny taught me in my hands now. See the world as it really is. To touch a rattlesnake, to hold it in your hands, to speak to it and *know that you know* it understands you, that is the truth of things.

And that's what I do. I pick it up, I hold it out, and keep my eyes on its dead gaze, even as its tongue flickers and its rattle rattles.

I turn, holding it high above my head now. Monty is naked and wide-eyed. For the first time ever, he regards me as something other than a girl, a body he wants to fuck. I'm powerful now. I am more than a girl, more than material.

"Get your ass back down the trail," I say.

He doesn't argue, but he does trip going for his clothes.

"Forget those."

"What?"

"Leave the damn clothes." I step forward, thrusting the snake at him and the damn thing strikes out at the air, and I realize it's inside of me, it reads my thoughts now, my heart, my pulse.

Monty leaves the clothes in a pile and starts walking back the way we came, following the stream. I can't help but laugh at the way the early moon shines on his bare ass. It's a scrawny ass, and he looks so much like a little boy now I can't believe he was ever a threat.

"Faster," I call. I sense the snake in my hands getting restless. We've made a pact, but that pact doesn't last indefinitely.

The dusk is nearly gone, replaced by a moonstricken dusk, the kind that opens up shadows and creates a hazy light among the trees.

"You're a rapist," I say.

"No," Monty says. He might be crying. "No, I ain't. You promised me."

"You only heard what you wanted to hear. Most of the time that's what rapists do. And you know what makes it worse?"

He turns to me, probably to see if I'm still holding the snake. I glance up too, just to see what it's doing in my hands. It's back to nonchalant, its rattler drooping down my wrist, its slinky form a dark inkblot against the early moon. My arms are tired, but I don't dare move them. I hold them up in worship to the god of the sun and moon and the god of the creeping dusk and to the snake itself for listening.

"That you're my goddamn uncle."

He sucks in his breath at this and starts to cry. I thrust the snake at him, goading him forward.

As we approach the trailers, I can tell something's wrong. No surprise there. Billy coming back when he did has the potential to fuck everything up. But for some reason, even that can't quite make me worry. This must be how Granny feels all the time, the confidence in her so bright it's like a second sun.

Up ahead, there's yelling and the baby's screaming its head off again. As the dock comes into view, a man in a cheap suit stands on the dock. He's got Elijah backed up against the edge of it, a pistol in his hand.

HOLY GHOST ROAD

Nobody else seems to even be paying much attention to the two men. Trudy's watching from her chair, but her face shows no emotion or interest in what's happening. The twins have fishing poles and stand on the other side of the dock, watching the lake water rush underneath. I don't see Ralph. Is it possible Monty actually told the truth about him being hooked on pain pills? Missy and Grandpa are in chairs near Trudy, both of them smoking dope. Missy's the only one who seems to even notice the gun, the standoff between Billy and Elijah. She's also the first to see me and Monty coming.

The snake is twisting in my hands, writhing like snakes do. I just hold on, trying to tell it with my mind it won't be long now.

Missy's hand falls to Grandpa's shoulder and he turns and sees me too. I swear he looks like he's seen a ghost.

Or a snake. Or probably just a girl carrying a snake.

Billy shoves the gun at Elijah and Elijah flinches so hard, he falls off the dock and into the creek. Billy laughs loudly, and I hate him all the more for the sound of that laughter. For a minute I don't think Elijah's coming back up. I hope he's just playing possum, trying to take a moment for himself, but it worries me when he vanishes beneath the brown water.

"Hey!" I shout. And hold the serpent out in front of me.

Everybody turns to see me now. It's like my voice is controlling them. I call, they turn, and the power I feel in this moment, is a power that can move mountains, escape devils, stare down Ruby Jewel, see the world true.

I step into the creek, and the cold water comes up to my knees, soaking the bottom of Trudy's blue jeans.

"I want the key to one of these boats." This snake is a mess now, twisting and writhing, squirming to get free.

Hang on, hang on, hang on, I tell it.

Elijah comes up from the creek. He's like a dead man coming back to life, revived by the twilight and my power. I'm doing magic now. I feel my body thrumming with it.

"The keys," I say very calmly. I'm almost to the dock, almost to the place where Billy stands.

He raises the gun in his hand slightly, as if trying to decide whose weapon is more deadly.

"Go on," I say. "Try it."

It's a ridiculous thing to say. It's clear he has the advantage.

Isn't it?

Maybe not. Maybe me holding the snake gives me more power than I've suspected.

He's staring at the snake, as if he can't believe it's real.

And then Edie screams. Something about the scream seems to bring him back. I see the change in his face. He's about to shoot me. So, I don't give him the chance. I throw the snake and dive out of his line of sight. He gets one shot off before the diamondback hits him.

Somehow the beast gets wrapped around his arm and ends up biting his neck. Billy stares at me, shock written all over his face. He fires again, but this shot doesn't even come close. Then he drops the gun, continuing to stare at me as the snake bites him over and over.

My attention turns to Edie. She's lying on the dock as naked as Monty. "Get her," I tell Elijah.

HOLY GHOST ROAD

"What?"

"You heard me. Get the baby!"

I don't wait for a response. I stride forward and climb up onto the dock. The snake is slinking away from Billy now. I reach into his pocket and pull out some keys.

"Which boat?" I say to Missy.

She points to the one I was hoping for. It's newer and in better shape than the other two. The pontoon. The snake is on the dock, moving toward the child. I come out of the creek and step up onto the dock, grab the snake from behind its head and throw it back on top of Billy. Just in case.

I pick up Edie's pacifier and put it in her mouth. She starts sucking it, content at last. "Elijah?" I say.

He's still standing in the water, staring.

"Come on."

I turn to Trudy, expecting a fuss about me taking Edie.

But sometimes folks surprise you.

"Go on. Take her." Her eyes are sad. Her face is old. She not pretty or jealous or anything except sad. It's the way a person looks who has failed and knows it.

I should tell her I can't take a baby. I'm only fifteen, and I've got trouble following me, but *should* doesn't seem as important as it once did.

"Elijah?"

"Yeah?"

"Get in the boat." I pick up Edie and turn to Grandpa. He nods at me, and I can tell he's impressed.

"Your son," I say. "That one over there." I point at Monty even though he knows which one I mean. "He's a rapist. He tried to rape me."

I don't wait to see Grandpa's reaction. I figure it will be one more sad thing I'd rather forget.

Instead, I step into the boat, holding the baby. I sit in the driver's seat and start the engine with my free hand.

Elijah comes to join me. He's shaking a little. Probably from being in the water. We came to this place wet and cold, and it looks like we'll leave it the same way.

No, not the same, I think as I pull the boat from the dock and out onto the wider lake, its flat darkness waiting for us to cross it again.

The Second Barn

1

WE'RE ABOUT A mile gone when it hits me.

I turn to Elijah, who is huddled in the back of the boat, trying to keep the wind off Edie. "Can you drive?"

"Sure."

I slow the boat and switch places with him. He hands me Edie and I sink into the bench seat that smells like beer and dead fish and start to cry.

I can't explain it. It's just the adrenaline. I held it together back there for so long that now it just comes rushing out.

Elijah can't hear me cry over the wind, but Edie hears it, and she gets quiet and watches me, as if she's learning something about the world, something secret, something desperate, and I hope she is. I want her to see how filled with miracles and sadness we all are.

"Where to?" Elijah calls over his shoulder.

The question I've been dreading. I want to go straight under the interstate, get out on the Cullman side, but we don't have his phone yet. Or his car, and I promised him I'd help him find it.

"We can get my car later. I think you need to get you to your grandmother's first."

I nod, thankful for his generosity, his help. I want to tell him, but it's too loud with the wind and the outboard motor running. I cry some more about that, and then decide I'm done with crying. It's not that crying's bad or anything. No, I'd say it's just the opposite. *Not* crying is the real issue. Sometimes the emotions overwhelm a person, and you've just got to let them out. Lord knows, I wish Ben had cried more after what he went through, but instead, he just bottled up the tears, stamped them down deep, until he found a different outlet over at the Miller's place.

Like a lot of boys around here, Ben didn't do so well in school. It wasn't because he was dumb. Far from it. Ben was too smart for school. Now, I understand when people say things like that, other people tend to roll their eyes. But I'm serious. He really *was* too smart. His problem was you couldn't pin his kind of smart down with a test. In fact, he rarely finished the tests he took, often leaving a bunch of the questions blank. When Mama started to catch wind that this was happening more and more, she told him he was lazy and needed to work harder. Ben nodded and promised her he would. But time and time again it happened, and we both knew Ben was trying. In what would turn out to be about the last good thing Mama ever did, she made him an appointment with a doctor who ran some tests on Ben. Turns out he had severe attention deficit disorder, and simply could not focus on tests. They put him on some medicine that fucked him up right away. Made him sleep all the time and stop eating. But his grades did improve. Turns out, he was always getting the answers right of the ones he was completing, and now that he could actually finish the tests, he was pulling A's across the board. The downside was he lost weight and fell into a depression.

There was a brief period where I thought he was getting better. The grades were up, he seemed more like himself. We were having fun again, out in the woods, climbing trees, going to Granny's on the weekends, everything I loved about life and about Ben, but then he brought home his report card and it had two F's on it.

He admitted he'd been flushing his pills instead of taking them, and then told us he'd decided to join the army.

He was seventeen, about to turn eighteen, and Mama said it was his decision. Hell, I think she liked the idea. There's people around here who think the military is a way out, but Granny taught me about that too.

"Maybe it is," Granny told me once. "But it's like saying the fire is a way out of the frying pan."

I begged him not to go, but his mind was made up. He told me he wouldn't amount to nothing here, and the army gave him a chance, at least.

He made it nine months. Nine months before getting shot and shipped back to us with a healed body, but a mind that couldn't seem to start itself anymore. The ADD had somehow gotten worse. He lived in another world, a space world that didn't coincide with the material one too often. He'd spend an hour or more in the morning trying to make it from his bed to bathroom, and afterward he'd wind up on the couch, just sitting and staring at the television. Half the time it wasn't even turned on.

Months of this, and we only had one real talk. He told me something had finally grabbed his attention. It was something no book or test had ever been able to do.

"I keep seeing it," he said.

"Seeing what?" I was scared to ask the question, but I was scared not to ask it too.

"There was a bomb," he said. "And these children." He turned and his eyes focused on me for the first time in ages. "The children there are so sweet. Sometimes I would look at them and wonder how people could go from that to where I was, and then I'd wondered how I'd made that damn transition too. It's like that's what life is. Making the transition from something wonderful to something horrible. Some people can do it with dignity, but I don't think I can."

"Forest?"

I realize I've been drifting. Not quite into a dreamwalk, but a place that's adjacent to it. I'm still holding Edie, and she's being so good, so quiet, so still.

"Forest, there's something happening to the boat."

"What?"

But then I hear it. The engine is sputtering. We're slowing down.

The engine stops.

"Turn it. Turn the boat. Aim to the shore."

Elijah cranks the wheel hard and points the front of the boat toward the other side of the lake. Our momentum pushes us along about another five hundred yards, but eventually, the boat slows to stop in the still lake.

HOLY GHOST ROAD

It's dark now, and the shore is still far enough away to be lost in the gloom. It's got to be a hundred yards, or maybe more.

Neither of us speak. What is there to say? Edie is asleep. She's peaceful, and the moon lights her face in pale fire. I lay down on the bench seat, holding her on my stomach. She'll wake soon enough, and we'll have to figure out how to feed her, how to get off this boat and onto dry land. But, for now, being in the still silence of the lake with an infant, with Elijah, seems like a blessing that would be a sin not to appreciate.

Elijah must sense this too, because he comes to the rear of the boat and lays down across from me on the other bench seat.

For a long time, I keep my eyes open and watch the moon above us. When I began this journey, the moon was full. Now it's diminished, waning, one side of a smooth circle collapsed.

Edie breathes softly on my chest, and I think of Ben, what sadness he brought back from the war, what sadness we all must endure.

2

WE WAKE UP when the boat hits the bank on the other side of the lake.

Edie stirs first, whimpering slightly in my arms. I stand, the boat rocking beneath me, and nudge Elijah with my foot.

A few minutes later we're standing on the wooded bank, no sign of houses or life or roads anywhere. 278 can't be far from here. It runs along this side of the lake like a seam on a pair of pants.

Elijah takes Edie from me and grins down at her. He's obviously infatuated. I am too. Babies always bring out the truth about people. If your instinct is to neglect or even take advantage of a baby, well, I reckon that says just about everything there is that *can* be said about you.

I scan the bank, thinking. "Dollar General."

"Dollar what?"

"Dollar General. They're all over the place. Four between my house and Granny's. We can't be too far from one. If we hurry, we can break in and get some food and…" I glance at Edie. "…baby stuff before it even opens."

"Right. Okay." He seems shaken. I don't blame him. I'm shaken too.

"You okay?"

"No."

"Wanna talk about it?"

"How did you…"

"How did I what?"

"Do the thing with the snake?"

"You won't believe me."

"Tell me anyway. Tell me the truth. As you know it."

He looks completely worn out by the thought of more unexplained phenomenon, but he's asking for the truth.

"I talked to it."

He shakes his head. "No. I changed my mind. I don't want to hear it."

"You said the truth."

He's still shaking his head. "I don't believe any of this. It's like I'm experiencing some kind of drug-induced hallucination."

"What drugs did you take?" It's infuriating to talk to someone who fools themselves so easily.

"I don't know. Maybe they gave me drugs at the Ramsay place. That woman cooked me supper before I went into the barn."

"So, you think everything that has happened to us has been because of drugs?" The anger in my voice is like the edge of a blade.

"I don't know. Look, there's no way you talked to that snake."

"And there's no way that barn was haunted either."

"Almost certainly."

HOLY GHOST ROAD

"And this child?" I say, putting at the baby in his arms. "What of her?"

He shakes his head, confused.

"Is she not a miracle?"

"She's beautiful, but it's all just biology."

I start through the trees, knowing 278 will be somewhere on the other side of them, and when we find it, we'll truly need a miracle to avoid Nesmith and his minions.

We continue through the trees. My mind turns to the dreamstone again, as I remember Granny's request and how I'm no closer to finding it than I was when she mentioned it to me two nights ago.

I wish I understood why I needed it so much. Why *she* needed it. I know one thing; I can't go back home for it. I just can't. Surely Granny understands this too. In which case, the dreamstone has to be somewhere else.

But where?

Shit. My head hurts, thinking about it. I decide I'll call her again first chance I get.

"I still can't believe it," Elijah says almost to himself. "I wonder if it'll ever really sink in."

I wonder things too, like if I'll ever get out of Winston County, but mostly I wonder if the world will be more or less the same somewhere else? Will I always be caught between the heaven of youth and the hell of adulthood? And what of the dreams in between, what of dreamstones and snakes, forest canopies, and hills scarred by lightning? Is there a place among all of these where magic can linger? I reckon there has to be, otherwise how can a person like Granny exist? Somehow, she still has the heaven of her youth. She's kept it, held it, *protected* it like I wasn't able to do with the dreamstone. There's nothing more essential than that, I realize, as I walk into the deeper woods. Nothing more essential than finding a way to keep the magic you already have. In fact, that might be the greatest magic of all.

3

WE FIND A Dollar General around six-thirty, according to Elijah's watch. The door says it opens at eight, and Elijah figures that gives us about a thirty-minute window to get in and out before somebody shows.

"There's going to be an alarm," he says. "So we need to get in and out quick."

"No problem."

He sucks in a deep breath. "We killed a man."

Has the same thought been plaguing me? Well, yes and no. I mean, a man is dead, and that's heavy. But I really don't think *I* killed him. Maybe I'm wrong, but he's the one who brought it on himself when he aimed that gun at me.

But Elijah's been through enough lately he can't explain, so I decide to keep it simple. "If anybody killed him it was me."

He nods. "Or the snake."

"Yeah, if you want to get technical, it was the snake."

"I still don't understand how that happened."

"Let's focus," I say. I'm holding Edie and she's starting to squirm. I feel like she's getting hungry, and I'm afraid to bring up my fear: that Dollar General may not carry formula and bottles.

"Okay," he says. "Let's go around back."

We walk to the back of the store. There's a dumpster, a back door for deliveries, and a single, high window, barely large enough for me to crawl through. Elijah finds a two by four leaning against the dumpster. He pulls himself up to the top of the dumpster and takes a whack at the window, cracking it on the first swing. He shifts the two by four in his hands, so he can push it like a pool cue and slams the end of it into the splintered glass, shattering it. A few more strikes and he's got most of the shards cleared.

No alarm. At least not that I can hear. He climbs back down, and I hand him Edie.

"How's your ankle?" he asks as I start to climb.

"Hasn't hurt since I picked up that snake."

4

DOLLAR GENERAL DOES carry formula and bottles. The only problem is the formula is supposed to be mixed with water and warmed up. I grab several packets, a bottle, and some diapers. I also take some granola bars and two giant bottles of water. I stuff all of it in my bag and head to the clothes section. It's a risk, but I still feel weird wearing Trudy's clothes.

I strip off right in the store and grab a one-piece bathing suit and put that on. Just in case I have to swim again, I'll be ready. Besides, it works fine as underwear. I pull on some athletic shorts with a drawstring I tighten as much as possible and then grab a t-shirt and a sweatshirt in case the weather turns cold again. I put them both on, so I'll have less to carry.

I'm about to head out when I remember Elijah still needs shoes.

I'm trying to decide between cheap flip-flops and cheap sandals when I see the police cars in the front lot.

There are two of them, and they've pulled up parallel to each other, their front ends facing different directions so the drivers can talk with the windows down. Both officers have coffees and seem pretty relaxed. As long as I can manage to not set off an alarm, I'll be okay.

I grab the sandals, stuffing them into my already overfilled backpack, and then head to the break room and the window I climbed in through.

In the break room, I pull out the bottle and the formula and mix some according to the directions. My hands are only shaking a little, and it seems like this might work out. I just have to get the temperature right, and there's a microwave, so I put the bottle inside it and turn it on for ten seconds.

It counts down, the seconds themselves lingering as if they are aware I'm waiting for them to pass, somehow enjoying the attention.

The countdown reaches five, and I hear something from the front of the store. Because of course I do.

Opening the microwave, I grab the bottle and shove everything into my backpack. I step up onto the desk and reach for the window when the voice speaks.

"Haven't seen anyone around, officers." It's a female, who I can only assume is here to open the store.

"Well, they're desperate. As far as we can tell they don't have money or any means of transportation. So, make sure you keep your eyes open."

"So, why are they on the run then?" the voice says.

"That's none of your concern. Just be sure to keep an eye out."

"Are they dangerous?"

I wait. I want to know the answer. If it's yes, then that may mean Missy or Grandpa has reported what happened on the other side of the lake. A no could mean the opposite.

"Just let us know if you see anyone matching their description, okay?"

"Sure."

I toss the bag through the window and climb out.

Once I'm on the ground, I thrust the sandals at Elijah and gesture for him to get them on quickly.

I take Edie and decide to wait on the bottle. She's got her pacifier in her mouth and is quiet. Still squirmy, but quiet.

"Hurry," I hiss at Elijah. "Cops inside."

His face is pure terror. "Shit. We're screwed."

"We haven't done anything wrong."

"Murder? Kidnapping? Breaking and entering? This is a shitshow."

"Don't worry about any of that, okay? Worry about Nesmith. That's the concern. If he catches us, he'll kill us or worse."

"You keep saying that. What's worse than killing us?"

I shake my head. Mostly because we're getting too loud, but also because I don't know what's worse than killing us. Well, I *know*, but I can't exactly explain it easily. Worse than killing us is making us one of them. One of those people who find their drug and take it until it kills them. Mama's people across the lake take one kind of drug, but Mama and so many people on this side are taking another kind. I don't want the drugs because the drugs are worse than death. The drugs are the hell people bring upon themselves because they're scared of the reality of this world. It's crazy, but to so many people, hell seems safer than living.

I don't want to be one of those people.

But that's still not all of it. There's the shadow goat, the way it seemed to look at me, as if waiting. But what's it waiting for?

"Car coming," Elijah says.

I hear it too. One of the police cars, circling around to the back. Elijah and I step behind the dumpster and listen as the car slowly comes around. The engine purrs softly, and then downshifts to idle.

Elijah shakes his head, his eyes wide, and that's when I remember I left the backpack on the ground on the other side of the dumpster.

A door opens. Something beeps followed by static and a voice. "Here at the Dollar General on 278. Address, 2145. I've found what appears to be a backpack stuffed with items from the store."

I grab Elijah's arm and squeeze. His face is drawn, and I can tell he doesn't have a plan. All it's going to take is a couple of feet in this direction and the officer will see us.

Edie squirms again and spits her pacifier out. I've learned that this is what she does right before going into full tantrum mode. I grab it and stick it back in, not really giving her a chance to reject it.

She sucks it a few times contentedly and then her face creases into a rage and she spits it back out. Or tries to. I hold it in place. Her face breaks and her mouth opens wide. She screams at me.

"Hold up," the officer says into his two-way. "I hear something."

I step out from the side of the dumpster, holding Edie up to cover my face.

"That's my stuff, officer."

He looks at me, stunned. "Who are you?"

"Pauline," I say, using a named I've always thought was pretty. "I'm sorry, that's my bag. Well, *our* bag."

HOLY GHOST ROAD

I try to stand up straight, to be taller, older, to be somebody else, somebody named Pauline whose husband got too physical with her last week and has been on the run ever since. I need to buy time, but not much time. I'm hoping, praying really, Elijah can use the element of surprise to get us back into the woods before the other officer drives around. But even as I attempt this ruse, I'm pretty sure this is the end of the line for me.

For us. And that hits me hard. It's one thing to imagine the end of me and Elijah. Quite another for this baby.

With the snake, I felt so much power. So why has it left me now? It's been replaced by pure desperation, a miserable sensation that feels in every way the opposite of what I'd felt when I lifted the snake over my head.

The officer eyes me closely. He seems suspicious, but a little unsure of what to do about it, which shows how dumb he is, I guess. Or how caught off guard, maybe?

"Can I have it back? My backpack? I was waiting for the store to open and had to feed her, so I went around behind the dumpster for privacy." *Be confident,* Granny whispers. *Believe what you say, and nobody can question you. Ain't that what everybody else in this godforsaken world does?*

I can tell the talk of breastfeeding is confusing to him. Like many men around here, anything women do with their bodies that isn't sex tends to confuse them, to strike half of them dumb with silence.

"You got any ID?" he finally manages to say.

That's when his two-way buzzes again. Someone is calling him. It's also when Elijah figures out what I'm buying time for. He comes barreling out around the side of the dumpster and throws his shoulder into the officer's midsection. He drops the two-way onto the concrete just before he falls on top of it. He reaches for his gun, but that's what I'm waiting on him to do. I step on his hand right before he touches the gun and grind his knuckles into the concrete.

"Get his gun," I say.

Elijah scrambles over on his knees and grabs the officer's holster, but the gun seems stuck.

The officer swings at Elijah with the hand I'm not standing on, and the blow is solid enough to knock Elijah away from the gun. He gets the gun out and aims it at me.

I step off his hand.

"Please let us go. Please."

I'm aware of Elijah groaning in pain to my right. The sun is fully risen now. The day is already warm, bordering on hot. The policeman's face is riddled with complex emotions I don't attempt to decipher.

The gun wavers and I step over to Elijah and kneel to see if he's okay. His face is bleeding, but his eyes are clear. He nods and stands up.

We both stare at the officer. He's still on the ground holding the gun.

"He's not going to shoot us," I say. Then, thinking I should probably not take that for granted, I meet his gaze. It's a careful gaze, a gaze that wants to do the right thing for reasons of his own, but is afraid of what could happen, afraid of how the right thing will fit into this world of wrong things. I can see all of this very clearly, and though he says nothing, I know I have to acknowledge it.

HOLY GHOST ROAD

"It's okay," I say. "I know what you're feeling. Nesmith has got it all twisted. If more people will do what you're doing right now, the world will straighten itself out from the way he's got it tangled."

"I need you to leave the bag," he says. "Please. I already called it in."

I nod, fairly confident if we took the bag, he still wouldn't shoot us, but I also feel like it's only right to leave it with him.

"No," Elijah says. "We need that."

I glance at Elijah sharply.

"We need it," he says again. "For the baby."

The officer lowers the gun, and as he does, he follows it with his eyes, as if he's unsure exactly why he's holding it, what kind of man he is.

"What's the plan?" I ask.

He shakes his head. "I don't know a plan. We just got your picture and word from the sheriff to bring you in. Didn't say nothing about any baby."

"And you shouldn't either," I tell him quick. "You know that bad feeling you get whenever Nesmith is around?" I'm making a leap here, but I've got to believe in the goodness of this officer and try to nurture it.

He nods. "You're not the first person we've been asked to track down."

This shakes me a little. There have been others?

"How many others?"

"A half dozen or more. Most of them are veterans, men and women who don't buy his bullshit or people he wants to use who don't like it. Who aren't willing…,"

"Willing to do what?" I say. I can't help but wonder what it is he wants me for, exactly.

"Who the hell knows? But when he wants them, he always gets them. You know that big guy that's always with him?"

I nod. "Helmet?"

"Yeah. He tried to get away too. Now, he's wrapped around Nesmith's finger."

"Thank you," I say. I pick up the bag, hesitating to see his reaction. When he nods, I nod back and begin moving toward the woods. Elijah follows.

"You got lucky," he calls after us. "I have doubts. The rest of them are all in."

"It was meant to be," I call back.

"The river," he says. That stops me at the edge of the woods.

"What?"

He turns over and shakes out the hand I'd been standing on. "I heard Sheriff Sutter say something about the Tuskahatchee being where they'd get you."

"I don't understand."

He seems frustrated by my confusion. "They're going to set up a road-blocks on all the bridges. You're gonna have to find another way across."

"Thanks," I say. "We'll figure it out."

"Don't tell them I helped you."

"We won't."

Then we're running through the woods again, free as we're likely to be until we can think of a way to cross that river.

5

EDIE TAKES THE bottle easy. Sucks the hell out of it and wants more. I mix her some in a gas station bathroom right off 278. Use the hot water from the sink, shake it good, and she coos like crazy when she sees the nipple again. I smile, watching her. I can't help but think how much Granny is gonna love her too. Eventually, she might have to adopt her officially, but I don't think that's going to be too much of a problem. An image of Trudy's angry face flashes through my mind suddenly. Maybe it will be a problem. No point in worrying about it now. Right now, I'm living with only one future in mind, and that's stepping onto Granny's sixty-four acres in Cullman County. After that, I'll be able to handle anything. Until that, I can't afford to worry about anything else.

I come out of the bathroom, my head down, moving fast for the door. Having Edie helps. It's obvious none of Mama's people have filed a report yet, which means nobody's looking for a young couple with a baby. Hell, one thing comes clear pretty quickly—people don't look at young girls carrying babies much at all. It's almost like it makes them feel ashamed. I suppose that in itself says something about the truth of the world, though I can't make out exactly what, not on first blush anyway, but I promise myself to think on it as we travel.

Speaking of traveling, we've made a plan. It's a good one, but it'll take some nerve. I'm going to get us to the Ramey place and recover Elijah's keys. Once we do that, we'll find his car and I'll climb in the trunk and let him go across the bridge with the baby in the back seat. He'll have a story just in case they do stop him, but we both agree with the baby in the back, they're most likely to just wave him on.

The one issue Elijah brought up is a car seat.

"It's unsafe to drive with a baby without one," he says.

"Seems like the least of our worries."

"May seem like that, but it's still a concern. Not only for the safety of Edie, but also for our plan. A baby in the backseat without a harness is going to raise suspicion."

He's right, but it feels like something we'll figure out when the time comes. That's another difference between me and Elijah. He's a planner. I'm an adapter. I can't plan nothing out because I don't know what the world is going to do anyway. I guess Granny taught me that, what with all her advice to just let understanding come when it comes. Meanwhile, Elijah feels pretty certain about the world. It's part of his logic/ science shit, which I guess does have its uses, but not here. Not in a world ruled by subtlety and lies, by the two kinds of magic—one kind pulled out of the world and directed, while the other is the kind that just connects a person to the earth, the kind you can use to direct yourself.

HOLY GHOST ROAD

Maybe I should ask him about him dreamstone? Get his take. Logic could be useful, especially when I don't have a clue.

I decide to let it ride a little longer. I like the silence and the walking, the way the wind blows on my face, the way the trees wave gently against the glare of a nearly white sky. We cross 278 around four that afternoon, waiting until the road is completely clear in both directions before sprinting to the other side. I know a road—a narrow, two-lane county highway, that should take us straight to the Ramey Place.

The sky has been on its own journey, going from pristine blue to a ragged, cloudy gray, and with the clouds has come a mugginess that feels more like summer than mid-October. I've passed Edie to Elijah, mostly because I need a break for my ankle's sake. The pain has returned, and the euphoria from my moment of power is all but diminished completely now. We've been walking all day, which wouldn't be so bad if we hadn't had to backtrack. We're actually moving away from the Tuskahatchee at the moment, and part of me wonders if heading closer to the barn, *another* barn—considering where this all began—is a mistake.

There's power in place. Granny's made that abundantly clear. Our house has been infested with the wrong kinds of power lately: first with the power of uselessness Ben came back from overseas with and then with the dark powers of greed and selfishness that arrived with Brother Nesmith and Ruby Jewel. Whatever I saw in the barn was likely some kind of physical manifestation of those powers.

We have diapers but not wipes for Edie, so we do our best to keep her clean with the various creeks and streams we cross on the way to

Ramsay Place. Weirdest thing is how content she seems. She likes traveling. Probably just the constant, comforting feel of our movement. Mama says I was the same way as a baby. She couldn't never put me down unless it was in a swing or a car seat. I needed to be moving, and I guess that hasn't changed too much. Only place I really like being still is high in a tree, where every place I could go is far beneath me, and easy to forget about.

It's nearly dusk before we arrive at the long, rutted road leading to the Ramsay Place.

"There," Elijah says and points at a hunter green SUV parked on the side of the road.

He shakes his head, dismayed. "All of this because I didn't want to get mud on my tires."

I glance from the vehicle to the long, muddy road I'm going to have to walk alone. But not yet. First, I've got to ask him about the dreamstone.

"Granny says it ain't enough just to come to the farm," I say, and then get quiet, waiting for his reaction.

"Well, I could have told you that. In fact, I think I've tried."

"You don't know Granny." My voice is hard. As mean as I can make it.

"Sorry," he says, softening. Maybe remembering what I'm about to do for him. "I'm sure your Granny is great, but I'm just struggling to see what she's going to do to help."

"She'll be able to help," I mutter, and suddenly I don't even want to mention the dreamstone because now it'll make her look weak, it'll confirm what he's already thinking.

HOLY GHOST ROAD

But he's not going to let it go. I can tell. I haven't known Elijah long, but the time we've spent together has been charged with something electric. I feel like all the stuff we've already been through has sort of fused a piece of me with a piece of him, and now we can read each other like siblings or something.

"So, what else does she want you to do?" Elijah asks.

"Find the dreamstone Nesmith took from my room." I realize as soon as I've said it, there's no doubting it was Nesmith who took it. But where would he keep it?

Once again, the thought of backtracking to the house makes me feel deflated.

"I'm not even going to ask what a dreamstone is," Elijah says. "I'm pretty sure the answer is going to be something I don't believe in anyway. But why would Nesmith take it?"

"Because it's supposed to keep me safe in my dreams, and apparently, he's been…" I trail off, as I realize what should have been obvious from the start. He's been messing with my dreams.

"He's been what?"

"He's been disrupting my power."

"Your power?"

"Haven't you been paying attention at all? My dreamwalks. That's my power. It's Granny's too."

"Oh," Elijah says. "What about the thing with the snake?"

I shake my head. I don't know about the thing with the snake. Hell, I don't *really* know about the dreamwalks. Granny can be so fucking cryptic sometimes.

"That was something else. Or maybe not. It's all related, but can we stay on the subject, please?"

"The subject?"

"Where would Nesmith put the dreamstone? Use your logic or something."

"Well, if this dreamstone is something he didn't want you to recover, he'd probably destroy it."

"I don't think you can."

"Sure you can. Remember the sledgehammer and the lockbox at the lake house? Anything can be destroyed if you put enough muscle behind it."

"Not magic stuff. The stone was given to me by Granny."

Elijah looks like he wants to laugh, but then maybe he remembers what I'm about to do for him, and how maybe he's not always as rational and logical as he wants to be, and just shrugs. "Okay. Fine. So, he would hide it somewhere. Let me think… I would say it's probably *not* at your house."

"Why do you say that?"

"Logically, it wouldn't make sense. It would be easier for you to find there. Common sense suggests he would hide it away from you, somewhere else. Does he have another home? Like before he moved in with you guys?"

I shrug. It's honestly never crossed my mind, but it does make sense. He would have had to live somewhere before moving into our house, but where? I have no idea.

HOLY GHOST ROAD

"Find his other house," Elijah says, seemingly pleased with himself, "and you'll find the dreamstone."

"Logic, right?"

"It never fails."

6

I LET THE thoughts of dreamstones and where Nesmith might have hidden mine, slip away as I traverse the muddy lane heading toward the barn.

The barn.

Legend and fact are often fighting sisters in Winston County, but everybody I know agrees that on a night in the late 1950's, an entire family was murdered inside the barn by at least two men, possibly more, who were never caught. The family consisted of the parents, an aunt that lived with them, and three kids.

Legend and fact get pretty twisted up concerning the details. Some stories hold that each family member was forced to tie their own noose and loop it over the rafters. Then, the murderers made the family take turns in order from oldest to youngest, stepping out of the hayloft with the nooses around their necks. The old-timers tell this version, mostly. I'm pretty sure if I was to have asked Grandpa or Missy, they would have sworn this to be the case. This version goes on to talk about the young boy from the farm a couple of miles away, coming over to check on the family because the kids had missed school for over a week, and walking into the barn and seeing all six of them hanging from the rafters. His name was Andy Satterfield, and Mama told me once they sent him to the nearest asylum a few years afterwards because he couldn't stop thinking about what he'd seen.

Other stories claim the hangings happened over a series of years, starting with the family matriarch, Bella Jean, and followed a year later by her sister, Francis. After that, the rest of the family did the same, until they were all gone.

Both versions give me the creeps, and if pressed, I can't begin to choose which one is worse. The only consistent detail appears to be the part about Andy Satterfield. In this second story, he finds the youngest Ramey boy hanging in the barn and ends up in the asylum.

And *that* I can totally believe. Seeing something like that is enough to send anyone to the crazy house.

Like Ben, I think, and then shake my head. I don't need to complicate my thoughts right now. Instead, I need to be clear-headed and fast because I still have a dreamstone to find, and a very, very long way to go.

7

———

I FEEL LIKE I might be in a fairy tale. I learned a little about those in school, about how they've changed to be more parent-friendly, and how most of the time when people think of fairy tales, they aren't even in the same ballpark of what they started out being. Ms. Jefferson, my 9th grade English teacher, shared some of the real ones with us, and they often involved kids running away from dark entities or evil men, running into or out of the woods, getting lost, and sometimes easing down dark lanes between darker trees, heading toward the very thing they should be running from.

I feel it as I draw closer – the selfish kind of magic, the kind Nesmith uses, the kind Granny warned against.

There are those who want it, but it always wants something back. And once you call something out from the dark places and it sees you...

My mind flashes to the goat demon's shadow. It's fathomless eyes studying me while I was in the tree. It's already seen me. So, what happens after the evil sees you? Granny never said. It was as if there was no putting into words the devastation waiting on a person in that situation.

My situation.

I remind myself it's going to be okay. I'm so close to the keys, and once I have those, we'll be across the river in no time. I'll be with Granny, and she can help me sort through all of it: Nesmith, the demon, what happened on the island, and what I'm going to do with Edie.

Hurry, child.

Hearing Granny's voice gives me a chill. It sounds as if she's a few feet behind me, so I turn quickly, sure I'll see her standing there, nodding her head at me like she does. Tremors, she told me once, is what causes her to nod like that.

But she's not there. Of course she's not. Granny hasn't driven in three years. Granny's even different in that way. Most old folks put up a terrible fight about giving up their independence, their ability to get where they want to go and when, but Granny decided on her own to sell her car and depend on others to get her around. Not that she goes anywhere. She's got everything she needs right on her land. Good milking cow, chickens, and a garden that grows the best tomatoes and peppers you've ever tasted.

I keep walking as the lane narrows, and the waning moon makes an appearance over the tops of the bare trees. I can't help but think the tree branches look like thorny wands, divining rods, beseeching the dark, hoping for answers, just like the rest of us.

In and out, I rehearse. Grab the keys, the wallet, the phone. In and out. Quick. Don't even look up. If you don't look up, you can't see a family hanging. You can't see anything.

By the time I see the Ramey house, the sky above me has turned a darker blue and all the trees are pure black, conspiring to create jagged gaps in the firmament of the dusk. The house itself is nothing too special, nothing intimidating. Just a white cottage with an addition on the back. Through the windows, I can see light, and a man and woman moving in the kitchen. Should I go there first, knock on the door, ask for someone to show me to the barn? Ordinarily, I would. Having company would make it much easier, but what do I really know about the Rameys? They seem nice, but they go to Nesmith's church. Sit in the front, all happy looking on Sundays.

I can't take the risk of letting them see me, so I slip off the lane and follow the trees, sticking to the long shadows and hollow places in between.

The barn stands off in a pasture by itself. A story I heard about it once comes to mind suddenly, vividly.

A kid on my school bus, a few grades below me, talking shit like most of the kids on the bus do. He said something about why they never tore the old barn down. Said they tried, but every time they'd knocked it down, the next day they'd come back to clear the rubble and wood and there it stood again.

I didn't believe a word of it when he told the story, but now… Now, I'm not so sure.

First of all, with its history, why wouldn't you tear it down? Makes no sense. So, maybe, just maybe, the kid was right. Maybe this is a place so filled up with that kind of selfish magic there's nothing in this world that can touch it.

Hell, Forest, you've got to stop. I've managed to work myself up over nothing. In and out. Wallet, keys, phone. Don't look up. That's all, that's it. I've got bigger fish to fry. Just one more step to Granny's. That's all this is.

The barn's got kudzu growing straight up the sides of it, and an owl is sitting on the roof peering at me with orange eyes.

The red paint of the barn is peeling and blotched green and black. Looks like mold. The large sliding gate door is partially open, and a tongue of dark air lashes out into the pasture. When I'm close enough to touch it, I stand still and say a prayer before going in.

"Make my eyes see only the truth," I say.

I'm just through the door when I get the flashback. God, it's strong, so damn strong I can't help but think the two barns are connected somehow.

I'm in the barn behind my house again. Dreamwalking. Shadows gather near the stacked hay. It's dark, but these shadows do not need light to be visible. They are the absence of light, darkness personified. There's a moment when I'm so deep in the dreamwalk there's nothing else, no waking world, no memory, just a single moment in time drawn along a string.

Nesmith is alone in the barn. He motions me forward, and I move as if compelled. That's when I notice he's naked. He reaches out and touches my shoulders, guiding me to my knees, and at first, I'm sure he's about to make me do something sexual, but instead he turns away and kneels beside me and begins to murmur a prayer. The words sound like they are in a different language, one I don't recognize.

I feel my consciousness quaver slightly as I try to wake myself up. I don't want this to happen, but I'm a prisoner here. I'm stuck inside the dreamwalk.

HOLY GHOST ROAD

Nesmith turns to me. "Stay asleep," he says.

I obey—and hate myself for it.

He continues to pray, and as he does, the demon goat manifests in front of me. No, that's not completely accurate. It manifests *from* me.

And that's when I feel myself breaking. I'm lost inside the dreamwalk. Not just trapped, but truly lost. I'll never find my way back to the surface.

The goat thing is my shadow and then it becomes something more than a shadow. I can feel the delight radiating out from Nesmith as the entity becomes whole.

I can see it clearly now. Its horns are no bigger than two pencils, but they have spirals that make them thicker and stronger looking, and they are black. Nesmith raises his hands in worship.

I lose time in the dreamwalk. There's more chanting, more worship, and I feel two claw-like hands grip my shoulders and shake.

Nesmith shouts out in surprise, and I'm awake.

I fall back onto the dirt floor of the barn and scramble away. The demon goat fades into the shadows.

All of this comes back to me as I enter this second barn. It takes my breath away. Nesmith had been about to kill me until someone woke me up, ended the dreamwalk, made the black-horned goat disappear.

But who?

Granny.

There's no question about it. She entered my dream. She pulled me out before Nesmith could kill me.

Before I can truly process what this means, I hear something moving in this barn, in the present.

I try to focus on the gathered darkness in the rear of this barn, trying to see what's making the sound.

There's nothing now. Just silence.

Enough. I need to focus. In and out. Quick. Like a thief.

This barn is so dark, I can't see anything. I go back to the door and slide it open wider, and that does the trick. Twilight floods through and reveals a mattress and some clothes laying out in the middle of the space. There's some hay too. Not stacks of it like in our barn, but just some scattered about, like carpet on the ground. The ladder to the hayloft is just behind the mattress, but I don't follow its wooden steps to see where it leads. If there are six bodies hanging above me, I won't know, and that feels like a small blessing.

But then something moves again in the very rear of the barn, underneath the hayloft, behind the ladder. It moves slowly, whatever it is. All I can make out is a single piece of dim white fabric, drifting across the back of the barn, and I wonder if it's a sheet tied up somehow and maybe a draft is blowing through the front door, rustling it. Except, there's no wind. Everything is still. The air is flat, stagnant, and the smell from earlier is stronger. Like something dead that's been wallowing in shit.

I remember the phone and step toward the mattress. I lift the blankets and see the mattress is bare underneath. Light is fading fast in the barn, and I badly need some kind of light source. An idea comes to me. Maybe there's a window under the hayloft like in our barn. If I could find it, and open the shutters up, that might allow enough light for me to see by.

HOLY GHOST ROAD

Yet, I hesitate. That's where most of the darkness is. It's also where I saw the movement. Probably my imagination. But imagination can be an extremely powerful thing when you're by yourself and it's dark, and all you know about a place are the stories you've heard so many times you figure at least some part of those stories must be true, and even if they're not, you feel pretty certain your imagination is strong enough to make them true, not to mention it feels like I'm in a dreamwalk somehow, that I'm in a world where anything can happen.

I leave the barn and walk around to the other side to see if a window exists, if there's one I can open from that side to let in some of the fading light. I jog because the dusk is slipping away with each passing second. The backside of the barn faces west, so there's a sliver of sunlight remaining here.

Just as I expected, there are shutters on this side. They're supposed to be opened from inside the barn, but I suspect if I push on them hard enough, they'll open. Then I can sprint back around into the barn to see if I can find the phone and keys.

As I'm reaching my hand up to push, I hesitate. A strange feeling comes over me. It's more than just a full body chill. It's an *extra* body chill. The air is charged all around me. Pressing my hand against the wooden shutters, I lean in and push with all my strength. Something cracks and the shutters fly open. Last light streams into the barn and the dark shadows at the rear are revealed.

The phone and the keys aren't too far from the mattress. Hell, I could have grabbed them from where I was standing if I'd only known to—

Fuck!

What was that?

Something moves again, except this time it's not slow. It's fast, and it scurries past the window where I stand, a figure in a white dress.

Or...

I peer in again, leaning back at an angle to keep my body from blocking the sun. Nothing.

Or... I just imagined it.

No. *Trust your eyes, but don't be afraid of what they show you.* Another one of Granny's sayings. She doesn't believe eyes play tricks. Only the mind, and the mind is *always* tricking us in order to make the things we see easier to take.

"So, what's happening?" I say it aloud, as if Granny were here with me, right beside me.

That's when the cellphone rings.

It's the same ringtone as Mama's, and it's coming from inside the barn. Is it possible Elijah's phone still isn't dead? Maybe. I've heard these newer phones can last for days.

I decide it's as clear a sign as any and break into a run for the front of the barn.

The phone is still playing its little tune when I reach the sliding door. The setting sun has finally slipped away, and no illumination comes through the back window anymore. The cell phone is on the ground, a single light in the middle of the now dark barn.

Running across the hay-scattered floor, I reach it in what seems like only a second, but as soon as my hand touches the device, it feels cold and alien. I pick it up and answer.

HOLY GHOST ROAD

"Hello?"

The voice is all static and distortion, and I know that I *know* it's the demon's voice.

Granny's dead, the voice says. *Dead.*

"Liar!" I shout —and end the call. It immediately rings again, but I ignore it and instead focus on the movement at the rear of the barn. It's happening again.

Footsteps. Coming toward me from the darkness. I brace myself for anything: demon goat, a family of ghosts, even Ruby Jewel, but whatever it is doesn't reveal itself yet.

I reach down for the keys, sure they must be nearby, and my hand falls on them. I scoop them up in my free hand, as the movement begins again, and something finally emerges from the darkness.

I don't run. I *can't* run.

Instead, I try to close my eyes, to shield my face from the thing I am sure will be the black-horned, upright goat, but I can't do that either. The only way is to face it, to *see* it true.

What I see doesn't need light to be visible. It eats into my field of vision just as it eats into my ears and nose and mouth, and even burns past layers of skin. It consumes me and enters me, but not before I recognize its terrible face.

And it is indeed a terrible face, more terrible than anything I could have imagined. In front of me, attached to a crippled and malformed body, is Granny's face. It's blotched with purple and red markings, and her eyes are sunken almost past being visible, nearly hidden under a sharp, clavicle-like brow. She opens her mouth, and the foul air that flows from it is enough, finally, to make me move, even if that movement is only to fall back onto the hay. I peer up into the darkness and see her face looming over me like some deflated moon.

Drool falls from her slack lips onto my cheek as she tries to speak again.

The words are wet with her saliva and her voice scratches the darkness like nails scratch skin.

"See the world true."

"You're not my grandmother," I shout at the thing, which I know is some trick of Nesmith's or more likely the goat's, some zombie, demon-haunted spawn made to look like the woman he fears more than any other.

Her eyes go wide at my accusation, and her head lolls to one side like she can't understand what I mean, or why I would say such a thing.

The phone in my hand rings again. I ignore it and slide back across the hay.

The thing with my grandmother's face watches me, and I swear there's a sadness in its eyes, and when I see that, I begin to cry.

The tears come fast. They come from nowhere. Nothing prompts them, but they arrive anyway, as if they are on some schedule, and they are bound to follow it no matter what emotion I am feeling. My disgust and anger get twisted inside me and changes over to match the tears. Sadness, grief, and desolation overtake me, and I turn my face against the hay and sob.

HOLY GHOST ROAD

Some time passes. It's not possible for me to say how much. What I do know is when I turn over again, the barn is empty. The barn is silent. I'm alone.

Slowly, I stand and brush off my bare legs and look at the phone in my hand. Somehow, there's a little battery left. Two percent battery life.

Without looking back, I leave the barn, sliding the door shut behind me as I do. I key in Granny's number and listen as it rings. I pray the battery won't die on me before she answers.

8

"**HELLER?**"

My whole body goes limp. I nearly stumble but manage to stay upright as the relief rushes through me. It's a heavy thing, relief, and it makes me feel like crying all over again, but for different reasons than before.

"Granny?"

"Where are you?"

"Near the Ramey Place. Not too far from the barn, you know the one where the family was killed."

"That's a dangerous place. You shouldn't go in there unless you're ready for it."

"Too late."

"What's that?"

"I already went in, Granny."

"Well, I reckon you survived it."

"I saw something. I *remembered* something."

"The truth, more than likely."

"The memory, yes. The rest was lies."

Her end of the line is silent. And for a moment, I fear the phone is dead. But then she clears her throat, hawking the mucous out like she does sometimes when her allergies are acting up.

"Well, sometimes a person has got to make up their own mind about truths and lies, but in the end, the truth will shine. Ain't two ways about that. Only question is when's the end?" She laughs and hacks some phlegm again. This time, I hear her spitting it out. Maybe into her sink. She's only got one phone, and it hangs on the wall of her kitchen. I've seen her stand and talk to a friend or relative for hours on end, grinning and nodding, occasionally clearing her throat in that irritating way of hers. I hate when almost anyone else in the world does that, but with Granny, for some reason, it's always been a lot more tolerable.

"I don't know," I say. "When is the end?"

"Everything and everyone's got a different end. You'll know when you know."

"Granny?"

"Yeah?"

"What does it want with me?"

"I reckon you mean the thing from your dreamwalk?"

"Yes."

"It's not what it wants *from* you. It wants you."

"I don't understand." As soon as I say the words, I regret them. She's just going to explain to me how understanding is overrated, how you can't rush it, how people understand when they understand and no sooner, but in typical Granny fashion, she has one more surprise.

HOLY GHOST ROAD

"You're the conduit, Forest. You're the doorway."

"How is that—»

"The dreamwalks. Be careful when you sleep. And around dusk and dawn. In pastures and borderlands. Forgotten places. That's when he'll come for you. But it's also when you can best fight back. But you need that stone."

I suck in a deep breath. "Okay. But I don't know where to look for it."

"Well, you're gonna have to figure that out."

"Granny..." I want to plead with her, to tell her she's supposed to know these kinds of things, but there is a resignation in her voice that makes me afraid to say anything. If Granny can't handle it, how can I?

"You'll find it. Just keep your eyes and ears open, and you can't miss it."

"I need your help," I say.

"Of course, baby. I'll always be there for you, but I'm old, and these bones don't have any get up to them. You've got to get it. Once you do that, bring it on over. And then you'll be ready."

"Ready for what?"

She's quiet for a moment. No hacking, no breathing either, and again I'm pretty sure I've lost her, but then I hear her voice, and I swear it cracks just the slightest bit as she speaks. "To face it."

The lines breaks up. Static and then sudden silence. Her voice comes back, garbled.

"It's nice here. I can see the sky from where I'm sitting, and hear the birds..." The phone cuts out, and her voice slides underneath the noise. She says something else, but I can't make sense of it.

John Mantooth

"The sky, Granny? The birds? What are you talking about?"

But there's only static that fades into silence. This time when I take the phone from my ear. It's dead.

9

I RUN THE rest of the way back out to the main road. The night has cooled off, and for the first time since I started this journey, it feels like fall. I'm hungry, tired, and my face is swollen and heavy from all the sobbing, but despite these issues, I feel light on my feet, as if I could run forever.

The cool night air burns my lungs, as I reach the old highway. The trees here form a tunnel over the road that is just now being illuminated by oncoming headlights. Ducking back into the woods, I wait as the vehicle goes past. It's a pick-up truck, of course, and its driver is a grim-faced man with his windows down. His eyes go right past me, but they are roaming eyes, the kind hoping to find something, or somebody.

Me. The kind hoping to find me.

Once the taillights of the truck are tiny red embers in the distance, I step free from the woods again and call out to Elijah.

When he doesn't answer, I head toward the place his car was parked. At first, I think it's just too dark for me to see it, but as I get closer, I am hit with the reality of the situation.

The car is gone.

John Mantooth

But how? Maybe someone towed it?

It's the only thing that makes sense.

I call out again, louder this time, hating the note of panic in my voice. "Elijah?"

No answer, just the truck downshifting a little further on down the road.

He promised me he'd wait, that he'd stay right here. And I believed him.

Call me naive, but I can't think of a single scenario in which he would break that promise. He needs me as much as much—or more—as I need him. And even if he doesn't need me, even if he's been playing me all along, I can't imagine a world in which Elijah doesn't really want to stick around to get his cell phone.

No, he was forced to flee. Or he was abducted by whoever moved the car. Those are the only explanations that make sense. I'm both relieved and distressed to come to this confident realization. Relieved because the thought of being abandoned by Elijah is just too much for me to take. Not to go all poor pitiful but being abandoned by men is sort of a theme with me. First my father died when I was four. Sure, not his fault, but he was once here and now he's gone, which feels an awful lot like abandonment to me. Then Ben. He abandoned me for drugs, for a hazy, zombie-like existence in which he could focus on never thinking about those kids in the Middle East again. Even though in both cases, these men had to contend with factors beyond their control, the end result was still the same: I was left alone. I don't think I can deal with the same thing from Elijah.

HOLY GHOST ROAD

Now I've got to figure out which direction he and Edie went. I search both sides of the road for clues, but the night has gone cloudy, and the moon glow is soft, so soft, I can barely see. I call out his name again and again, thinking maybe he and Edie are asleep, but there's never any answer.

I'm alone. And suddenly the tiredness, the hunger, the emotional explosion from the barn... all of it hits me at once. I sink to my knees beside the empty highway and lean forward, placing the side of my face against the warm asphalt shoulder of the road. I lay like this for some time, clinging to the warmth at the edge of the highway.

As I am about to fall asleep, I hear a car coming, or maybe I *feel* it coming. With my face flat against the road, I can pick up on the vibration, a humming that signals danger. When I look up, the headlights are rounding the bend up ahead. I stand and am about to head into the trees again when I spot something illuminated on the ground a few feet away from me. It's Edie's pacifier.

Granny says signs and portents can be anything. It's not the thing as much as what you make of it. She says most people think a sign is from God or fate or something, but sometimes, it's just reading the world for what it says. *Signs are all over, in the ordinary multitude of things and most of the time we miss them. They ain't so special like people think. The special part is being able to see them.*

Like so many things Granny taught me, I pushed her on it, tried to pull back the veil of obscurity she seemed to layer over all her advice.

"How do you know when you're seeing a sign or just something ordinary?"

A playful smile stitched itself across her mouth. "What's the difference?"

So, the pacifier is a sign or it's not a sign, it doesn't matter. It only matters how I perceive it, and how I react to it. The soft, nipple part seems to be pointing into the woods. I follow where it's pointing to and see there's a part in the trees, the barest hint of a trail.

The headlights, meanwhile, are getting ever closer and I can sense the vehicle slowing. Maybe it's just because the driver doesn't want to hit me, but maybe because the driver's trying to find me.

I'm on my feet and running then, pausing only to grab the pacifier in my fist before darting between the trees and onto the trail that probably isn't even a trail.

Except, I guess it is now.

10

WHOEVER IS IN the car must not have been looking for me because it doesn't stop, and instead speeds up again, taking the next turn far too fast. I decide to keep going. Trusting the sign seems as good a plan as any.

The woods are impossibly dark. I hold out my hands as I walk to fend off trees, but still manage to run into two of them anyway, knocking my right shoulder against the hardwood both times. I keep going, oblivious to the pain in my shoulder and my ankle, which is acting up again.

I don't want to think about what I saw in the barn, but I do. And what's the deal with barns anyway? First the black-horned upright goat and now the zombie Granny. Not to mention the memory that flooded back to me inside the second barn.

Nesmith had been about to sacrifice me to the goat. Or at least that's my best guess. And now he wants to finish the job. But apparently, he's not the only one who desires that. According to Granny, the demon is still after me too. And at some point, I'm going to have to face it.

All that scares the hell out of me, but at least I can make sense of it. And at least I have a goal: get to Granny's before either one of them catches me. If I can do that, I won't have to face either Nesmith or the demon alone.

What makes a lot less sense is the zombie Granny.

Granny's not dead. She's not evil. So, what could it possibly mean? It has to be some trick, some deceit played against the dark of the barn to make me weak, to make me lose my mind and myself, and if that one's a deceit then wouldn't the first one be too? And if it was a lie, if I'd simply dreamed it and then fled, what could that mean?

The night swarms around me as I run, and as I get more exhausted, it's harder to think. The air, once cool, now feels like it's been supercharged with a blast of heat. I'm sweating.

Staggering to a stop, I realize I'm not too far from 278, but I need some food, or rest, or both.

I press on, hoping to find some shelter or something to eat, but all the trees here are pines and none of the branches are low enough to grasp, and there's no way in hell I'm finding something to eat out here.

Slowing to a walk, I drag myself along, panting and groaning for what seem like hours until I can see the road. 278. Smoke swirls into the sky and dissipates before reaching the waning moon. The same fire from the other night if I had to guess. The realization fills me with an appalling sense of regret. So much effort and so little gained.

The feeling is simply devastating. This *must* be a dream because real life just couldn't possibly work like this. The road is empty.

I look around and find no sign of Elijah, but I do find a large oak not too far off the other side of the road in a small pasture of cows. I have to climb a fence with some barbed wire on top, but I make it over no problem. From there I pass several cows who appear to be dozing as they stand in a small cluster. One of them spots me and shuffles her feet like she means to come over, but then she drops down on to the ground, exhausted, ready for some real sleep.

Grabbing hold of the lowest branch, I pull myself up high into the oak until I find a good, sturdy limb, wide enough to sleep on. The moon is visible again through the nearly bare branches. Somehow, at least for a moment, the world doesn't seem so bad. Which is weird, right? Because I've pretty much failed at everything I've tried. I've made very little real progress in getting to Granny's, nor have I made any progress in figuring out what's real and what's not. Still, the moon is visible again. The clouds are gone. I held a snake and saved a baby. I saw a sign.

I'm still alive.

The Crossroads

1

___

I SLINK ALONG the tree line for hours, hungry, cold, and scared. I reckon it's Thursday, or maybe Friday. Time has slipped. I hear Edie crying. Every car that blows past me out on the highway is Nesmith's Cadillac, Ruby Jewel in the passenger seat, staring out at the world with those blind eyes. When I hear noises off in the woods, I'm sure it's Helmet, dead eyes and all, come to scoop me up and carry me on his shoulder. I'm so tired, it doesn't sound half bad, the shoulder part anyway. Being carried.

Because my mind isn't right, and because I'm hearing so many things, seeing so many visions, I almost miss the sound of the car slowing down behind me.

I'm mostly covered by the trees, but I realize it's still possible someone with sharp eyes might have spotted me. It's not until a car door closes nearby that I finally stop dragging myself along and turn to see what it is.

Elijah is standing on the shoulder of the highway, not far from where 31 bisects 278 heading north. He's holding Edie and she seems content.

Her face is calm, her clothes have been changed. Even Elijah looks fresh, like he had a decent night's sleep for a change.

"What's happening?" I say through the trees.

"We came to get you."

"Where did you go? You were supposed to wait for me."

"We tried. A car came by, and a man got out and said he wanted to help us. He was able to get my car towed. I got scared and ran. We came back for you, but we must have missed each other." He looks down at Edie, as if she might confirm his story, but her eyes are on the sky, and she sucks on her new pacifier contentedly. "I got lost."

"Oh," I say, thinking that actually makes sense. I've never known a man—or woman—who had a worse sense of direction.

"Anyway," he says, turning and pointing across the road. "I've got a van now."

On the other side of the road is a plain white van, the kind you usually see with a ladder on the top or a slogan painted on the side that says "On Time Service" or something like that, only this one is just plain white and there's no ladder.

"Where'd you get it?"

He shifts Edie, so I can see her face. "Gas station up the road. Guy left the keys in it."

"*You* stole a car?"

"I was desperate, Forest."

I lean around some tree branches for a better view of the van. There's about a million reasons this doesn't seem right, but the one that stands out the most is Elijah doesn't seem right. I could imagine him stealing a van if it was the absolute last resort, but I don't think it was. Besides, how would he know the guy left his keys in the van? It's not like a car, where you could easily look in the window and see the keys hanging there. The van is too high up. And then there's the clothes change. How in the hell did they both change clothes?

"This is bullshit," I say.

"What? No."

"Why are you lying to me? Did *he* get to you?"

"Listen, Forest…" He sucks in a deep breath. "Okay. Fine. I'm lying, but only because I want you to see reason."

"Reason? You lie to me and then say you want me to see reason?"

He glances at the van, as if he's checking to see if anyone is there. "Look, they sent me over here, and told me to talk you into coming to the van."

"They?"

"Nesmith and your mom."

I start to back up, already planning my route in my head. I'm exhausted, but the adrenaline will get me where I'm going. I know it will. But I can't quite pull the trigger, not until I understand how they've manipulated Elijah.

"Please don't run, okay?"

I say nothing, keep an eye on the van.

"The Helmet guy grabbed us last night. He took us to your house. They fed us. They got me my car back. I don't have a key yet, but you do. I'm going home. You can too. Brother Nesmith is confused by your actions. He doesn't understand why you're running. What you think you saw. He's worried about you."

"He ain't confused. And he ain't worried."

"He doesn't know what you think you saw in the barn, but he's worried that you might be losing it. Your mother too. She told me about what happened. What keeps happening."

No. This is the absolute worst thing. I back up some more, deeper into the woods, but that's when Edie cries and I realize I can't leave her. She had it bad across the lake with the Gazaways, but it will be hell for her growing up with Nesmith and Ruby Jewel.

"Let me have her, Elijah. You don't know what they're like. You don't know about their lies, the way they make reality whatever it they want it to be. In the barn… it was a devil, it had black horns and stood upright. I was on my knees. He was going to kill me, or… or worse."

"It's just the dreams, Forest. The trauma from what happened."

"Nothing happened, okay? They lie all the time, and it's just more of their lies."

"Your brother never came back from the Middle East, Forest. Ben died over there."

"No, that's a fucking lie. That's Nesmith. It's his lie. His way of controlling us, of making me feel like I don't know what I know."

"And since then, you've been sleepwalking and having these odd dreams, sort of fantasies. Look, Forest. You're a good person. Good through and through, but you've got to stop running from the truth."

HOLY GHOST ROAD

The lies. The fucking lies. I feel like they are tearing through my skin and jabbing my flesh, looking for places to take root and to become a part of me like they've become a part of the rest of my family and this community. I won't let it happen. I will continue to see true. I will continue to run from the lies and run toward the river, so one day I might cross it and make it to Granny's again.

But I can't leave that baby. I don't even want to leave Elijah. What he's saying about me is actually true about *him*. He's a good person, just deceived. He's deceived by a world that believes logic is a sturdier than wonder, that material destroys mystery.

And the sad part is how right he is. But it doesn't have to be that way. That's what Granny has taught me. You have to resist.

"You saw what I did with the snake," I say. "You saw that. That was magic. That was from the Holy Ghost. The real one."

"I saw you take a risk, and while it may have been brave, it was also foolish. You got lucky." I can tell as he says this, there's a small, very small part of him that is doubting himself

"And the police officer. What was that? He let us go. You know why? I was praying. I prayed."

He nods. "I think you should come with me. They don't want to hurt you. They want to help you."

My mind spins. Only two options, but I seem stuck between them. Stay here and try to convince him to come with me, or bolt. It's the baby, Edie that makes me feel stuck. I want to get her to Granny's as much as I want to get myself.

"Come with me," I say. "I got your phone."

"My keys?"

I nod.

"The barn… Did you see anything?"

"Yeah. I saw something and so did you."

His reserve falters a little.

"Come with me," I say again. "Granny will explain it all."

"What did you see?" he asks.

For some reason I think of lying, of making something up because what I really saw, I don't even want to talk about, but I decide to go ahead and tell the truth. That's all we both want, isn't it? The truth? Hell, I think that's all anyone wants.

"I saw Granny. She was…I don't know…a zombie? She seemed dead. She said something to me. It's something she always says. 'See the world true.'"

Elijah glances back at the van again. This time there's something happening. The back door slides open. Nesmith climbs out and holds his hand to help Mama step out too. No Ruby Jewel. No Helmet. This is a different tactic. Nesmith will be in preacher mode, the concerned pastor, trying to bring back one of his wayward sheep, and the worst part is Mama will eat it up like it's goddamn chocolate pie.

Mama hands Nesmith his cane, and they wait for a big rig to blow past on 278 before she takes his arm and walk over.

"They lie," I say, while they're still out of earshot. "Whatever they say, it's going to be a lie."

"Well," Mama says. "I'm proud to see you're okay."

"I've never been better," I say.

"Forest," Nesmith says, his voice buttery smooth. "I'm very sorry you've felt the need to run, and I'm especially sorry our friend Ronald may have gotten a little rough with you. You know he fought in the mideast, just like your brother."

"Don't you mention my brother."

"I apologize," Nesmith says. He pokes his way a little closer, and I find myself backing up on instinct. There's a smell Nesmith has, and he can't seem to cover it no matter how much cologne or deodorant he wears.

He places a hand on Elijah's shoulder and peers down at Edie and smiles. Elijah flinches just a little when he feels Nesmith's hand.

"Elijah here has explained to us that you believe you saw something in the barn the other night."

Mama shakes her head. "Forest, you know you were sleepwalking and whatever you see when you sleepwalk can't be the truth."

"It is the truth. Look at him, Mama. When he came to stay with us, he was in a wheelchair. Now he's out. He looks younger too. Why do you think that is?"

"Prayer," Mama says without missing a beat. "And clean living."

"Bullshit. I saw him in the barn. With a demon. He was going to kill me. As a sacrifice."

Nesmith gasps and turns to Mama. "I'm sorry you are having to witness this. She's losing it."

Mama nods. "Listen to yourself, Forest."

And for a second, in the clear light of day, with so many other people staring at me, I do feel some doubt. What if I am just losing it? What if it's all a lie? What if there's nothing more, nothing out there, no Holy Ghost, nothing that separates us from any other material?

"It's too much time with her grandmother," Nesmith says. "She's rubbing off on her."

And that's all I need to bring me back. The mere mention of Granny reminds me I'm not alone.

"I woke up," I say. "I dreamwalked out there, but I woke up. I saw the demon goat, but I didn't need to see that. I've known it all along." I point at Nesmith. "He's evil." I turn to Elijah. "Come on. Let's go."

"And where do you think you're going?" Mama says.

"Granny's. The only place him and his demon won't be able to touch me." I jab my finger at Nesmith as I say the last part, and he flinches just enough that I know there is some truth there. Granny will protect me. I know it, and he knows it too.

"Oh, that's perfect. And what happens when you run out of money and can't feed yourself, much less this baby?" Mama says.

"You know," Nesmith says, "kidnapping is a very serious offense. I'm sure my friends at the sheriff's office will be glad to overlook it considering you are a minor and in a bad place emotionally, but you'll need to come home and apologize to the mother. If you continue to run and show no remorse, then things could get... tricky."

HOLY GHOST ROAD

I step back, because as he's been talking, Nesmith has been creeping forward. "I'm never coming home," I say. "Never. That's not my home anymore."

He sighs. "Dear girl, do you know how much this hurts your mother?"

Before I can answer, he reaches into his pocket and pulls out a bottle of pills. "At least let me give you these."

"I don't want them. But I do want the other thing you stole from me."

His face changes just enough for me know he knows what I'm talking about.

"Forest," Mama says. "Where is this going?"

"He took the stone Granny gave me."

"That rock? Who even cares about that?" Mama says.

"It was mine. He took it because he knows it would have protected me from the demon."

Mama's eyes go wide, and I realize I've miscalculated.

"I told you," Nesmith says. "This is exactly what I was talking about."

"You need help," Mama says.

"I need my fucking dreamstone."

Mama gasps, but I swear Nesmith smiles, just a little. He likes that I'm desperate, that he knows he's made my life more difficult.

"You need to come home and stop this nonsense, now." Her voice softens a little and she adds the kicker. "Maybe being off the meds has hurt you more than you realize, baby."

"No. I'm done with that medicine." All at once, I understand something that should have been obvious to me from the beginning.

John Mantooth

Nesmith was—*is*—behind the medicine. It was his idea. If I'd just paid attention, I wouldn't have been so blindsided, but I missed all the clues. I don't understand all his motivations or what he's even trying to accomplish, but the truth of his actions resonate inside of me. It's like what Granny means when she says sometimes magic and truth are the same thing. You don't have to understand either one. You just have to *recognize* them.

Before either Nesmith or Mama can say anything else, Edie's eyes go wide. She sees something in the woods behind me. I turn quickly, but there's nothing there, at least not that I can see.

"I'm sorry, Mama," I say. I mean it too. I'm sorry for all of it. For Nesmith, for Ben, even for Dad. She didn't deserve any of it. Except maybe Nesmith. She *chose* him.

"Sorry isn't good enough. You need to come home. Clean up your act. Get your head out of the clouds. Come back to church and get back on your meds."

Now Elijah sees something too. He gasps and calls out to me, but it's too late. By the time I turn, Helmet is already charging me from the woods. He scoops me up, for the second time, and throws me over his shoulder.

"Put her in the van," Nesmith says.

I beat on Helmet's back with my fists, but just like before, he doesn't seem to notice.

"You said it would be her choice," Elijah says. "You lied."

"Look," Nesmith says as Helmet climbs the steep incline toward the highway. "You're free to go. Thanks for looking out for her. We'll take Edie."

HOLY GHOST ROAD

I strain my neck to see them behind me now as we march toward the highway. Mama goes over and holds out her arms for Edie, but—thank God—Elijah refuses.

"No, I don't think that's a good idea."

"Hold it," Nesmith says to Helmet. Helmet stops, one foot out in the highway.

"Run!" I shout at Elijah.

"No, not without you."

Helmet turns to face Elijah who, still carrying Edie, walks up to stand on the shoulder of the road too. I kick and pound Helmet, but he's impervious to the pain.

"What are you doing?" I say. "You're going to get caught, and then Edie will be caught."

"He's going to have to put you down to take me," Elijah says.

Helmet doesn't react at all to Elijah's claim. Instead, he just starts walking toward the van. I crane my neck around Helmet's right side and see Elijah standing in the road. A car flies past, brushing us back, barely slowing. I wave my hands at it and scream in case someone is looking in their rearview, someone who might be willing to help, maybe somebody from out of town heading to their lake house for a weekend of quiet solitude. But the car just keeps going, and soon vanishes from view.

Helmet continues across the road. I strain my neck and see Nesmith and Mama are following him. Elijah is still standing on the side of the road with Edie. I shout at him to run, but he's frozen, seemingly unable to move at all.

When he reaches the van, he tries to open the door, and when he does, I grab his elbow and pull with both hands, holding his arm back. It's no use. He's too strong. I'm going in the van, but as soon as that realization hits me, the seed of an idea enters my mind. It's a chance, or maybe it's more than that. It's a probability, as long as I can focus my energy, my attention, my will. As long as I can see the world true.

The van door slides open and he all but tosses me inside. I land on the old carpet that smells of cigarettes and piss. He slams the door behind me, and I am the thing that moves through the world like an arrow. I am a star, burning toward a distant planet, causing plants to grow and animals to thrive. I am the one true thing in a world of deceit, and I move like a flash of lightning, scrambling into the front seat of the van, my hands grasping the wheel and then going underneath the steering column, trying to find the keys. Blindly, I pat down the steering column until I feel them. Keys, at last.

I crank the hell out of that van, twisting the ignition with the power of pent-up anxieties, fears, and pain, letting it all loose through the power of my wrist, and through those keys, so that the energy roars into the engine and thrums beneath me. Dropping it into drive, I floor the van. It lurches out into the road, and I have just enough presence of mind to strap myself in before I cut the wheel hard—too hard, because for a terrible second, the van feels like it's going to leave the ground—but then it stabilizes, and I've made the turn. In front of me, Helmet is on one side of the road and Mama and Nesmith on the other. Elijah stands nearby, holding Edie, staring at me like I've lost my mind.

HOLY GHOST ROAD

And maybe I have, because I nudge the wheel to the right just enough to aim the van at Helmet. He turns and sees me coming. Really sees me for the first time ever. And I see him too. Behind the cold, machine-like eyes is something else, something I saw in Ben before he turned to painkillers that killed him.

Whatever I see in those eyes is enough. At the last minute, I jerk the wheel to avoid hitting him. *Am I seeing true?* I ask myself as the van leaves the road and goes airborne toward the tree line. Is this the sacred magic?

And where is the Holy Ghost? Why can't I see it? Or feel it? Or even know it?

As ever, the question goes unanswered. Instead of an answer, I see something in my rearview. In the back of the van, all along.

Ruby Jewel.

She's coming this way, stumbling and slouching, some great shambling beast with too much make-up. I only see her for a second before the flight of the van pulls my attention away from her.

The van doesn't flip, but it tries. The front-end noses into a ravine, and I am snapped back from the windshield by the seatbelt.

Ruby Jewel isn't so lucky. She flies forward between the seats like a missile and cracks the windshield with her forehead. Blood streaks the spiderwebbed fissures in the glass, and Ruby Jewel's head lays on the dashboard, her make-up smeared by the blood oozing out from the gash on her forehead. The engine revs as the front wheels spin for purchase against nothing. The ravine is only about a ten-foot drop, but inside the van, with

Ruby Jewel's body laying across the center console, her head on the dash, it might as well be a thousand.

I try my door, but it's jammed shut against the trunk of a pine tree.

Ruby Jewel's bloody cartoon face smiles, splitting the wound open even more, but she doesn't seem to mind. Despite her blindness, she reaches for me, both of her hands going for my neck. She's a sleepwalker, trying to touch the world from the other side of sleep. I lean against the door with all my strength, but it's not enough.

Her hands are as strong as they look, and they form a seal around my neck. I try to scream, but my breath is gone.

"You hurt me," Ruby Jewel murmurs, and it's clear she isn't concerned about Nesmith's admonition to take me alive.

I try to say, *it wasn't my fault,* but because I can't breathe, I only think it. Yet, she seems to hear me anyway.

"Not my head," she said. "This is nothing." She tightens her grip on my neck, and I feel like I'm getting closer to a darkness that has been waiting for me for a long time. It's a shadow world, the one I walk through sometimes in my dreams. I can see it on the other side of the pain.

And perhaps Ruby Jewel isn't ready for me to go there yet because she eases her grip, and I can breathe again. Just enough to keep me on this side.

"The snake," she says, and she hisses the word. "That hurt me."

"What?" I manage.

And as if in answer, I am hurtled back through the timeline of the last few days until I'm at the base of Lightning Hill again, and I find I have a stone in my hand, I slam it down onto the snake's head and Ruby Jewel screams out in pain.

Her hands tighten on my neck. "I want you to suffer for that."

"Please…" I manage, as her hands squeeze life out of me, and the world begins to darken. Just before it goes completely dark, I focus on the keys hanging from the ignition. There's several on a big loop. One of them catches my eye. A round sticker on the end of the key says *Amp Cellar*. I don't know what it means, much less why I keep focusing on it, but it's the last thing I see before the darkness is complete.

2

I GO BACK to the dreamwalk. I go back to a ledge, overlooking a ravine of black water, smooth as dark glass. I'm traveling here, the lake on one side of me and strong wind on the other. There's only one place where I can live, and it's on this tiny ledge, following this single path.

To my left are three barns. The doors of all three are flung open wide, and the first two are filled with light. As I walk, I look inside them. The first is a scene that might almost seem innocent if not for the details. A man kneels before an altar of hay and grass and bones. It's Nesmith, of course. Standing behind the altar is the black-horned thing. His face is the face of a billy goat, and his horns have sprouted into antlers strewn with vines and leaves and every small piece of the forest. He holds a cup, a very, very large cup, more like a bowl in both of his hands. The demon goat thing stares at the cup where a head is bobbing gently in thick blood. I can just make out the eyes over the rim of the cup. It's Ben. But that's not all. Beside his head is a floating rock, a smooth stone, polished to a dark sheen.

The dreamstone.

The goat thing sees me looking and smiles.

I look away. Keep walking.

The next barn is flooded with light too. Zombie Granny is standing there, a phone held up to her ear. She's speaking into it, but I can't hear what she's saying. It's as if her voice is gone, dead like the rest of her. As bad as the first barn was, this one somehow seems worse, and I turn back to the black water on my right as I continue to walk. In the water's reflection is Ruby Jewel's gruesome face, her dead eyes somehow filled with determination as she bears down on me.

The final barn. Through the mouth of darkness, I can't see anything at first, but whatever is in there is the worst of all possible visions. I know that. I *feel* that as a giant, throbbing emptiness inside me. I strain my eyes, but this barn is completely dark, impenetrable. The barn door slides shut as I try to see inside. There's a loud clang that pulls me back up out of the dreamwalk and into the van again.

3

FIRST THING I see is the key again. *Amp Cellar.*

I still can't breathe, and I realize I am about to die. The pain is gone. The desire to breathe is even floating away. I feel ethereal, content, but I can't stop looking at the damn keys.

Amp Cellar.

The door on the passenger side opens. Helmet is standing there, his face as impassive as ever. He sees me and then his eyes take in Ruby Jewel, splayed out across the space in between the seats, her hands around my neck.

He reaches for her, grips her around the midsection and pulls her toward the door. She doesn't let go of my neck, and the darkness is there at the corner of my eyes, a dusk just waiting to drop again. This time, it will be the final dusk.

I drop away for a second. Everything goes dark. No dreamwalking now. No earthwalking either. Just shadows. But then light rushes in and it's followed by a great wallop of air that I choke on. I cough and sputter and ache, and finally breathe again.

Opening my eyes, I see Helmet dragging Ruby Jewel out through the passenger's side door or trying to. She's fighting him with everything she's got, her hands still reaching for me.

I pull myself into the back of the van again, falling over the center console between the seats because I'm so out of breath, and plant face first into the carpet. I suck in a deep whiff of piss and cigarettes and reach for the sliding door. It opens easily and I tumble out onto the ground, right next to where Helmet and Ruby Jewel are struggling. I run, darting past Nesmith and Mama who are picking their way through the trees toward the van and out onto the road, where Elijah and Edie are still standing there in the middle of the two-lane. Elijah's eyes are as vacant as Helmet's or even Ruby Jewel's.

"We've got to go. Now," I shout.

Elijah's eyes flash back to life. "How did you…"

"Just go. We can talk later."

But he doesn't go. He stands right there until I reach him. Then he hands me Edie and wraps both arms around me, us. All three of us embrace, and just like that, we become a family, the strangest and best family I've ever known.

"I'm sorry," he says. "So, so, so sorry."

"It's okay. You were scared."

He nods. "I still am. None of it makes sense."

"I know." I break the embrace and shift Edie to my right arm and grab his hand with my left. I pull him out of the road toward the trees on the other side. We have to disappear, and quickly.

HOLY GHOST ROAD

As we make our way down a steep incline, into what some of the densest trees yet, Mama yells for me to come back and listen to reason. I'm more sure than ever there is a certain kind of reason that can damn a person, just as surely as other kinds can save them.

4

WE RUN THROUGH the woods until I can't run anymore. Elijah has a little more energy than me, but the truth is, we are all hungry. Edie too. We have to find a place to get some food and some formula, or we won't be able to keep moving. It's that simple.

So, when we come to the old dirt road deep in the trees, I have an idea. Back when Mama was in one of her drinking spells, she used to take me and Ben to the bars with her. Except in Winston County there aren't really bars, at least not officially. Winston is dry, so mostly people bring their own alcohol in. If you do want to go sit in a bar and drink yourself silly, you've got to find one in the woods. Mama preferred this method as she was a binge drinker and never has liked to drink it regularly. She taught us how to find the backroads like this one and look for the signs posted to trees that signaled where the bars were. It will give us a place to regroup, to rest. Most importantly, to think.

Amp Cellar.

It doesn't take me long to spot one of the signs just off the road. It simply says, "Water—a mile ahead, on the right."

"There," I say and point at the sign.

Elijah frowns. "Water?"

"It's a bar. They may have food."

He nods and checks on Edie. "We need to get some formula too."

"I know. Maybe they'll have some milk we can warm up."

"Can a baby drink cow's milk?"

"I reckon this one can. She's tough."

That causes Elijah to chuckle a bit. "Has to be. Hell, we're all pretty tough at this point."

We continue along the road in silence. A mile shouldn't feel like such a long way, but when you're as tired as we are, it feels like traveling to another country.

"We ever going to make it?" I say.

"You mean to your grandmother's?"

"Yep. To salvation."

Elijah keeps walking. Doesn't answer. Maybe he's thinking it over.

"Ben ain't dead," I say after some time.

Elijah turns to me. "Okay."

"I'm serious. That's Nesmith's doing."

"I don't understand."

"When Ben wouldn't get clean, Mama lost her shit and said he was dead to her." I wince a little, remembering it. "Nesmith goes into Ben's room and tells him he's dead. Just like that. This is when Mama is gone, of course. She's down in Birmingham for the day. The scary part is when Nesmith was standing at Ben's door, Ruby Jewel was right behind him as usual, and I felt like he really wanted him dead, that he might kill him himself, if it came to it. Ben was asleep. He was always asleep during this time, and the only way to wake him up was to, you know, shake him. So, Nesmith, he steps aside and Ruby Jewel steps in." I remember her hands around my neck, the strength of them, crushing me, and the memory makes my neck hurt. I'm pretty sure she's permanently damaged my neck, but I can't worry about that now. I can breathe, and I can swallow. That's enough for the time being.

"What did she do? Ruby Jewel?" Elijah asks. I haven't told him about my experience in the van yet.

"She walks over to his bed and drags him out onto the floor. Ben wakes up. He's groggy from the painkillers, but not too groggy, you know? He can understand what Nesmith says to him."

"And what does he say?

"He tells Ben he's dead."

"He's dead?"

"Yep. Says it like he's making it come true, like it's some kind of spell or something. This is after Ben spent several weeks at Nesmith's facility. You don't know this, but Nesmith's got this place where he helps vets out. Except he didn't help Ben any. And then it was like he was done with him. He might as well have been saying 'you're dead to me,' but he just said he was dead. I can tell Ben wants to argue, and maybe he would if not for, you know, the pills, but instead, he just slowly gets to his feet and throws his stuff in a bag. He tells me he's sorry and then he walks out of the house. I follow him down to Macon Freeman's trailer, where he goes inside and lays down in the dark den. Macon smiles at me and asks if I want some pills." I'm crying now, remembering it, the darkness of the trailer, the *death*ness of the place, and in a way, I realize for once Nesmith wasn't wrong. Ben *is* really dead.

"And that's where he still is?"

"As far as I know. Last time I went to check on him…" I hesitate, not wanting to remember this part.

"What?"

"Never mind. He's still there."

"And what did Nesmith tell your mother?"

"That he's dead, just like she said."

"And she believed him?"

"Of course she believed him. That's another spell. I don't know how he does it, but she can't think for herself anymore."

"I'm sorry."

"It's okay. If I can get across the river, I'll leave all of this behind forever."

"But what about—" He stops himself.

"What about what?"

"Your brother."

I don't answer him, mostly because I can't. I don't know how to. I've thought about Ben, but I've also thought about how sometimes a person has to save themselves before they can save anyone else. And if I'm being honest, it's something I planned to ask Granny about when I get there. She'll know what to do, how to fix it. Anyway, we're rounding a bend and there, hidden among some tall pines, is a little shack. There's a pickup truck and two sedans parked outside. The place itself is made out of cedar shake, with a tin roof and two boarded up windows. There's no sign or anything out front, but it's clear this is the bar we've been looking for.

5

PEOPLE IN THESE places are serious about drinking, and no one pays us much mind when we come into the poorly lit bar. A generator hums somewhere and every few seconds it hiccups and chokes, and causes what dim light there is inside to flicker, but no one seems to notice that either. Three people are at the bar, all men. The bartender is also male, though there is a female voice I hear call out from the other room that must serve as a kitchen. A jukebox in the far corner plays a song about black velvet sung by a woman who sounds like she's trying to seduce a man. The bartender taps his thumb on the bar and nods toward us, as if to ask what we'll be having. He doesn't seem at all surprised we are carrying an infant or that the infant is screaming her head off.

"We don't have any money," Elijah hisses at me, over the sound of Edie's desperate cries. She's been doing this off and on since we saw the sign. I reckon it's on account of her needing to eat. Elijah says the last time he fed her was early this morning before leaving the house with Mama and Nesmith.

"You don't have any in that wallet I got back for you?"

"No cash. Just a debit card." He shrugs. "Something tells me they aren't going to take that here."

"We'll worry about that when it comes time to pay," I say. "I've got to eat. Edie has to eat."

"Okay." He nods and we walk to the bar.

"Whiskey or beer?" the bartender says.

"We were hoping to get something to eat," I say, trying to sound confident, trying not to sound too worn out, too hungry. I fail. The desperation in my voice is hard to miss. The bartender takes it in stride. I guess desperation is the norm in a place like this.

He points at a crude, homemade sign behind the bar that reads, *Menu-Meal 6, Sandwich 7*. "We got eggs and bacon," he says over the painful sobbing coming from Edie. "We can put them on bread and that's a sandwich. We can put the bread on the side and that's the meal."

"Why is the sandwich more?" Elijah says.

"Sandwich has got mayo," the bartender answers. He smiles at the baby. "She got a name?"

"Edie," I say.

He nods. "My oldest used to cry just like that. Would drive a stake through my heart every time." He shakes his head. "What's it going to be?"

"Two meals," Elijah says.

"Fried or scrambled?"

Elijah looks at me.

"Fried."

"Two fried," Elijah says.

HOLY GHOST ROAD

The bartender calls our order out to the woman in the back. "Also," I say. "You wouldn't happen to have any milk you could warm up, would you?"

He looks at the baby, looks almost like he's about to ask for our story, but then seems to think better of it. "I can round something up. Got a bottle or something?"

I shake my head.

"She gonna drink out of a cup?"

"We'll try."

He makes a face and heads to the kitchen.

I stand to walk with Edie. She usually cries less when we're moving. I go from one end of the tiny bar to the other. Elijah sits and watches me, his face still contorted by what I can only call confusion. Edie doesn't stop crying. In fact, the movement seems to agitate her more. She screams like she's on fire, and the bartender is right, each one of those screams is like a stake going right through my heart.

"You gonna get that damn kid quiet or what?" a man says from the end of the bar. He's thin, angular, with long black hair and a scraggly beard. He's got tattoos on his face, dark splotches below his eyes and on his forehead, symbols of something I can't make out. Mostly it's his voice, though. His voice cuts through the screams, a slurred knife, and the sound of it makes the bar go quiet. Even Edie quiets, seemingly waiting to see what such a sound could mean.

"She's hungry," I say. "She'll be okay when I get her some milk."

The man shakes his head and peers down the bar at Elijah sitting there. "You with him?"

"He's a friend."

"Is that what they're calling it nowadays?"

"What else would you call it?"

I turn, surprised to see Elijah is speaking up. He's shown courage on this journey, for sure, but never much willingness to engage in confrontation.

"He speaks," the man with the tattoos says.

A woman comes out of the back, carrying an actual bottle, thank God. She seems to sense the tension in the bar and pauses, scanning the men sitting at the bar, her eyes finally falling on me and Edie.

"See if she'll drink this," the woman says. "It's a bottle got left here a while back. It's been cleaned." The woman's in her fifties, I guess. Pretty with gray hair and clear skin. Her eyes are blue. She wears a pair of old jeans and a button-down men's shirt.

I take the bottle from her, and Edie perks up as soon as she sees it. Her eyes grow wide and she coos. Something about that sound sort of breaks my heart and puts it back together all at once. It's a wonderful thing.

But she doesn't want it. Well, she does at first. At first, she drinks greedily, but after a moment, her face contorts as if the liquid she's swallowing is some poison. She spits and sputters and chokes, and then begins to cry again. What starts as a gagging whimper soon turns into a full-throated shriek, as she flails and knocks the bottle out of my hands.

"Goddamn it, can you shut that retard up?" the man says.

Elijah comes off his stool and heads down the bar. The tattooed man stands up to meet him.

HOLY GHOST ROAD

"It's a goddamn baby," he says, his face inches from the man's unreadable tattoos.

"Elijah," I say. "You don't have to do this."

"What are you even?" the man says. "Some kind of mixed breed?" He shakes his head. "This is why the races should keep to their own. Cause when they don't, you get this." He says it as if he's speaking to an audience, as if the entire bar is captivated but I'm the only one watching. The woman has returned to the kitchen with her husband, and the other two men at the bar are staring hard at their drinks.

"Fuck you," Elijah says. He barely gets the words out of his mouth when the tattooed man takes a swing. The punch lands on Elijah's jaw. It's a good punch. He's been in fights before. Hell, from the look on his face, right now, he fights a lot. He seeks out conflict like he seeks out alcohol, wherever he can find it, no time like the present.

Elijah—to his credit—doesn't go down. He buckles back against the bar but holds himself up. I'm looking for a place to put Edie—still screaming--when the bartender comes out with a baseball bat. Tattooed man sees him too, because he steps back, holding up his hands.

"I'm good, Wallace," he says. "I'm good."

"I warned you about this bullshit," Wallace says.

"Aw, fuck, Wallace. The damn baby wouldn't shut up."

"It's a baby. That's what they do. Go on. Come back tomorrow with a new attitude, Greg."

Greg glares at me. "You oughta have just kept your panties on," he says. "Fucking slut." He picks up his whiskey and drains the rest before heading toward the door.

He's almost there when he stops. "Wait a minute," he says. He squints at me and then at Elijah. "Something don't make sense."

"Can you make him go?" I say to Wallace.

"I'm going," Greg says, "just a second." He looks at Edie now. "Don't you remember what Ronnie said earlier today?"

"Ronnie?" Wallace says.

"Yeah. About the girl they're looking for. She's supposed to be on the run with some man, some half breed."

Wallace nods. "That's right. I remember now."

"Hell," Greg says. "You still gonna make me leave? I'm a hero now." He turns and heads back toward the bar.

"Hold it," Wallace says.

"Hold nothing," Greg says. "I'm making the call."

"No." It's the woman, Wallace's wife. She's come back from the kitchen carrying a shotgun, which she's got aimed right at Greg. "You're going to leave."

Greg doesn't react at all like I'd expect him to. That's when I recognize the thing that's in him. It's something Nesmith and Ruby Jewel carry too, a kind of knowledge of how things are gonna go. It's a knowledge most of us don't have. Lord knows I don't. But some people can just see it all laid out, and because they can see it, they can act in ways the rest of us can't. Maybe it's a dark gift from the black-horned thing. Maybe it's there for all of us if we but learn how to snatch it out of the air and use it. Whatever the case, it's in his eyes. It's a light, or hell, a lack of light that moves him, powers him like he's a machine running on some dark energy.

HOLY GHOST ROAD

After the brief pause where Greg's eyes change, he walks slowly to the bar. He reaches over and pulls out someone's cell phone from beneath it.

"Did you not hear what I said?" Wallace's wife says.

"I heard you." He begins to dial.

"We've got to go," I say.

"I'm going to shoot you," the woman says. But the sound in her voice is the opposite of the look in Greg's eyes. The sound makes it clear she has no idea what will happen. It's a sound of doubt.

"Hey," Greg says into the phone, "I've spotted that girl and her friend."

I don't ask again. I hand Edie to Elijah and reach over the bar and grab the bacon from the plate and stuff one piece in my mouth, saving the other for Elijah. Then I pick the bottle up from the floor.

"Let's go. Now," I say to Elijah.

Elijah seems shaken. Not just by the punch, but by everything.

"Come on."

He nods and follows me toward the door.

"They're leaving now," Greg says into the phone. Then he speaks louder to the other two men at the bar. "One of you. Stop them."

One of the men rises. He's as big as a tree trunk, and has dark, sad eyes that haunt a long face. His beard is touched with flecks of gray that look like steel wool. I take Elijah's hand and we flee out the door and into the night.

6

"**I WANT TO HELP**," the man calls.

He's been pursuing us for a hundred yards or more. We're back to the main road now, and Elijah doesn't want to stop, but there's something in his voice, something I don't hear very much. It's courage. Or concern. Maybe both.

I grab Elijah's arm. "Wait. Let's listen."

Elijah stops. We're both breathing hard, but Elijah manages to shout to the man to keep his distance.

"Fine," the man says and stops. It's too dark to see him very well now. He's just a shadow on the road, and for a moment I'm pretty sure he's not real at all, but instead, he's a messenger from God, or maybe he's the Holy Ghost himself.

"I was going to tell you this when the time was right, but then Greg got started and everything went bad, and you had to leave..."

"Go on," Elijah says.

"A man came through earlier. They call him Ronnie. He's not a cop, but he's a security guard. Works over at Looney's where the services are held. Anyway, he knows a lot of cops. Most importantly, he's in Brother Nesmith's inner circle."

"Inner circle?" I ask.

"Yeah. Four or five men. They meet under the amphitheater before and after services. Men only, well, except for Ruby Jewel, but she and Nesmith are connected a the hip. Where he goes, so does she."

He's right about Ruby Jewel, but I focus on something else he said instead. *Underneath the amphitheater.*

"Anyway, he comes in sometimes and he always creeps me out. And he likes to talk. He talks a lot."

"Sorta like Greg?" I say, shaking the bottle to give Edie some more milk. She's whimpering at the sound, so ready to eat, she's lost her voice.

"No. Greg's just an asshole. This guy's in."

"In?" Elijah says.

The man steps forward, closing the distance on the dark road by ten, maybe fifteen feet. I still can't see his face, but I can see he's probably not the Holy Ghost, but then again, wouldn't the Holy Ghost be able to take whatever form it wanted? Wouldn't it be able to jump from one body to the next like a kind of virus?

Elijah reaches for my hand. I let him take it. It's sweet. I've decided there's something good about Elijah. There's some bad stuff too, but the goodness is really good. It shines through, like a lantern in the dark woods.

"I guess when I say, 'in,' I mean he's taken the pill, drank the Kool-Aid, whatever. He says Nesmith's got a vault underneath the amphitheater with all the money people have given him, you know donations and tithes. Says, he's got other stuff too. Wonders upon wonders." The man shrugs. "I don't know if I believe that or not, but Ronnie believes it sure enough. Ronnie's a true believer, thinks Nesmith is somehow the answer to a question that suddenly everybody's asking."

I feel a chill at the man's words. "And what question is that?"

The man, the Holy Ghost, whatever, nods his head. "I think the question is really a bunch of questions. Who are we? Why are we here? Where the hell are we going?" He pauses, looks around as if for answers and lowers his voice. "Why does it all hurt so much?"

"If Nesmith is the answer to those questions," I say, "I think I'd kill myself."

The man laughs. "Me too. But he's got something, some kind of power. There's no denying it. Maybe people like us are just immune to it. You know, like people can be immune to certain kinds of sicknesses."

I feel Elijah tensing up at this. It's a line of conversation he doesn't like. Elijah doesn't like the questions because they remind him he's supposed to have the answers.

"What else did this Ronnie say? We can't stand here all night."

"Right." the shadow says. "He said a lot of stuff. Said you were dead in the water, that even if you did make it where you were going, you didn't have what you needed to beat Nesmith."

"The dreamstone," I mutter. Mostly to myself, but the man hears me.

"What's that?"

"You're talking about the dreamstone. Did he say where this thing was that I didn't have?"

"No, just that you needed it."

"Damn," I say.

"It's just a stone," Elijah says. "If it's got any power at all, it's only mental."

"Only mental?" the man who I'm really starting think might be the Holy Ghost says. "*Only* mental? Man, that doesn't even make sense. What's more important than your mind?"

Elijah doesn't have an answer for that. He wants to. I can tell by the way he shuffles his feet and tightens his grip on my hand, but in the end, he says nothing.

"He also said that they would catch you eventually when you crossed the Tuskahatchee. Said they had all the roads blocked. They're checking cars."

"We already knew that," Elijah says. "We were hoping someone could let us ride in their trunk or something."

"I think that's a bad idea. They've got dogs, apparently, and they have the girl's scent. They're letting them sniff the cars, pretending it's about some search for drugs or something."

"Damn," I say. "Goddamn. We'll swim then. We've done it already."

"No," the man says. "That's what I come to tell you. There's another way."

7

HE TELLS US we'll have to skirt the lake until we reach the train tracks. Those will lead us to an old trestle that crosses the river.

I've heard about the old train trestle from Ben. He and some of his friends used to go down there and jump into the river for fun. This was back when Mama was still a mother, and worried about him. She'd tell him it was dangerous, not just the jumping part, but that the trestle itself was cursed. People who went there sometimes didn't come back. Or worse, they came back changed. Ghosts of themselves.

I reckon in a way that happened to Ben too. He'd become a ghost of himself, though that ghost seemed to be made in the Middle East, rather than suspended over the Tuskahatchee River. Or maybe it was made both places. Maybe I'm making my own ghost right now, and it'll arise out of me on that very train trestle, sending my physical body crashing into the rocks below. Maybe then I'd be a Holy Ghost my own damn self, and the idea doesn't even seem too bad. A wandering Holy Ghost, haunting the Nesmiths of the world and helping folks like Elijah and Edie sounds pretty damn good, as a matter of fact.

But it's Elijah who brings up another danger. Leave it to him to think of the one made of steel.

"Do trains still run across it?" he says as we find the tracks about an hour later.

I don't have an answer to this question. Maybe they do, maybe they don't. I never heard of any train in Ben's stories. Mama never warned of one either, but then again, there's some things that seem too obvious to warn a person about.

Truth of it is, I can't make myself focus on the train tracks. I've got the dreamstone on my mind.

"We can't cross the river without it," I say.

"Without what?"

I just look at him.

"Oh, Jesus. The rock."

"That's right. The rock."

"Well, it's kind of tough to get a rock when you don't know where it is."

"Maybe we already know."

"What?"

"I mean, maybe it's in front of our face, but we're missing it. Granny says the hardest thing to see is the thing that's right in front of your face."

Elijah sighs and sits down on a stump. "Granny says a lot of shit, you know?"

"Yeah. I know."

HOLY GHOST ROAD

I take Edie from him and walk around with her, bouncing her the way she likes. I'm hoping the movement will help me think.

"You said it would be at his previous home, right?"

"It's a possibility."

"Well, what if he didn't have a previous home?"

Elijah shrugs. "Maybe his church then?"

"The amphitheater?"

"I don't know. Is that his only church?"

"Yeah. Not a lot of places…" I stop. I'm about to say, *not a lot of places to hide it there,* but then I remember there's one very good place. And the Holy Ghost was trying to show it to me all along.

Amp cellar.

Amphitheater cellar.

"What's today?" I ask.

Elijah leans back, his face to the sky. "What?"

"What day of the week is it?"

"Why's it matter?"

"Damn it. Do you know or don't you?"

"Friday, I think. Yeah, 'cause I came down on Tuesday. Spent the night, well, part of the night. Got lost. Ran into you Wednesday. We slept in the cabin Wednesday night. Then we spent a night on the island. That was Thursday. And then last night… he trails off, likely remembering the way he almost betrayed me last night.

"Never mind," he says. "I was wrong. It's Saturday. Tomorrow's Sunday."

"Perfect."

"Perfect for what?"

"We got to get back out to the road. Double back, not too far, just a few miles."

"Why would we do that?"

"Because I know where the dreamstone is."

8

"SO, NOW," ELIJAH says as we leave the train tracks behind and head back out to the road, "we're going to Nesmith?"

"To his church. Or near his church. We'll find a place to sleep, in a tree or something, and then wake up in time for early services—"

"Did you say, 'sleep in a tree?'"

"Yeah, don't you remember how we met?"

"Sure I do, but I didn't think that was a regular thing."

"Whatever. That's not the point. The point is we wait until sunrise and go underneath the amphitheater."

"For the dreamstone?"

"Yes."

"I have a lot of questions."

He's being sarcastic, which I take as a good sign. It's better than nervous or scared.

"Go ahead," I say, figuring there must be at least some truth behind the sarcasm.

"Why sunrise?"

"Easy. Nesmith has sunrise services every Sunday. Means he and Ruby Jewel will be occupied."

Elijah nods, and I can tell he likes my thinking. At least for a moment. Then his brow furrows and he looks constipated. "What about Helmet?"

"We may have to deal with Helmet."

"I don't like that."

"Better than Ruby Jewel or Nesmith."

"If you say so."

"I do say so. What are your other questions?"

"Why do you think the dreamstone is underneath the amphitheater?"

"That one I'm less sure about. But a couple of things. First, what you said about him putting it somewhere else, and not keeping it at the house. That's logical. Second, the Holy Ghost Man we met outside of the bar—"

"Holy Ghost who?"

"Sorry, that's how I think of him. Granny says you'll often meet the Holy Ghost as a traveler on the road. Or as someone you least expect. I think maybe that was our Holy Ghost."

Elijah's sarcasm has faded. Now, there's just a look of concern on his face. It's sort of how I imagined some of Granny's old parishioners might have looked when she started talking about this stuff.

I decide to press on. "Anyway, he talked about the wonders Nesmith had stored under there, right? If it's safe enough to store those, then it's safe enough to store the dreamstone. Logic. You can appreciate that, right?"

I decide not to mention the thing that sealed it for me, which was seeing the *Amp Cellar* written on the piece of paper taped to the key.

HOLY GHOST ROAD

Elijah shrugs. He's just too stunned by it all to argue. And when I say, 'by it all,' I mean everything. The barn he was supposed to disprove, my story about Nesmith, the goddamn snake on the island, and now this. It's a lot, I suppose, for most people. But Granny prepared me for it. She spent her life showing me a lot of the time the stuff that seems impossible is because we want it to be.

Let's be honest, we all want a world that makes sense, that we can figure out, that we can somehow hold, like a scene in a snow globe. A world we can shake up when the scene needs to be refreshed; or leave alone when we want it to stay just how it's always been.

I take Elijah's hand. "You're gonna have to trust me on this one."

He nods. "It's not a bad conclusion. I mean, I refuse to believe this stone has any power over Nesmith. But I suppose if he took it, he must at least believe that it does, or believe you believe it. Putting that aside, yes, I do think you're on to something regarding where he would keep it, not to mention the best time for us to try to get it."

It's not exactly a ringing endorsement, but I'll take it. Normally, I don't give a damn if anyone's with me or against me (well except for Granny), but the fact that I care now about what Elijah thinks is significant. And I gotta say, it's pretty scary, too. Don't get me wrong. I'm not pining after an older man. That's not something I could ever do. Even if I did find him attractive like that. And I don't. I do find him attractive as a friend though, and sometimes that can be an even rarer thing.

9

ELIJAH IS AGAINST climbing a tree with Edie, and I reluctantly agree it's probably a bad idea. Instead, we bed down for the night (or what's left of it) on a hill just above Loony's Tavern. It's a good thing we decided not to try to infiltrate the underground portion tonight, because the place is buzzing with activity.

Workers are setting up props on the stage. Most of them are crosses of some sort or another. There are also large pieces of furniture that take three men on each side to move.

We watch in the otherwise still night as the men move like ants far below.

"Do you see the way to the underneath?" I ask.

Elijah shakes his head. A willow branch hangs in his face and when he moves his head, it moves too. We're pretty well hidden, I think.

"No. I'm still looking."

For a man who believes in so little, he's intent on helping me, and I don't know exactly why. Maybe he's just got a good heart. Yeah, that's got to be it. Misguided as Elijah might be, he's definitely got a heart that sees true, and even if your eyes and mind don't, a true-seeing heart can make all the difference.

Just then, Edie decides it's time to wake up. She screams at the top of her lungs. I move fast as I can and scoop the bottle off the ground. I stick it in her crying mouth, and she settles for a moment before sputtering and screaming again, most likely at the milk's cool temperature.

"Easy, easy baby," I coo at her, and she settles down some. I try the bottle again, and this time she accepts it, though her face is still frozen in a look of pure disgust.

"Did they hear?" I hiss at Elijah.

He's standing now, peering down at the amphitheater. "Maybe the first one, but they've gone back to work."

My heart slides out of my throat and settles back into my chest. Edie is squirming and mad as all hell, but in this case, her hunger overrides every-thing. If she finishes out the bottle, she'll almost certainly go to sleep. I close my eyes and concentrate on the bottle in my hand, the weight of Edie's head in my other one, and pray she'll sleep.

It works. A few minutes later she's fallen into a fitful sleep. I'm afraid he can't go on like this much longer. She needs a crib and regular feedings. Diapers and wipes.

"Hold on, little girl," I say. "Granny will fix you right up." I smile at her, and for a moment, everything seems like it will be okay.

Then Elijah speaks. "I found the way to the underneath. That's where they're getting the props from."

"Yeah? Where is it?"

"There's a door at the bottom of the stage. In the very front. Looks like it leads to some kind of cellar or something."

10

HOW DO YOU sneak past an entire congregation, a preacher who is trying to kill you (or worse), his blind sister who can in fact *sense* your presence, *and* a Gulf War vet who moves like a goddamn robot built to seek and destroy? And how do you do all this while holding a very tired and hungry baby?

Short answer: you probably don't.

Long answer: you hand Edie to Elijah and trust him to distract the congregations while you slip inside.

That's it. That's all we have. It occurs to me we probably should have planned an escape route too. But by that time, I'm already moving alongside the amphitheater, making my way to the stage from the right, waiting for Elijah to get everyone's attention from the hillside.

I have no idea how much time it'll buy me, or if Elijah and Edie will be able to make it to our rendezvous point or not.

I'd probably obsess over it a little more, but I've managed to creep into the amphitheater now. I'm so close I can smell the strong perfume the women wear. I kneel beside the stage, just hidden by several crates a few feet from the first row of chairs. I can barely see Nesmith up on the stage as the sunlight rises over the hill. He's standing behind his lectern wearing a red robe, something he started doing once he left the wheelchair. No one ever questions it even though it looks exactly like something a cult leader would wear, and not even a very creative cult leader. He seems to delight in what he can get away with in plain view.

"But for you who fear my name, the sun of righteousness shall rise with healing in its wings. You shall go out leaping like calves from the stall," Nesmith booms out over the congregation. It's a quote from somewhere in the Old Testament. One of the ones he uses to begin the sunrise services. He's got other ones he uses at the eleven o'clock and sunset services.

The congregation responds with a rousing "Amen," and Nesmith smiles, completely confident in his place at the head of the church he has created.

Nesmith raises his hands as if beseeching the morning sky. He closes his eyes and begins to pray. Ruby Jewel is behind him. Her forehead is bandaged from where she cracked it against the windshield the day before. She's wearing her best dress—a shapeless flowered number—that covers her ankles. Her eyes are shielded by large sunshades, and her mouth—caked in that garish crimson—is slack. She may well be asleep, which would be a small blessing.

A tall, solemn, unshaven man stands on her right. I've noticed him before, but don't know his name. Ronnie, maybe? It's possible. To his right is the sheriff, his eyes shut tight, his face enthralled by Nesmith's words.

I want to vomit.

HOLY GHOST ROAD

Instead, I slide away from the stage until my back is against one of the crates keeping me just out of view of the congregation. From this angle, I can see Helmet too. Good. Knowing where he is, means I can act more confidently. His face is neutral, so unlike the other faces that seem enraptured by Nesmith's words.

Next, I turn my attention to the door in the bottom of the stage. I can't make it out from here, at least not in any detail. Only a slight bump in the solid wooden base of the stage I assume must be the door.

A terrible thought hits me like a finger to the eye. What if it's locked?

What if the moon falls from the sky? What if the sun don't rise? Granny's voice gently mocks me. It's what she used to say when I was little and liked to ask *what if* about everything.

What if everything goes right and is perfect from now until the end of time? She used to say, as a way to break me out of my *what ifs*. It usually worked, and it works again now. Besides, *what ifs* are more Elijah's territory than mine.

Nesmith finishes the prayer, and the choir comes up behind him. Though I can't see them, I hear them begin "There is A Fountain Filled with Blood." According to Nesmith, it's the hymn that was playing when he was a boy and had his conversion experience. Ruby Jewel loves it too. She always stands as the song rises into the refrain of "...away, away, away, wash all my sins away." This morning is no exception. She rises, holding her hands to the sky, letting the bright rays of the sunrise bathe her and for just a moment, I can almost believe she believes in some higher power, some God who bled for her.

And maybe she does, but it's not any kind of God I want to be a part of. Her God is the God of blood, of control, of power.

The song winds down, and Ruby Jewel turns her palms over to the sky, as if inviting some ancient power to come and refresh her. She sits back down as Nesmith rises and approaches the lectern. The time is close now. Hopefully, Elijah is ready.

"I know I've spoken at great length about the way that song has influenced my life," Nesmith says, his voice coming from some deep place inside him. I wonder if he could have done the things he's done in this county without that voice, without the tone of assuredness that blasts forth with full-throated confidence. It's the voice of a man who knows how things will go.

And I hate him for it.

"It was the first song I heard the day after Ruby Jewel saved my life in the pond. You all know the story… but I like to tell it just the same." He grins like he's telling a joke we are all in on. "Ruby Jewel died on that day. She saved me and she died. I didn't know what prayer was then. My parents weren't faithful people, and there is a great sadness I suffer because of that. Friends, I have no doubt they are in hell." He pauses for dramatic effect. No one seems to care how sick this statement is, how dismissive, or how fucking unchristian.

"But God put a will in me to pray for my sister. And so, I did. I prayed and I prayed, and I prayed. Brothers and sisters," he says, his voice rising, "I am here to tell you that prayer works. Ruby Jewel stood up on the banks of that pond and lo, she had been struck blind, the girl that had drowned that day, was saved because she saw the face of God, hallelujah!"

The congregation loves it. They all stand and clap. Some people are whooping and calling out "amen," while a few begin to vibrate in an almost sexual manner. I can't actually see them from where I'm crouched by the crates in front of the stage, but I've seen them all before. I know how these things go.

But I also know this time is going to be different. Nesmith is about to be interrupted. I'm about to go underneath the stage, into the bowels of Nesmith's world, and who knows what I will find there to see true.

It's during this long dramatic pause, when the congregation finally falls silent, that a voice calls from the hillside. It's faint, barely audible, but if I can hear it, so can the others.

"Nesmith," the voice calls. Nesmith grins and cocks his head to one side.

"Hey, asshole!" Elijah calls again, and this time it's loud enough to grab Nesmith's attention. A murmur runs through the amphitheater, and much as I'd like to stick around and see how this plays out, I have to move now, or risk being seen.

I dart forward, out into the space between the first row of seats and the stage. Nesmith's saying something now, something about "chickens coming home to roost," but I can't really pay attention to it. I'm focused on the door. As I grab the door handle, and it turns, I wonder at what logic made us think this was the best time to attempt such a move.

"...And where is our wayward friend?" Nesmith says.

John Mantooth

The door opens with a creak, and even though every story I've ever heard says not to look behind you, I can't help it. Just before heading underneath the stage, I see the whole congregation, backlit by the newly risen sun. Thank God, no one is turned toward me. They are all facing Elijah on the hill. My heart sings with the hope of victory. It's a song I've heard before, but usually just the opening strands.

I turn back to the open door and slip inside, shutting it behind me.

11

THE DARKNESS MAKES every sound seem louder. Above me, the stage creaks as Nesmith adjusts his stance. His voice comes out like a warble shot through a megaphone. It's loud, but I can no longer make out the words.

I move forward, hands outstretched, as if I am really sleepwalking, and who's to say this isn't one long dreamwalk? This whole journey sometimes has had the logic of dreams, the overwhelming sense that as we move, we move along horizons shrouded in mists, and walk in and out of different worlds, until it becomes one jangling chorus of a world that connects my despair to salvation and back again.

And now, this dark place.

I just wish Granny were here with me, that I could hear her voice now, that her cryptic sayings could provide a light, no matter how dim, inside this underworld.

I've gone no more than ten yards when I see a light. It's coming from the ceiling, and it illuminates the path in front of me. It is a narrow, stone corridor, like a path in a dungeon. Moss or lichen or something green and wet grows along either wall. There's a grate far above me. It's been built into the stage, perhaps for an actor to see and hear their cue.

And through this grate, I hear Nesmith again. He's on fire now. "And the wicked shall be crushed under the heel of the Lord our God, and they shall be brought to account for their sinful ways. An affront to me and my ministry, to everything I've worked so hard for, brothers and sisters."

He pauses, and I pause, taking in a deep breath, almost afraid to move because if I can hear him so clearly, can't he hear me? Or what about Ruby Jewel? Is she still sitting on the stage?

As if she can read my mind, and thus locate me, I hear the stage creak. Footsteps. Heading toward the rear of the stage. I don't know how I know, but I know that I know that *I know* it's Ruby Jewel.

A terrible thought hits me. If this is where actors waited for their cue, there must be another way up onto the stage. Which means there's also a way for Ruby Jewel to come down.

I step past the grate and hurry forward down the corridor. Sure enough, there is a set of stairs only a few yards in that direction. I can't see up them because it's too dark, but the footsteps are coming toward the place where there must be a door leading to the stage.

Briefly, I consider running up the steps and trying to bar the door from this side, but that's when light floods the stairwell. I shield my eyes against it, and try to see to the top, but I can't. It's too bright. I'm about to run back to the exit the way I came in and take my chances the congregation is too enthralled by Nesmith to notice me, when I spot another door, off to my right. I can see it because of the light coming from the top of the stairwell. Without thinking, I reach for it and pull it open.

Another set of stairs. This one leads down. I slip inside and close the door behind me. It's totally dark, but the fact that these stairs are carpeted, and the walls seem finished makes me think there might be a light switch. I touch both sides of the wall near the door until I find it.

A single bare bulb is illuminated out over the steps. It hangs at eye level, and I have to duck under it as I descend.

I count fourteen steps to the bottom, where I come out into a large open room. I search around for another light switch and find it.

The room is filled with crosses, podiums, tables, and chairs. This isn't it. There's got to be another place where he keeps the important stuff.

The door at the top of the stairwell opens.

I look up and see Ruby Jewel standing there, her nose turned upward as if smelling for me.

Suddenly, I realize how stupid I've been. I'm trapped down here. She's got me just where she wants me.

"You've been such a bad little slut," Ruby Jewel says as she begins to drag her giant body down the steps.

Look around. It's Granny. Her voice is calm. The opposite of the way I feel. *See this place true.*

"I can't," I say out loud. I don't mean to. It just comes out.

"You can't what?" Ruby Jewel says.

But I ignore her and make myself turn around slowly. There are four wooden crosses, a couch, two chairs, and folding table. There's also a large podium pushed tight against the back wall.

Ruby Jewel is almost to the bottom of the steps.

"What brings you here, girl? Let me guess. You figured out you needed that little rock?"

I back up toward the podium. There's a small crack between it and the wall, and I can feel air coming through it.

"Cat got your tongue, Forest? It don't matter if you say anything or not. I can smell the slut on you. Going with that half-breed. Trying to play house with him. I know just what you're up to, girl."

She can smell me, sure. But I can smell her too. Rosewater and powder, barely masks her body odor. But as much as that makes me want to vomit, it's her appearance that's most upsetting.

The bandage on her head has slipped so that the wound is fully visible. Her forehead is a raw collection of veins, gore, and ragged skin, and the light from the bare bulb behind her makes it all appear translucent, like a cross-section of a cadaver under the harsh lights of a laboratory. The rest of her isn't really any better. Her lips are a deep red gash across the pale powder of her face. Her eyes are dead and covered in a blurry film. Eyeshadow runs down either side of her face, tears that don't match the manic joy of her smile. She's a juxtaposition, a figure that could only exist in a place like this, a place of final darkness and cloying despair. I could almost just stare at her, fascinated as she moves closer and closer...

Closer.

Forest!

It's Granny again, her voice sharp now, breaking me from the hypnotic spell Ruby Jewel has cast on me.

HOLY GHOST ROAD

I lean against one side of the podium and push with every ounce of strength I can find. The podium slides across the floor, and I feel more air rushing into the room.

Ruby Jewel pauses. "What have you found?"

I keep pushing, but now the podium feels stuck. It won't move.

Ruby Jewel sniffs the air. "That room belongs to my brother."

"He took something that belonged to me."

Mistake. Maybe she can smell me but smelling is one thing. Locating me is another. Now that I've spoken, she lurches forward, grasping at me. She grabs the podium instead of me and shakes it. Angered, she shoves it aside, and I am again reminded of just how damn strong she is. A dark opening in the wall appears, barely large enough for me to slip through. I waste no time and dive headlong into the opening.

I'm almost in when I feel Ruby Jewel's hand clamp down around my ankle. She starts to haul me back out, but I reach around blindly for something to grab on to, and my hand falls on something rough, like a rock, but this rock is far too large to be my dreamstone. I reach forward with my other hand and grab something wooden. Splinters dig into my hand, but I hold on.

Whatever I've grabbed is either heavy or bolted to the ground because Ruby Jewel pulls me hard. My body stretches until I hurt, but I hold on anyway.

For a long time, it seems we're in a standoff. Will I let go before she tires? Will my body break or will the thing I've grasped move? I close my eyes, determined to never let go.

Ruby Jewel grunts and takes one hand off my leg, perhaps to get a better grip, to grab me somewhere closer to my midsection, but it's all I need. I jerk myself into the hole. Her other hand slips down my ankle and is left holding my shoe.

I crawl across a stone floor and into a circle of light. Far above me, the sun shines through what appears to be a grass roof.

I blink my eyes and see what I was holding on to. It's an altar. Stone on the bottom, gnarled, unfinished wood rising out of that. The wood comes together, creating a flat table. On top is the head of a goat, pierced through the right eye with an impossibly long nail. A bowl sits beneath the head, and blood has collected in it.

Ruby Jewel is crawling through the opening. She's so big she appears to have gotten stuck. I try to imagine a scenario in which Nesmith would have created a place Ruby Jewel couldn't access, but I can't do it.

Which means there's another way in. I look up again at the light coming through the grass roof.

There's a rope ladder hanging down. I could climb it and be at the top in seconds, but I still don't have the stone.

There's nothing here except the damn altar. Is this where Nesmith comes to do his real prayers, the ones that brought forth the goat demon?

Suddenly, I remember the bowl of blood from my dreamwalk, the one when Ruby Jewel had her hands around my neck. What was inside the bowl of blood? Ben's head, of course, but there had been something else too.

I step forward and stand before the altar. The goat's head looks at me with one glassy eye. Behind it, shadows gather and writhe just above Ruby Jewel's blind face as she continues to force her way through the hole.

Vaguely, distantly, the strains of "Nothing but the Blood of Jesus" swells toward its refrain: *Oh! Precious is the flow…*

I reach for the bowl and plunge my hand into the blood.

…That makes me white as snow…

Ruby Jewel grunts and emerges on this side of the hole, panting on the ground, her hands twitching to grab something.

…No other fount I know…

My hands are soaked in the goat's blood. It's thick and somehow still warm and the longer I feel it on my hands, the more the shadows behind the altar take shape.

My fingers touch something smooth and solid.

…Nothing but the blood of Jesus…

As I attempt to grab it, the shadows become more solid and the goat's head on the altar shifts slightly, its good eye coming to life.

I shriek and pull my empty hands out of the blood.

Ruby Jewel stands up.

The shadow goat retreats slightly, and the head is as still as the blood inside the bowl.

Ruby Jewel grabs for me, but I step out of the way, and plunge both hands into the bowl this time. I feel the stone immediately, and when I do, I shut my eyes to keep from seeing what might be threatening me- and pull it out.

It's not easy. The blood feels too thick, and my hands seem to be stuck for a terrible second.

There's a shriek from right in front of me that hurts my ears. I don't know if it's Ruby Jewel or the shadow goat or if it's the goat's head.

But I don't let go of the stone.

Granny says I need it.

My hands come out of the bloody bowl, clutching the stone. I open my eyes and see Ruby Jewel's face, inches from mine, her hands hooked into those familiar claws. Behind her, the shadow goat watches, waiting to see what she will do with me this time.

Her hands seize me around the neck, but my hands are still free and in one of them is a bloody stone, the size of my whole fist. I slam it against the raw place on the side of her forehead. She holds on anyway, her eyes bulging, so I hit her again, harder this time. The stone causes something to collapse in her face, caving in the side of her forehead.

She still doesn't let go of my neck.

I can't breathe, which makes what I need to do even more difficult, almost impossible. I tighten my grip on the stone and slam it down into the crook of her right elbow. Her arm bends, but her grip remains solid.

Again and again, I slam the rock down into the crook of her elbow. Eventually, her grip begins to loosen. She takes a hand off to try to wrestle the stone free from me, but I'm too fast. I smack her in the face again, deepening the wound I've already made. She howls and lets go completely.

I'm smoke. There and gone. Turning to find the ladder and scampering up toward the sun and the grass covered roof. It's not until I force my way through the thick vines and feel the sun on my face again that

HOLY GHOST ROAD

I fall down. I only lay there for a second because Ruby Jewel can't be far behind. Catching my breath, I rise and sprint back toward the place where Edie and Elijah wait for me. As I run, I squeeze the dreamstone in my fist like a tiny, pulsing heart, that powers me onward.

The Sacred Magic

1

THERE'S AN EERIE quiet as we move across the trestle in the late dusk. Elijah and Edie have been waiting for me by the tracks, and when I arrive, we don't waste time with small talk. Instead, we move quickly along the tracks, arriving at the trestle as the sun dips to the other side of the horizon behind us.

I carry the stone in my right hand. It has some of Ruby Jewel's blood on it, but I don't care. I did what Granny asked me to do. Now, I just have to finish the job and make it to her house. Once I do I feel confident Nesmith can't hurt me. How could he? Granny will be there.

As we cross the trestle, I notice the scaffolding on either side of us has huge gaps in it, so it would be easy enough to make the leap off the trestle and into the fast-running Tuskahatchee a hundred or more feet below us. I go first with Edie and Elijah following a few feet behind me. Every now and then, I glance back to make sure he's still coming, that he hasn't given up, chickened out. He's been so quiet since we met back up, almost as if all his energy is devoted to a private conversation he's having with himself.

Edie is solemn too, not asleep, but content to lay in Elijah's arms and watch the moon with big eyes.

The sky is close here, and the half moon seems to bob as if it is some stage prop suspended by strings, or a balloon not quite filled with enough air to float free. Above all of this are thousands of stars. The river smells ripe, a scent that would stink anywhere else, but here it turns into a wondrously complex and enchanting odor, one I'll probably miss one day when it's gone.

Speaking of gone, there's been no sign of Nesmith, Helmet, or Ruby Jewel since I left the cellar of the amphitheater, and it feels too quiet, almost like we are walking into a trap.

"Only your imagination," Elijah whispers when I mention the feeling to him.

"Maybe," I say, "but I can't shake it."

"An illusion, then," he says, and I can tell he likes this version best. "Feelings like that often have environmental explanations. Like swamp gas or something. People report it all the time, swear that they saw something beckoning them to follow, fairies or whatever. Never is, though. Always an explanation. You just have to look for it."

He sounds pleased with himself, so I don't argue. Truthfully, I'm just glad he's talking again, but it doesn't last. We continue on in silence. Edie falls asleep, and her face is calm in the moonlight. It's a magical calmness. A sacred calmness, and it makes me think maybe the Holy Ghost is here with us, maybe her presence is hovering over us, keeping us safe, clearing the way.

But I can't shake the feeling there's something amiss, that getting the dreamstone, and making it to Granny's is only a small part of what I have left to do. But what else could there be?

"Almost there," Elijah says.

But almost there or not, I need to deal with what's nagging me, and maybe it's not about Granny at all. Maybe it's about Elijah.

"I never told you what I saw in the barn," I say. "The second one."

"You said you saw your grandmother, that she was a zombie or something."

"Right, but there's more."

He's silent.

"You want to hear it?"

"Fine."

"I saw my grandmother, but I also saw more clearly what happened to me with Nesmith."

"That's it?"

I nod.

"Thank God. Oh, thank God."

"Why do you say that?"

"Don't worry about it."

"Wait, what did *you* see? The night you ran from the barn?"

He walks on in silence for a bit. The river grows louder beneath us. We're so very close to the other side now. The moon shines against the smooth side of the tracks.

"What did you see in the barn?" I ask again.

"I saw myself," he answers. "Another one of me. A different me."

"And that was scary?"

"Are you kidding? It was horrifying."

I nod and think about how the most terrible things in life are the most intimate, the ones that are inside you, the ones that are you.

"The other me… he could fly."

I almost laugh but stop myself. Thank God. Not the time or place, Forest. "Fly?"

"Yeah. I woke up. Saw myself up in the hayloft. The other me was grinning, like so happy it was scary. At first, I thought I saw a rope around my neck, but that was just what I *expected* to see because of all the stories. Instead, the other me jumped, and instead of falling down to the ground where I was, he flew. I mean really flew. That's when I got up. That's when I started to run."

"I can see how that would be frightening," I say, but actually it sounds far less frightening than what I'd expected him to say.

"I'm not finished. I'm opening the barn door when I hear the other me gasp. I turn to look and there's an expression on the other me's face that's the most horrifying expression I've ever seen, and that's when I under-stand –he's seen me too. And there's something about me that makes him deeply unsettled. He crashes then. Crashes hard. Slams into the side of the barn. Hits the ground in a heap. It was so real. The sounds, the way the barn shook with the impact. I just got out of there. Didn't stop running until you called out to me from the tree."

He pauses, seemingly rendered speechless by Edie's dreaming face.

"And now," he continues after a time, "I've come all this way trying hard to find something that would dispel what I saw, but everything that keeps happening makes me think it's real."

"Maybe because it was real," I say, my voice a whisper.

He nods. "Okay. Maybe. So what does it mean?"

I put a hand on his shoulder, and then decide it's not enough. I pull him into a hug, and he hugs me too, Edie in between us. She looks up at our faces, and for a moment I pull a Ruby Jewel, and I'm inside of her, inside of Edie, I see through her eyes, and what I see is me and Elijah, our faces framed by moonlight, our eyes shining, our jaws set to something I can only think of as wonder.

"It means what it means, and when you're ready to understand you will. Don't rush. People are always in such a hurry to understand that they never do." As soon as I've said it, I realize I quoted Granny. Well, not quite. The part at the end was my own thought, but it could have been something she said. That makes me feel good. I know she will be proud when I tell her.

After the embrace, I peer out at what lies ahead. Twenty or so more feet before the other side, before I'm in Cullman County, Granny's county, the place where Nesmith has no dominion.

When I step onto the solid ground, I feel so overwhelmed with emotion, I lay down in the cool grass.

"I'm so tired," I say, surprising myself a little, but it's true. I've been too determined to cross the river to notice before now, but now that we're across, it hits me all at once.

"You're kidding. How much farther from here?"

"Maybe three or four miles."

"Let's knock it out."

I shake my head. "I have to rest."

"Here?"

"Why not?"

He looks around, staring back out over the river and shrugs. "I don't know."

"Don't tell me Mr. Rational has a case of the shivers."

"I'm fine."

"Good, then we crash here. Leave at first light. Be there for bacon and eggs and biscuits."

"Sounds good. She knows we're coming, right?"

"Yeah."

"And why didn't she send help?"

I shake my head. "Life is different for Granny. She's out in the country. She doesn't have a car or a phone, and it's difficult for her—"

"Wait, what?"

Elijah is looking at me like I've insulted him. "What did I say?"

"You said she didn't have a phone."

"I did?"

"Yeah."

"Well, I misspoke. Obviously, she has a phone. I meant she didn't have a cellphone."

"Right."

There's an awkwardness that rises up between us after that. I don't know why. Truth is, I'm a little too tired to care. "Can you handle Edie?" I ask.

He nods and stares down at her sleeping face. "Handled," he says, "But better hope she doesn't poop tonight. No diapers."

I nod. I'm fading fast, but just before I slip behind the wall of sleep, I remember the dreamstone. I reach for it, placing my hand on it and fall asleep.

2

FIRST TIME GRANNY ever saw me dreamwalk was when I was ten. She'd come to stay the weekend with us, something that was a regular event in those days. She was still driving then and didn't mind the trip at all. She'd always bring fresh blackberries from her farm, and I remember when I woke up from the dreamwalk, I had blackberry juice all over my face.

Granny was sitting at the kitchen table, grinning.

"Well, it's good to know you won't ever get far starving yourself. You'll just eat when you're sleeping."

I was too disoriented to follow what she was saying, but that only seemed to make Granny laugh more. Eventually, she stood and held onto my arm as she guided me back to bed.

"What was it you were doing?" she asked. "Answer quick before it fades."

I don't remember what I told her because just as she'd suggested, the memory of what I had been doing in my dream did fade. That was before I started writing them down. Granny suggested that.

"It'll teach you how to go back to the dreams. And pretty soon, you'll get so good you won't know if you're asleep or if you're awake."

"That doesn't sound like a good thing," I remembered telling her.

"Sure it is. You'll have powers that other folks only dream of."

"I don't understand."

"Pshaw, you're young yet. Give understanding time to get ripe. You can eat it then. People spend half their lives trying to understand. It's a waste of time. When you understand, you'll understand. Simple as that."

She put me back to bed and kissed my head.

The next day is a little clearer. It was the argument she and Mama got into over me and the dreamwalking.

When Mama found out I'd done it again, she got up on her soapbox, and started saying she needed to take me to a sleep doctor.

I shrugged, which was pretty much what I always did when Mama mentioned taking me to doctor for something. I wasn't opposed to it, but I didn't really take her seriously. She was always saying I needed to go to the doctor for one thing or another, but the proof was in the pudding. I'd been twice when I was really little, but that was it.

"A doctor?" Granny said. "Why in God's name would you do that?"

"She's got a problem," Mama said. "Sleepwalking can be dangerous."

"So can regular walking," Granny countered.

"Oh, come on. This is not your area, Granny."

That had been Mama's favorite line whenever Granny would try to contribute to a family discussion. Apparently, Mama considered Granny's area to be limited to vegetables you could grow in a garden and the weather. She'd hush the whole family whenever Granny had something to say about the weather.

"That woman is never wrong," she told me once. "She says rain, and by God it's gonna rain."

But sleepwalking wasn't weather, and Mama didn't want to hear from Granny about it. Usually, Granny would defer in these types of situations to keep the peace, but this time she didn't back down.

"It is my area," Granny said. "I've dreamwalked for most of my life. People come to my house for help with things. I use dreamwalking to contact them in a different place. Her daddy did it too. I taught him how to handle it, and I can teach her."

"Dreamwalking? Is that what you call it?" Mama said.

"It's what it is."

"Well, I'm going to get her some help, so she doesn't kill herself."

"Kill herself?"

"I read a story just the other day about a man who sleepwalked right out his bedroom window. Cut an artery in his leg and bled to death."

"That's sleepwalking not dreamwalking. I can help her with the dreamwalking. A doctor will just screw her up."

"I think this is one you need to stay out of," Mama said.

Granny ignored her. "Now listen to me, Forest. When you dream-walk, it's like a dream, except you're bringing the two worlds together."

"Two worlds?" I said, glancing at Mama nervously. I was afraid she was going to make me go to my room or something while she and Granny argued. But she was just staring at Granny like she was curious as to where this was going.

"There's the waking world. That's the one most people identify with. It's what most people would call the real world. But it's only half the picture. There's also dreams. That's the other half of the world. A dreamwalker can walk through one world while experiencing the other. They merge the two. Sometimes dreamwalkers are artists or prophets. Sometimes they're just people who have access to something most refuse to see. They are used as conduits sometimes too, so you do have to be careful about that."

"I've heard enough," Mama said.

Granny turned and looked at her, as if she'd forgotten we weren't the only ones in the kitchen. "Okay. Maybe you should leave then."

That did it. Later, Granny would tell me she regretted saying that. Not sure if she ever told Mama, though. Whatever the case, Mama lost it. Started screaming, telling Granny her son was gone, and she was doing the best she could, and she'd appreciate a little support. Granny listened to the rant before nodding and giving me a hug. I didn't see her nearly as much after that.

3

WHEN I DID see her, Granny made it a priority to tell me more about dreamwalking. She even started letting me stay in the room when people came over to her house for help. I learned that she could activate a dreamwalk pretty much whenever she wanted to, but each time she did it, the act took more and more out of her. The hardest part, she explained, wasn't just activating the dreamwalk, but actually moving from her dream into the person's dream she was trying to help.

"I've gotta retire from this," she'd say after helping someone and refusing payment. She always waited until the person she'd helped was long gone before saying this, of course.

"You always say that." I told her once.

"That's because it's true."

"If it's true, why don't you just draw the line and stop helping?"

"That's a good question. I reckon I can't stand to see people suffer. That, and God gave me this gift. I should use it until I can't."

"So, what's going to happen?" I asked.

She shrugged. "I'll have to pick and choose who I help more. But if I had to guess, one day I'll go into someone else's dream and I won't come back out. At least not on this side."

That scared me some, but I watched her closely over the next few years and she really did slow down. I saw her turn people away at her door on more than one occasion.

My own dreamwalking journey was curtailed when Nesmith moved in with us and talked Mama into giving me the Klonopin.

I hated it. At least at first. I was so sleepy all the time. But eventually, my body adapted to it, or it adapted to me, and the side effects became less severe.

According to Nesmith it would stop my "sleepwalking," which might have been true if that had been what I was doing. Instead, what seemed happen was it pushed me so far into my dreamwalks, I couldn't remember them the next day. It was around this time Granny gave me the dreamstone. I see now it was a countermeasure against the meds, against whatever Nesmith was trying to use me for, what he's still trying to use me for.

4

WHEN I STAND up, I float just off the ground, as if standing on some invisible platform. Elijah and Edie sleep in the grass, just beyond the tracks. A mist covers them like a blanket. I rise through the mist until I can see over everything. The fog is coming up from the river, and it shrouds the trestle like smoke.

Two people are on the tracks. Figures in the mist. From where I am on this side of the river, they look like me and Elijah, but how is that possible?

I start out onto the train trestle, still floating like I sometimes do in dreams. It's not exactly flying. Nothing so freeing as that. I still feel bound by gravity, tied to the earth, but my feet can't feel the ground. It's as if I'm walking on the air itself.

The dreamstone moves along beside me, floating at eye level, a comfort that cuts through the fog and absorbs all the light from the moon.

As I move closer, the two figures in front of me take shape. The nearest is Elijah. He's different than the other version of himself Elijah described from the barn. This version is solemn, calculating. He's staring down at the water, as if trying to determine the exact distance, should he fall. He kneels and touches the track, checking it just as the real Elijah had done when we first approached.

Except... It's not Elijah at all.

It's Ben.

He sees me coming, and lifts both arms to warn me away, but how can I stop? It's my brother, and he *is* alive, just like I knew he was.

As I get closer, I can see the other figure better. It's not a person. It's the demon, the black-horned, upright goat, and it's not a shadow here. Its form is solid, not shadow. Steam rises from its muzzle and blood is streaked across its horns.

"Ben?" I say. "Get away from there."

"I can't, Forest. I'm only here to help you."

"I don't understand."

He shakes his head.

"You've got to fight or wake up."

"Fight or what?"

"Wake up."

"How do I fight?"

"Steady. Strong. Brave. Face it down." The dreamstone twitches in the air beside me.

Behind Ben, are the red eyes of the goat. Everything about it is misery. Everything about it reminds me of how broken the world is, and I can't take that feeling.

"Please get away from it," I say.

He shakes his head, and his face is the saddest face I've ever seen.

HOLY GHOST ROAD

"Ben!" I shout just as I realize what he's planning. But it's too late. He jumps off the bridge.

My screams are cut short by the clomping of hooves. Fiery eyes glare at me through the mist. The goat is charging at me across the tracks.

Wake up or fight.

Wake up or fight.

Wake up or...

I can't do either. Instead, I try to turn and run, but now the air on which I stand gives me no purchase. I slip through the air and land hard on the train tracks. They thrum beneath me as the goat charges.

Standing up, I turn to face it. Smoke billows from its nostrils and its horns glow with a light the color of blood.

I can't run. My feet won't move.

Fight?

I can't win. Even with the dreamstone, I still need Granny. If I can get there, I'll face it with her help.

As it closes on me, its hooves pound against the tracks like they're made of steel. Mist gives way to smoke. The air is charged with energy.

The demon goat's mouth and eyes are pure light now.

I'm about to jump into the river, to follow Ben, when I hear someone screaming my name.

5

I'M FALLING, AND at first, I truly believe I jumped from the train trestle. The wind flies through my hair and lifts it like feathery wings. My heart flies into my throat and I open my mouth to scream.

Then I feel the solid metal of the tracks against my knees. My eyes focus on the river below me, and I feel my teeth shaking inside my mouth. I turn and look over my shoulder.

Light blinds me. Smoke fills my lungs.

The demon goat is a train now, and it's a few short yards away.

A voice screams at me. "Go. Go. Go!"

I run, not looking back. I can smell the train now. Diesel, smoke, the acrid tang of grinding gears. I can feel it too, its heat pushing me forward, the thrumming of the trestle beneath my feet, making my entire body vibrate like a tuning fork.

I saw true, I realize, as hot air from the train blasts me forward. I saw true.

6

I'M IN THE air, flying.

The train, or what looks like the train, is behind me, splitting the night open, pushing itself over the river, onto the land again. Train or goat, I've found a way to outrun it.

I'm flying.

For a moment, I believe a spell has been cast, a sacred spell, cast on me, so that I might be in the air and never touch the ground again. The dark night comes alive around me, the stars grow cradling arms, hands made of moonshine brace me and lift, bearing me like a wind I can feel in the deepest parts of my bones.

The magic is real. Maybe it's from the dreamstone, or maybe it's from inside me, but it's real.

But like all real things, it doesn't last.

The ground reaches up. Gravity reaches up. It pulls me down as if angry with me for forgetting its power. I roll, tumbling down through undergrowth and vines.

I hit the stump and my side explodes in pain. I'll never remember any of this as magic. I'll only remember the pain.

John Mantooth

And it's the first time I forge my own quote, one that I know I'll tell Edie one day. My own Granny quote: *People don't ever remember the magic. Only the pain.* Or even better: *Make sure you're a person who remembers the pain and the magic. Remember both, dear child, and in this way you will survive.*

7

I STAND AND stumble the last few feet into Elijah's arms as the train goes past like a wall of steel and steam, and then fades into the morning mist. Silence enfolds us up, as we wrap our arms around each other.

"What were you doing?" Elijah says.

"Dreamwalk. You saved me."

"Me needing to take a piss saved you."

I nod. "A miracle. Magic."

He shakes his head and lets go of me. He nods to Edie on the ground a few feet away, somehow still sleeping peacefully.

"What was the dream?" he asks.

"I saw the demon."

"The goat thing?"

"Yeah. I've got to fight it."

"Fight it?"

I nod. "But Granny will be able to help me." I look at my hand. It's holding the dreamstone. "And we have what she needs. We need to get moving."

Elijah checks his watch. "It's still a ways until morning. We should sleep some more."

He must see the expression on my face because he puts an arm around me again. "I need to sleep."

"Okay, I understand."

He lets go of me and goes back over to where Edie is asleep. He lays down and wraps the child up in his arms, to keep her warm. He's asleep so fast, it almost doesn't seem real he was ever awake.

8

IT TAKES US an hour to get back to 278, just in time for 8 AM rush hour traffic. The eastern side of the river is much more populated than the western side, which is mostly fields and the lake and the Bankhead National Forest. On this side there's gas stations and Dollar Generals everywhere you look. There's tons of traffic, passing us on the road too, but the cars have a different feel to them here. The drivers—I don't know exactly how I can be sure of this, but I am—aren't paying us any mind. We've crossed over to a place where Nesmith's power is weaker. This is a world Elijah is immediately more comfortable in. And I can see a change in him right away.

It worries me a little. Though he has been sort of desperate since the bridge, it had seemed like he was getting close to a break-through. But now I fear all that hard work might be undone. It doesn't take much for a man like Elijah to begin to doubt his own heart.

I don't have words for this breakthrough he was near, exactly. But it's clear our journey is more than just a physical one, right? I mean we're both going to Granny's, but we're on separate journeys too. I just wish I knew where.

But maybe it doesn't matter. Maybe these are the kind of journeys you take and don't understand until years later. Maybe they shift your perspective just enough to shift your life in ways you'll never notice.

Or maybe I'm making it too complicated, trying to explain things in the terms Elijah can accept. The simple truth is this: we've moved out of Nesmith's territory, a place of magic, that was very difficult for Elijah, and now we're in a place that mirrors the reality he's learned to accept. But we're also very close to Granny's farm, and it's a territory onto itself. A different kind of magic reigns there, but it's still magic. I don't want him to come apart again.

"There's a grocery store," Elijah says. "We need to get Edie something to eat."

"Right."

"And they'll have a phone. You should call your grandmother. Tell her we're almost there."

"Right," I say again.

The store has just opened and is mostly empty. I'm in the baby formula section before I remember once again, we don't have any money. I turn to tell Elijah, but he's wandered off again. Seems to be a habit with him lately.

A girl about my age leans against the cash register, scrolling through her phone. I decide to take a chance. No managers around. Only one other customer, a young man browsing over in dairy when we came in.

"Hey," I say, approaching with Edie in my arms. "Weren't you in my history class?"

HOLY GHOST ROAD

She looks up from her phone. "You go to Cullman High?"

I nod. "Well, I did, and then this little bundle of joy happened last year." I glance at Edie, hoping she's old enough to have been at the high school last year.

"Oh, shit. Wow."

"Yeah, what was your name?" I ask.

"Samantha."

"I'm Forest." I shift Edie to one arm and hold out my hand. She takes it tentatively.

"Shouldn't you be at school?" I ask.

"It's a holiday. Columbus Day."

"Oh." I realize October is already nearly halfway over.

"You want to buy that formula?"

"Yes." I hand it to her.

She scans it. "What's her name?"

"Edie."

"That's pretty."

"Thanks."

"Seven ninety-eight."

I reach into my back pocket and shake my head.

"What?"

"I left my purse at the house."

Samantha stares at me. "You didn't go to Cullman."

"No. How'd you know?"

"I would have remembered you. Besides, you've got leaves in your hair."

I run my free hand through my hair, and sure enough, two leaves fall out onto the counter, as if in payment.

"I don't have any money," I say. "And she's hungry. I'm not far from home now. When I get there, I'll be able to bring the money back."

Samantha takes a look around the store and shrugs. "Fuck it. You can have it. I don't care."

"Thank you," I say, and resist the urge to hug her. "Is there a phone I can use too? Pay phone is fine. I'll call collect."

The girl—Samantha—takes out her cell phone and hands it to me. "Go for it."

Again, I resist hugging her. When you're as desperate as Elijah and I have been, even the smallest acts of kindness seem like gifts of great consequence.

I dial Granny's number and she answers on the third ring.

"I got the stone."

"I knew you would."

"It was at his church. There was an altar there too."

"I don't doubt that. He's been working on this for a long time."

"Working on what? I still don't understand, Granny."

"What did I tell you about understanding?"

"It's overrated."

"And it comes when it comes. No rushing it. All will be made clear when you're ready."

"What does that mean? When I'm ready?"

"It's like dreamwalking. You started it when you were ready. Not one second before. And the same is true with understanding this situation. You'll be ready when you're ready."

HOLY GHOST ROAD

I nod, trying not to cry. It hurts to be so confused, to have been through so much with no answers, just a vague sense of dread I can't quite shake.

"I dreamwalked last night," I say, searching for something that will keep her on the phone, that will let her know how much I'm hurting. "The demon was there."

"As I told you it would be. What else?"

"Ben was there too. Is he okay?"

A long pause, maybe meaningless. Maybe filled with meaning. "He's okay."

"Good," I say.

"You're close?"

"Yeah. Real close."

"Let me talk to your friend. To Elijah."

"Why?"

"You'll know why."

"What?"

"Let me talk to him."

He's coming this way now. I motion him over.

"Granny wants to talk to you."

"To me?"

I shrug.

He takes the phone.

I smile at the cashier, who is watching all of this closely.

"Okay," Elijah says. "Yes ma'am. Yes. I will. Goodbye."

He hands me the phone back. I hand it back to the girl at the register and we start out of the store.

"What? What did she say?"

"She said to watch out for you. That the hardest part is still to come."

I shake my head. "Are you sure because that doesn't make—"

"I'm sure. That's what she said."

It doesn't make any sense unless it means there's still going to be an encounter with Nesmith before we get there. That has to be it. "Keep your guard up," I say as we leave the store. "I'm betting we see Nesmith again before Granny's."

9

BUT I'M WRONG. We arrive on Granny's land later that afternoon without incident.

She's got sixty-four acres, mostly woods and some pasture. A small pond that we call a lake is the first thing you see from the road. Granny's house is up the hill from the pond. A sloping pasture with six cows fills the space in between. On the other side of the pasture in the front yard is a tree I love. It's a white oak, and once a few years back, Granny had some people from the forestry commission come out and measure it. They determined it was the second largest tree in the state. They measured its girth at nearly 18 feet around, but it always seemed even bigger than that to me as a little girl. I remember hugging it, trying to spread my arms out against its hard bark, wishing I could somehow embrace the whole thing. Somehow, though, it always held me. I felt comforted by its massive size, its march toward heaven, the way it spread itself across the sky, the fullness of its life, so heavy and magnificent over the yard.

But something is wrong. I see it clearly as I approach Granny's long, winding drive past the pond and up through the pasture. The tree has been split open and part of it hangs out over the fence. Some of its branches lay flat on the sloping hillside. Birds alight on the broken branches and fly around like bees, tracing paths past the charred and open sore, a wound never meant to see the sun.

"Lightning," Elijah says, and he sounds content, like he's thankful he can name this great and astonishing power. Named or not, I want to tell him, the magic of it isn't diminished. Except for him, it actually is.

For me, it's something else. I ache upon seeing this destruction. The only saving grace, I realize, is it didn't split the other way and fall on Granny's house. Why didn't she mention this when I called? I try to remember the last time we had a big storm. A few nights ago, when Elijah and I had been so soaked. It must have happened then.

"You okay?" Elijah asks.

"Yeah," I say, trying to remember that I'm almost safe now, that once I feel Granny's arms around me, my journey will have ended at last. Is this the thing I feared, the thing I sensed about coming here? It's possible. This is a devastating revelation. I can't express the way seeing that tree broken makes me feel.

"Come on," Elijah says. "Edie needs a diaper change and a bath."

I nod and we start up the drive.

Edie's crying again by the time we reach the devastation of the white oak, and I feel like doing the same. I stop to touch the trunk, the burned part where the lightning opened it up, as well as the other side where it's still healthy.

Elijah points out to the road. "What?" I say, looking up from the tree.

HOLY GHOST ROAD

It's Nesmith's Cadillac. The car turns into the long drive. Nesmith is driving. Ruby Jewel is in the passenger's seat. I can't tell for sure, but it looks like someone's in the back. Helmet. It has to be.

And no Mama this time. This time, they've come to finish me once and for all. But they're too late. I'm here. I've made it. Their presence seems little more than a mild irritation.

"Let's go," I say, and start running for Granny's house.

10

WE ENTER THROUGH the utility room, the smell of shelled beans, blackberries, and old newspapers hitting me square in the face. I stop and just breathe it all in, savoring the scent of familiarity, of safety, of home.

"Granny!" I call, and streak through the long utility room, past her freezers of frozen vegetables and meat. Past the shower she uses after a long day in the garden. Past the little toilet I always preferred when I'd come to visit because it let me be around the smells I loved best, the smells of this utility room, the smells of the garden drawn into the home.

I swing the door open that leads to the kitchen, expecting her to be standing at the stove, pressing a spatula against the bread of a fried bologna sandwich. But the kitchen is empty. There's a pot on the stove, but its contents—some dried-up beans—are cold and a dozen or more flies hover over its rising stench.

Moving through the kitchen into the dining area, I see a glass of watered-down tea and some mint leaves lying beside it. Her old, marked up Bible is open beside the tea, a pen laid across the pages. Granny once told me it's a good book like people say, but most people read it like it's an instruction manual. That's always stayed with me, and I've learned to distrust anyone who tries to read it like that.

On a nearby notepad, she's scrawled a sentence in her shaky hand. It reads— *The stone which the builders refused has become the headstone.* Beneath this, she's written, "*Forest*" and underlined it about six times.

I get chills looking at it. I don't know what it means, but it means something, and it gives me strength. It gives me hope somehow, like a kiss on the head or a prayer murmured in the dark.

"They're here," Elijah says, but I already know that. I can hear the Cadillac's engine purr as it pulls into the carport. There's a click as Nesmith kills the ignition. Three doors swing open. His cane hits the concrete. Footsteps clatter as they approach the door.

"It's okay. It's okay." I'm saying it as much to convince myself as I am for Elijah, because I'm finally feeling like maybe it's not going to be okay. Granny isn't answering. "She's in the back," I say. "She has to be."

"What's she going to do anyway? I mean, seriously."

As if in answer, an image forms in my mind's eye. Granny pushing me onto her bed. *Clear your mind. Walk through the dream. We'll face them there together on the spiritual plane.* It's my best guess as to how things might go.

"She'll be able to handle it," I say. "Trust me."

They're at the door. It's okay. We still have time. Nesmith wouldn't know she always keeps it locked, only uses the utility room entrance.

There's the sound of frustration as they try to open the door and find it locked. Someone bangs hard on the door. A voice penetrates the heavy oak.

HOLY GHOST ROAD

"Little pig, little pig." It's Nesmith, and he already sounds victorious. Does he not know the power of my grandmother? His mind has been twisted by power. It's the only explanation.

"In back," I say, and lead the way down the short hallway to her room. Empty. Panic starts to twist inside me. It dislodges something. A memory from the dreamwalk. *Find me in the barn.*

Shit, why didn't I remember that?

"She's in the barn."

"Okay. How do you know?"

"She told me." And suddenly, I remember something else. The garbled bit at the end. *You're the doorway, the conduit.*

And then something else: *Dreamwalks take us to the in-between places, cellars, attics, pastures, barns. Outposts and waystations. It's where you can grow. It's also easier to have a dreamwalk in these kinds of spaces. Dreamwalks in the in-between places are powerful and dangerous things.*

Which is why she needs the dreamstone. I feel something like relief wash over me. Understanding is so close I can feel it.

"We need to get to the barn," I say, suddenly sure that's where Granny has planned for us to make our stand.

"Okay, how are we going to do that?"

There are only three ways out of this house. The carport, the utility room, and the front door. There's a battering sound coming from carport. Sounds like Helmet's trying to break the damn door down, which is something I know full well he's capable of.

"Under the bed. She keeps a shotgun. Grab it. It'll help us make it to the barn."

"Are you kidding me? I don't do guns."

"Goddamn it, Elijah. Take Edie then."

I pass Edie to him. Edie's smiling, apparently delighted by something. Maybe she knows she's home.

Dropping to the floor, I peer under the bed. It's too dark to see much, so I wave my hands underneath until I feel the wood stock of the shotgun. I pull it out, just as I hear a huge crash from the carport. The door splinters and Nesmith whoops loudly.

I pull the shotgun out and open the breech to see if it's loaded. Empty. Shit. I dive back under the bed for some shells. My hand touches a box up near the wall, and I grab it.

"Hey, Forest? Where's your Granny now?"

Nesmith is in the den. His cane taps the almost bare carpet as he makes his way toward the dining room and the hallway that will lead him to where we are.

Last time I was here, Granny brought me into her room and taught me how to load the shotgun. I didn't understand why. Hell, I was against it from the get-go, but she insisted.

My hands fly through the work, as I close the breech and lock the shells into place. I manage to load four in all, two for each barrel. I grab two more from the box and stuff them in the pockets of my athletic shorts along with the dreamstone.

"What was that?" It sounds like Helmet, in the hallway.

"What was what?" Nesmith says.

"I heard it too." Ruby Jewel. "They've got a gun."

HOLY GHOST ROAD

No one speaks. They're just around the corner. I can hear Ruby Jewel's labored breathing.

I'm on the floor, propped against the bed, the shotgun in my lap, aimed at the door. First person I see, I'm going to shoot. Or at least that's what I tell myself. Truth might be different. Could I really shoot Helmet? I'm not sure. I can't help but feel like he's a victim in all this too.

"Ruby Jewel's right," I call. "I've got a shotgun, and I will use it. You should leave."

No response.

Elijah and Edie are pressed against the back wall. I really don't want to shoot anyone. I hiss at Elijah. "The window."

The shades are drawn, but when he pulls them back, light streams into the room, and we can see the barn, down near the pasture, its wide entrance offering a cool, dark solace from the morning's heat.

He lifts the window and pushes out the screen. I nod at him. He puts Edie on the bed and climbs out. I stand, still keeping the shotgun aimed at the doorway and ease around to the other side of the bed. Slowly, carefully, I lay the shotgun on the bed and pick up Edie. I watch the door, wondering if somehow they'll be able to sense that now is the time to come in.

The answer is revealed immediately. Ruby Jewel, blind bitch that she is, turns the corner and walks in. I spin quickly, nearly dropping the now crying Edie in the process and hand her to Elijah. "Go," I say. "The barn. Go!"

I swing back around, just as Ruby Jewel is lunging across the bed. She has no interest in the shotgun. She reaches for me instead, her hands with those long and haggard nails clench the meat on my shoulders and jerk me forward, twisting me as she pulls. I land on my back, the shotgun pressed into the space between my shoulder blades. I have a perfect view of the sky through the open window and the branches of a tree I wish I was at the top of instead of here.

"Where's Granny now?" she says, her voice a rusted plough cutting through a tree stump. I manage to turn my head, to look up at her, and see that her face is still an open sore from where I hit her with the dreamstone over and over again. Her hands go to my neck again, and this time they mean business.

They take my breath from me with one determined squeeze, sucking out my life, closing me off from the world. My vision blurs, darkens, and I begin to see shapes in the sky that I'm not sure are my imagination or if they're really there. One of them looks like an owl. He's staring down at me, watching Ruby Jewel murder me through the open window.

Help me, I say inside my head, inside its head. *Please.*

The owl stares at me, its face so still, so indifferent, I can only close my eyes in disgust.

That's when I hear Nesmith's voice. He's chanting, his words taking on a weird, but enthralling cadence. "She's useless to me dead. She's useless to me dead."

Ruby Jewel lets go. Her hands don't want to. It's like they have a mind of their own, and they tighten against my neck reflexively, even as she pulls them away.

I gag and cough and keep laying there, my eyes still shut.

HOLY GHOST ROAD

"Get something to tie her hands," Nesmith says.

I wait just a beat longer before spinning around and going for the shotgun. Ruby Jewel senses the move because she gasps. But it's too late. I've got it in my hands and I'm standing up, aiming both barrels at her blind eyes.

"No," Nesmith says, his voice powerful. Calm. The tone hypnotic. "No, child, no."

I want to do it so much. I want to pull the trigger. I can already see her head exploding, disappearing.

"Look at me," Nesmith says.

I shouldn't. I know it's part of the plan. He means to hypnotize me, to put me under, to make me lose control.

It's working. I turn to l him. He smiles. "Now," he says. "Place the gun on the bed, Forest."

I put the gun down. I'm not sure how much I'm being compelled to do it and how much I just want to. Maybe that makes the whole thing even more insidious. I really want to put the gun down. I want to comply with him. I tell myself it's because I don't want to shoot anyone. I tell myself it's because if we slip underneath together, into the dreamworld, into one of the waystations where a person can finally see the world in truth; then I can fight him. But maybe those are just lies he's making me tell myself.

I lay the shotgun on the bed. It feels like a relief to not be touching it anymore.

"That's a good girl. See, there's no running, Forest. The one we've beckoned to us is not an entity you can run from. He's attached himself to us now, dear. His desire is to join us fully here on this side of the world, to become as physical as he was once. You're going to help me make that happen." He smiles. "I'll let you decide how that is going to be. You can be compliant and live, or you can continue to be the rebellious little girl you've always been, and I'll bring him forth from your dead bones. The Dark One is coming regardless. I think the saying is, we can do it the easy way or the hard way. It's really up to you, girl."

"I won't help you," I say, and am pleased to see I'm not completely under Nesmith's spell. This seems to startle him some, but he quickly recovers, his face going so smug with imagined superiority I just want to punch him.

Ruby Jewel laughs and the side of her face slides against the exposed bone of her temple, and I'm surprised when she speaks instead of her brother. "There's no refusing the Dark One, girl."

I'm about to say something when I feel a pecking inside my mind. It's the owl. I close my eyes and speak to it. *Help me. Please.*

"What's she doing?" Nesmith says.

Ruby Jewel sucks in a deep breath, and I open my eyes just as the feathery wings flap behind me. A fury of brown and white blazes in through the open window, past the side of my head, and directly into Ruby Jewel's face. She screams as the owl throws its wings wide like air brakes and hovers just in front of her already battered temple. She raises a hand to swat at it, but she's too late. It's already struck. The motion of its head seems almost supernaturally fast as it uses the small, sharp beak like a ball peen hammer against the round flesh of Ruby Jewel's right eye.

HOLY GHOST ROAD

The rest is just what I can hear behind me as I flee through the window. Ruby Jewel is howling in pain and horror. Nesmith just keeps calling his sister's name over and over. I don't look back as I go out the window and onto the leaf-strewn ground. My ankle flares with pain momentarily, but then it's buried under the adrenaline that surges through me.

I'm alive. I'm alive.

And I'm almost to the barn.

God, get me there.

Once I have my bearings, I find the barn in the distance and pull the dreamstone from my pocket and clutch it tightly as I start to run.

11

I SLOW AS I approach the shady mouth of the old barn. It used to be red, but now it's just brown with little patches of green in the places where the vines have threaded themselves through the broken spots in the roof.

Edie's cries draw me into the darkness. She's in Elijah's arms, and he's too agitated to soothe her. He's trying to rock her, but manages only to shake her instead.

"Granny?" I call into the darker recesses of the barn. The smell of hay and ancient cow shit is strong here, but there's a deeper, wilder smell too. Old bones decaying in the October air.

"I don't think she's here," Elijah says.

"Of course she's here," I say, and move quickly into the rear of the barn, and as I do, I step on something. It cracks underneath my shoe, and for a wild second, my mind flashes back to the second barn and the frail zombie version of Granny lying on the hay, the knuckles of her brittle hand cracking beneath my foot. But the image is gone almost as soon as it comes, and I kneel to investigate. It's a bird's nest, fallen out of hayloft probably, too heavy from the weight of the eggs, all of which are cracked now. Except one. Thank God. It's sad for the others, but at least there's a remnant left, a tiny blue oval, smooth and warm in my palm. Warm is good. I remember that much. Means the baby bird still has a chance.

"Granny?" I say again to the darkest part of the barn.

"She's not here," Elijah says. "What are we going to do now?"

"She's here."

"Bullshit. That's the problem with all your magical thinking. When it goes wrong. When you're fucking cornered like we are now, there's nothing left."

I turn and scream at him. "She's here, goddamn it!"

He shakes his head at me. Edie is a furnace of shrieking fury now. It's as if she's chastising us both for coming this far and falling apart. But that's the thing. I came this far for Granny. She promised she'd be here.

In the barn. Barns, barns, barns. Another of Granny's cryptic sayings comes to me. When she couldn't make sense of something, she'd often shrug and say, "Oh well, it's turtles all the way down anyway." Maybe it's not turtles, but barns. Barns all the way down.

I keep the bird's egg still in my sweaty hand as I move toward the darkest part, the area beneath the hayloft. I hiss her name as I approach the ladder that leads up.

I scale it with one hand, keeping the other away from the rungs while I hold the egg in it as gently as possible.

There's more light up here. Cracks in the roof directly above the hayloft allow shafts of soft light. There's also a single window, a round piece of framed glass about the size of a tire.

HOLY GHOST ROAD

Just below that I see her. Granny.

The relief that floods through me is exquisite. It's like nothing I've ever felt before or will likely feel again. Raw, pure relief. Don't let anybody ever tell you there's any stronger emotion. Talk all you want about sadness, hate, joy, whatever. Relief is the only one that can take you from empty to full in a hot second.

She's sitting, leaning against a bale of hay, staring at the oval window. Her gray hair is tied back with a red kerchief, and it looks shiny, like she just washed it. Her shoulders are stiff, maybe a little too straight for comfort, but I write that off to her arthritis.

"Granny?" I say.

She doesn't react, or if she does, I don't see it.

"I made it."

When she speaks, it's almost as if her voice is coming from somewhere else. Trick of sound in the cavernous barn. Acoustics. Speaking of sound, Edie has gone silent. It's Elijah I hear now. He's muttering something. It sounds like "shit, shit, shit, shit, oh God, holy shit."

I barely pay him any attention though. Instead, it's Granny's voice I focus on.

"I knew you would. Come on over. See."

It's an odd thing to say, and even more odd, I don't see her body move at all. Her head stays still. It's like her back is hurt or something, she's sitting so straight.

And why is she so calm? Surely, she's heard the commotion, Edie's screams for God's sake. Not to mention Elijah's cries going on right this very minute.

John Mantooth

I'm pretty sure this is the moment I know or let myself know that I know.

(I know that I know that I know that I...)

Fuck. I feel my body wavering. I'm going to pass out, and I'm stuck on a loop.

(I know that I know that I know that I know... what do I know? That it's barns all the way down? That understanding comes when it comes, and oh boy when it comes... I know that I know that I... Goddamn it, stop.)

I step back. Get some distance. Some perspective. Try to calm my mind.

God, help me calm my mind.

And slowly, I breathe again. I think again. And I realize that maybe, I've known it all along. Ain't it funny how a person can hide something from themselves? Maybe funny ain't the right word, exactly. Maybe the right way to say it is like this: ain't it sad how a person can hide something from themselves?

Granny's face is blue. Pale blue, like the color her eyes used to be. But now her eyes are gray, covered with a hazy film, and worst of all, they don't see me, or see anything. Her hands are clasped in her lap, and beneath them is a piece of paper folded into a neat square.

Her shoes are off, and I glance down to see that her toenails are as gnarly as ever, and seeing those toenails means she's really here, and she's really dead. I collapse into the hay beside her. For a long second, I go completely empty. I'm a husk, as dead as she is. My spirit leaves me, and somehow, I don't go with it. I'm nowhere.

HOLY GHOST ROAD

But then I hear her voice again.

This time it's clearly inside my head, not outside me at all. *Come back, Forest. Elijah and that baby need you.*

"I can't help them. I can't even help myself." I say this, but I don't know if I'm saying it with my mouth, my mind, or both.

Pshaw, Granny says. *You've been helping them all along.*

"But that's only to get to here. I'm done now. Spent. I need you."

Not anymore. Now, it's them that needs you.

This last statement grabs my attention. Not so much for what Granny says—hell, what else would she say, dead or alive?— but more for how her voice sounds when she says it. It sounds different. Familiar, yet different.

Now, you're close, she says, and I hear it again. This time, I latch on. It's not Granny's voice at all.

Go on, the voice says. *Go on.*

I raise my head and listen. Elijah is whispering now. It sounds like a prayer.

I stare at Granny's dead eyes, the way her skin is blotchy and raw and peeling. There's a smell too, a rotten, terrible smell. She's been dead for days, and I guess that thought should deflate me more, but it doesn't. Because I've finally recognized the voice. I finally understand.

The voice belongs to me. It's belonged to me for some time now.

12

"LOOK," ELIJAH SAYS and points out into the grassy run between the barn and the house. The thing he's pointing at is almost impossible to reconcile with reality. It's Nesmith and Helmet, of course. Nesmith is leading the way, the shotgun in one hand, poking along through the uncut grass and weeds with his cane in the other. Behind him, Helmet is dragging Ruby Jewel's body through the grass. He's got her by one of her arms, and it appears to have come out of joint. Her face is a mask of blood and gore. The owl didn't stop at one eye—nor two. It took her face. Blood flows freely down her neck, pulsing out in dark waves, pumped hard by a relentless heart. Every once in a while, she jerks as if she can feel the pain in her unconscious state, her legs vibrating out of synch with her torso and more blood gushes forth from the open wounds on what used to be her face.

Nesmith picks up his pace and yells over his shoulder for Helmet to do the same. They draw closer, and I think of swinging the big barn door shut, barring it from the inside, but I'm too mesmerized to do anything.

"Here," Nesmith says through tears, and I realize he's actually sobbing about what the owl did to his sister (what I did to his sister), and points at a spot on the ground about twenty yards from the barn.

Helmet drops Ruby Jewel's body and steps away from it as if disgusted.

Nesmith hands Helmet his cane and raises the shotgun.

"Shut the door," I say. "Help me."

The first shot is so loud I think the world has split open, that the second coming Nesmith likes to talk about is really true. It's here, and for a second, that sound is everything. I don't even know if I've been hit because I can't feel my body. Maybe that means I have been hit. Maybe that means I'm already dead.

But then there's another sound, a scream, from Elijah. I'm back. I'm whole. Above me, about eight inches from the top of my head, there's a splintered gash in the side of the barn. So much for wanting me alive.

"Forest!" Elijah yells again. He needs my help. Another shotgun blast, not quite as loud as the first. No second coming, just a wake-up call. I grab my end of the door and together, we swing it shut. Elijah is still holding Edie, who is so quiet it's a little spooky. He shifts her to his other arm and heads to the rear of the barn. He comes back with a hoe. He slides the shaft through the door latch, effectively barring Nesmith from coming in.

"Helmet," I say, but Elijah just shakes his head.

"It's just to buy us some time. Is there a back way out?"

"A window up in the loft, but I'm not leaving."

"What?"

"This is the place where I have to face it."

HOLY GHOST ROAD

"It?"

I nod. "The demon."

Elijah groans, but mercifully doesn't otherwise engage. Instead, he goes over to the front wall of the barn and peers through a large crack in the side.

He waves me over. "You're not going to believe this."

I almost reply that I'll believe just about anything at this point, but instead go over and look.

He's right. I don't believe it.

Helmet has Nesmith's cane, except now I can see it's more than a cane. There's a serrated blade that he's popped out of the end of it, and Helmet is using it to saw away at Ruby Jewel's chest. Nesmith has turned away, towards Granny's garden, not watching Helmet as he digs in with the blade on the end of the cane, his face emotionless even now, as he cuts bone and tendon.

"What is he doing?" Elijah says. He looks from me to Edie, his eyes lingering on the baby. Maybe when things go batshit crazy, it's normal to look to a baby for answers. I don't know. But Edie doesn't have any answers either. Or if she does, she's not sharing.

"Forest?" he says, and I realize he's still waiting on an answer. He needs somebody to explain this to him, to give him some piece of information that will make it make sense.

"I don't know," I say, but maybe I do. Not the specifics, but the general idea. He's going to try to pull the power out of her before it's too late. It doesn't matter. I can fight him. I can fight her, whatever power he draws from her dying heart.

John Mantooth

I've already beat Ruby Jewel once.

But nothing prepares me for what happens next.

Once Helmet has done his work, he stands and hands the cane back to Nesmith. Nesmith turns and examines the cavity in Ruby Jewel's chest. Blood is coming out of it now, and I can see the tip of her broken breastbone, sawed through and jagged, gleaming in the dying sun.

Nesmith sits down on the grass and leans over the opening Helmet has carved. He starts to roll up his sleeve, but then thinks better of it and just plunges his hand inside. His hand disappears. Then his wrist. His face is a mask of pure determination as he roots around for what he wants.

He never loved her. Or if he did, it was the most selfish kind of love, born from what she could do for him. He loved that thing –that gift she gave him– more than he loved her, and in the seconds before he pulls out her still beating heart, in the last seconds of her miserable life, I feel bad for her. That too, I realize, is the Holy Ghost, the most sacred magic there is in the world, the magic of empathy, even for those people who you understand the least.

When the heart is in his hand, he lifts it to the sky. I hate him so much in that moment. Especially because he seems younger then, taller, stronger. So much understanding floods through me in that moment. He's been using others—Helmet, Ruby Jewel, my mother, and most recently, me—to turn back the clock, to increase his own vitality while the rest of us suffer the consequences.

Elijah steps back and gags. Somehow, the heart still beats in Nesmith's hand, and I'm pretty sure it's the unreality of that detail that has made Elijah gag. The unexplained is very upsetting to him.

HOLY GHOST ROAD

I feel the egg in my hand grow warmer and shift. I've forgotten I've even been holding it. I open my palm just in time to see the tiny mouth of a swallow opening up to the dark sky of the barn. And just for a second, I understand. I see.

No, I don't just see, I see true. This is also the Holy Ghost. This birth, this sacred life in the face of so much profanity.

Will it live in my palm? Will I place it onto the ground so it might thrive? Will its mother return to save it, to help it in ways I cannot? The answer to these questions is almost certainly no, but the Holy Ghost is not diminished. The Holy Ghost bears all indignities, obscures all plans. The Holy Ghost has been here. I have seen it.

Now, I will never stop being able to see it, and this gift is the greatest gift Granny has left for me in the end.

I hold it in my palm, while Nesmith holds Ruby Jewel's dying heart in his.

"The birds," Elijah whispers.

I crouch down, adjusting the angle of my view, so I can see the darkening sky through the crack in the barn wall. At first, they are just one shadow, and I can't quite be sure what he means, but then as they flock down out of the sky, I can't tell one crow from the next. They fling themselves at the still-beating heart, making it disappear in a frenzy of beaks and wings and god-awful squawking. When at last these creatures part, there is no heart. The birds cartwheel and twist, spinning circles above Nesmith. He nods at them, pleased.

"I need you to hold this," I say, and extend my hand, cradling the newborn bird.

"What? Why?"

But then he gets a good look, sees that it's a baby like Edie, like us, because in a very real sense, we're all just babies too. Confused like babies, needing to be fed like babies, subject to the whims of others like babies. He takes it. "This is the sacred magic," I say. "Granny always said it was everywhere. That it was simple and easy once you could see it."

He nods at me, and holds both creatures like they are everything, like they are the very universe itself, all existence made flesh. Meanwhile the grackles still circle, building their momentum, as if they are stones in a sling Nesmith continues to pull back.

"He's going to have them take the roof off," I say.

"What?"

I shake my head. "The birds. The barn won't hold against them all. We've got to do something."

I try to think. I try to understand. God, it would be good not to have to wait on understanding for once. I need it now.

It's always been you, I hear Granny say. No, I hear *myself* say the words.

"I've got an idea." I glance through the cracks again. The swarm of grackles has grown to size of the sky itself.

It's time.

"What are you doing?" Elijah says.

I don't answer. I don't have to. I remove the hoe from the latch and pull the door open just enough to slip through, but not before dropping the hoe, leaving it in the barn. I close the door behind me tight and step into the oncoming dusk.

13

I'M THE SAME girl that dreamwalked into a barn nearly a week ago and saw Nesmith consorting with the black-horned upright goat. I'm the same girl who ran for the house, for Mama's keys, but found Ruby Jewel already had them in her hand, like she'd been waiting all along for just this moment. I'm the same girl that smashed out headlights and ran like mad for Highway 278, for the river, for Granny's. I'm the same girl that lost, and found, the dreamstone. I'm the same girl that crossed the Tuskahatchee on a train trestle, saw Zombie Granny in the barn, and convinced Elijah there were enough mysteries in the world to forget—at least briefly—about science and reason and come along with me.

I'm the same girl that talked to the snake and then held it high above my head, the same girl that saved Edie. The same girl that went under Nesmith's church *while* he preached his sermon of lies. But most of all, I'm the same girl who knew Granny, who loved Granny. Who learned from Granny.

And yet, as I emerge from the dark barn into the twilight, I am also a different girl. Not even just a different version of the other me, but a new creation. All of the past versions of me have added up to something greater, something new, something that makes me not afraid of Nesmith anymore.

But something has changed about Nesmith too. His eyes glow with victory. "We're going to do this now," he says. "With Ruby Jewel's heart, I've accessed the other side. The Dark One is impatient. He's ready. Your death will be enough to complete the ritual."

It throws me off. What a thing to say.

He must read the confusion on my face because he laughs and points to the sky, where the crows are flocking together into a seamless entity.

"You were my conduit, girl. To the other world. Your dreamwalks opened the portal for me. I was so, so close to accessing the true power of that world, but since you are no longer compliant, I'm going to have to improvise."

That's when I see something else in the sky. It's the black-horned goat, or at least the shadow of it, watching, waiting, sure one of us is about to die, and it'll be here to capitalize on it.

Nesmith nods at me, but he's also nodding toward the crows.

They drop out of the sky like black lightning, their wings tucked in, their beaks aimed at my face, my eyes.

I fall to the ground, burying my face underneath my arms. I feel the birds attacking my head and shoulders, but I feel something else too. One of the birds seems to be calling out to me, not unlike the way I called out to the snake and the owl. It's as if once a conduit has been open, there's no shutting it.

HOLY GHOST ROAD

Please, I say. Please make them stop.

But they don't stop. They continue stabbing me with their beaks and grasping at me with their talons. My hair is being pulled skyward, and I realize they are attempting to lift me into the air. It shouldn't be possible, but there are so many of them.

Please, make them stop. It's a prayer, a spell, a plea. I'm saying it to God, to Granny, to the birds, to this whole world, and I just need someone or something to listen to me.

There's a loud squawk that silences the birds. The ones who have tangled their talons in my hair let go, and I don't feel any more beaks against my neck and back and shoulders. Above me there is a wind, and it sounds like the breath of God herself.

I lift my head and see the birds have formed a great barrier in the sky between me and the demon goat.

One of the birds looks at me, and I feel my body surge with power. I'm inside it, and it is inside me. The door to the barn of my unconscious has been thrown open wide.

I look at Nesmith.

He's afraid. He's never expected it to go down like this.

"Now, my dear, dear girl. We should talk about this. If you kill me… the demon won't go away. It'll haunt you. Only I can take it from you."

"You've always been a liar." I lift my hand. The birds call out in one magnificent squawk that makes my skin turn to gooseflesh.

"You just need to wait," he says, turning to Helmet. "Can't you do something?"

John Mantooth

Helmet, for the first time since I've known him, shows emotion. His eyes darken and his brow furrows. He's afraid and angry, and filled with regret. It's like all the emotions he's been keeping at bay spill out at once. He looks from me to the mass of birds above us that are awaiting my signal and then turns and walks back toward the house.

Nesmith turns to follow him, but he doesn't have his cane, and as he begins to lope through the grass, he stumbles and falls.

I nod. The birds move as one.

14

I DON'T WATCH.

Instead, I head back to the barn where Elijah is still holding Edie and the baby bird. We swing the door open wide and let the dusk in. Sometimes it feels like dusk can last forever in this world.

Neither of us know what to do with ourselves. Not to mention the bird. Finally, I take it and build a small nest for it in the hay, hoping its mother will return. The Holy Ghost, I realize, has to be nurtured or it will fade from me again.

After that, I do check outside to see what's become of the other birds and Nesmith. The birds are gone. Nesmith is still. The now dark sky is empty. The goat demon is nowhere to be found. I head back inside the barn.

Edie has fallen into a gentle sleep and Elijah has built her a bed out of hay beside the makeshift bird's nest.

"There's an explanation," he says.

"An explanation?"

He nods. "For what just happened. I was reading about it. Just a few months ago. Bird attacks are on the rise. It's a climate change thing."

"Okay," I say. It's easy to see he's arguing with himself and losing.

"Are you okay?" he says, almost as an afterthought.

And it is very much an afterthought. I've barely even considered my injuries. I touch my neck. It's bleeding badly. In several places.

"I'm okay."

"Here," he says, and takes off his shirt. He holds it against the wounds on my neck, and I feel them come alive with pain.

"Thank you."

"We need to get you to a hospital."

I almost tell him no, I'm not leaving because Granny is here. She can take care of me. But then I remember.

"Okay."

"Do you think Helmet took Nesmith's car?"

I shrug, feeling all the euphoria of what happened with the birds draining away from me. The goat demon is still out there somewhere, waiting for me, and worst of all, I'm going to have to face it without Granny.

"Can you come up to the loft with me?" I say.

Elijah looks a little startled. "Why?"

"I want you to see her."

He swallows so hard I can hear it. "Okay."

We climb the ladder in silence, me first, followed by Elijah. Once we are in the loft again, there is more light because the window here faces west, and the sunset is bleeding through making it seem like the stained-glass of a church.

And maybe a barn is a kind of church. A temple to the in-between places, to the might have beens, to those that see true. I'm finally seeing true now as I look at Granny.

HOLY GHOST ROAD

She's decayed, and likely been dead for several days.

Elijah must certainly realize the same thing because he says, "Who did I talk to this morning?"

"Granny," I say.

He shakes his head. "No."

I put a hand on his shoulder. "Yes."

We stand like that for a long time, both of us seeing more true than we ever have before. It occurs to me there are so many kinds of ways to find the truth in this world, but with each way, there is also potential for hiding the truth too. Religion, science, family. None of them are perfect. So often, they are anything but.

"What's that?" Elijah says after some time.

He's pointing at the ragged piece of paper clutched in her hand.

I kneel down beside her, holding my breath because she stinks, and pry the paper from her hand. Once dislodged, her hand falls back into her lap. I can still feel the ice of her flesh on my fingertips as I unwrap the note.

Forest,

I reckon one way or the other you'll find this note, and when you do, you'll be about broken. Let me tell you that it's okay to be broken. You go on and break right in half, girl. Feel what you feel and feel it good.

I also imagine you may be reading this after escaping Brother Nesmith. Maybe you had to fight back. If you did, I imagine you won. Once he's out of the picture, you'll be tempted to feel relieved.

John Mantooth

Don't.

As I'm writing this, I'm preparing to break into your dream, to make sure that goat demon will not have its way with you. It's going to take all I have left, so after that, you'll be on your own.

This window is a good place to go to sleep. I never slept here once without dreamwalking. In all my years as a walker through my dreams and other folks, this window would get me there. Why? I don't know why, and I don't want to know why. The more you know, the less you experience. The inverse of that is true too. I want to know that I don't know. That's bliss.

Anyway, you're going to have to face that demon down. I can't give you any advice on that because I've never done it. My grandmother before me was a woman named Judith Marcus. She told of a time she had to face one, but I don't remember many of the particulars except she said it wasn't that tough if you went in with the Holy Ghost on your side.

That's it. That's all my advice. Truth is, you don't need it anyway. You've spent so many years looking for the Holy Ghost, and I always put you off, said you'd know it when you saw it. Well, maybe I put you off because I didn't really know it until I saw it either. Recognition—that's the key. Magic and the Holy Ghost are out there already. You've just got to recognize them.

And, as I sit here writing, I think I may have just recognized it, Forest. The Holy Ghost… I see it in you.

Good night, sweet girl. I'll see you one day in a dream we'll share.

Love,

Granny

15

THERE'S A KIND of sadness that in my experience is pretty rare. It's the kind of sadness that aches so much inside of a person it almost feels good. It's the kind of sadness that breaks you up into pieces, but also makes you realize breaking up into pieces might be the thing you've been needing all along.

It's a sweet sadness that makes you know without a shadow of a doubt you're alive. Or maybe it makes you know without a shadow of a doubt you don't really know anything, that life is just a surprise of heartache and joy from the moment you're shuttled from the womb to the moment you breathe your last.

I know that I know that I *don't* know a damn thing.

That's the way I feel when I finish the letter. I feel all of this and a thousand things more, until I am wrung out of tears and shaking. Elijah holds me as I shake, the bare skin of his shoulder against my cheek. He pats my back and then moves to check the wounds on my neck.

"You're not bleeding anymore," he says. "But I still think we need to get you to a hospital."

I nod, knowing he's right, but I also know it's not time yet. There's work unfinished. My journey has not yet ended.

"You and Edie should go. There's a phone in house. Call a ride. Get her to safety."

"And what are you going to do?"

"I'm going to take a nap."

"A nap?"

I nod, and that's when I see it floating in the air out in the middle of the barn. Not a family hanging from nooses, but instead the demon that started it all, its shadow, watching me. It's a demon that didn't start following me that night in our barn. It's been following me since birth, since my father died. It grew in strength each time something else terrible happened—Ben, Nesmith, Mama—and all Nesmith ever did was capitalize on the demon I'd already conjured, a demon that clung to me like a hook in mouth of a fish.

And seeing it hovering like it hovers now, I understand it will probably always follow me. But following me is one thing. It wants to kill me. It wants to drag me down with it, and I've got to make it clear such a plan is unacceptable. I won't be taken down by this thing.

I won't.

"We're staying," Elijah says.

I nod. "Okay. Thank you."

"In the morning, this is over, though."

"I understand."

16

THE SUN WAKES me in the morning, shining brightly through the single window. I blink it away and sit up. No dreamwalk? Can't be. Granny said...

My eyes drift over to where Granny's body lay when I went to sleep.

It's gone. Only the hay remains.

"Elijah?" I say.

No answer. The barn seems cavernous. My voice echoes back to me. Outside, a wind blows hard against the barn. Through the window, I can see storm clouds threatening to overwhelm the sky, the sun, the world. Thunder rocks the barn and rain begins to fall on the tin roof. It should be a soothing sound—I remember it as exactly that when I was younger, and Granny brought me out here once to play during a storm—but now the tin roof sounds like it's being assaulted by the rain. It's a loud, grating clatter that fills my ears with a wall of sound. I hold my hands over them, but it does no good.

That's the moment when I realize I'm probably dreamwalking. No matter how many times I dreamwalk, it's always a surprise at first to realize this isn't the real world. But that's not quite right. It actually is the real world, just not the version I'm used to.

I turn to face the darkened part of the barn, half-expecting to see the demon goat there, but it's empty, and somehow that seems worse. I'm completely alone.

"Elijah?" I call out to the darkness.

The darkness does not answer.

I move to the side of the hayloft and find the ladder. I start down, and I'm halfway to the bottom when my foot misses a rung. I try to hang on, but gravity jerks me too hard. I land in a heap on the cold dirt floor.

That's when I realize I'm in three different barns at the same time, that indeed there is only one barn in the whole world anyway, and each iteration is just a version of the same idea of a barn. And once I realize this, I stand up, more confident than before. I feel as if I've broken some code, as if some secret has at long last been revealed to me, and now I'm ready.

Something creaks overhead, and I can see them now, the family, hanging from their nooses, except it's not the Ramey's or whatever the real family's name was. Instead, it's my own family. I recognize my father from the pictures I've seen of him. He's handsome—his mustache is trimmed closely, his dead eyes an opaque blue—and he swings slowly, his body a tree shaken by a dark wind. Mama is next to him, and she's glaring right at me, her face a mask of accusation. Somehow, she's not quite dead, and her body twitches as she swings.

On the other side of her is where it gets really bad. Ben. He's holding his own rope. One end is looped around his neck, and the other is in his hand, which he has extended as far as it can stretch. He's dead and he defies gravity.

Above them all is something else – a great hand, except the hand is half hoof. Three giant and crooked fingers extend from the hoof and from each finger hangs a rope attached to a body. Somehow Ben both holds his own rope, and the hand holds it too. There are no contradictions in dreamwalks, just things as they really are.

The clatter of rain on the tin roof grows louder and the wind howls into the barn. I turn and see the front door to the barn has blown open wide. I peer out into the rain and see the long run of grass leading up the house. Granny is coming toward the barn, making her way slowly, but steadily through the storm.

I feel relief flood through me. She's here with me again.

As she draws closer, I notice the rain bounces off her body, and there is a strange sheen to her skin, a slick splotchy darkness, but I write it off to the dreamwalk that she is both dead and alive here.

In my excitement, I head out to meet her but when she sees me coming, she waves me back. "No need to get wet. I'm coming. Be patient."

I nod and start back toward the barn, but not before I realize there is something else weird about Granny. I didn't notice it before, but there's a raven perched on her shoulder.

"Don't mind him," she says. "He's my pet. Remember the bird you saved. He's grown here. You gave him life."

"Okay. Granny?" I say, standing in the doorway of the barn now. "What's going to happen? Why are we here?"

"So many questions. Just trust me, child. Nothing for you to do but trust me."

I nod, so thankful she's here. Granny has never let me down. Even in death, she's there for me.

She slips past me into the barn, and the raven gazes at me before sort of blending back into Granny's shoulder.

"Why are they there?" I ask Granny, pointing up toward the rafters of the barn. I don't look because I can't make myself.

"Why's who there? This barn is empty, girl. Me and you and the bird."

"No, I…" But she's right. When I look up again, my family is gone. The cloven hoof holding the ropes from its fingers is gone. Suddenly, the rain stops on the roof. The thunder dies away. The sun pokes back through the window in the loft, and the barn smells like sweetness.

"It's over, baby."

"Over?"

"Yes. Over. Well, almost. You've just got to come up to the hayloft one more time."

"The hayloft? Why? I thought you said I had to face the goat?"

"That's what we're doing. You face it up here. With me, with the light through the stained glass."

"Like church?"

"That's right."

"You said church isn't a place."

"Maybe I did, but a barn is a place. This barn is a place, a special place, and that light is a special light."

HOLY GHOST ROAD

She climbs the ladder first. It's strange to be going back up into the loft again, stranger still when I see another bird on her, this time staring at me from her back as she climbs.

Once we're both in the loft, she points out to the open air.

"All you need to do is step out here."

"Out where?"

"Off the loft."

"Why?"

"Because once it sees you do that, it'll leave."

"The goat?"

"It's not a goat. That's just what you saw."

"What is it then?"

"It's just your fear manifested. Show your fear that you're not afraid, and it'll leave you alone."

"But I am afraid."

Granny seems frustrated. A raven flies up into the air, coming off her.

"Never mind that," she says. "Dreamwalks don't always make sense. The things inside them can throw you off. Focus on me. My voice."

I try, but there's another sound coming from beneath the loft. It sounds like the creaking of bones.

"What was that?"

"Step off and you can see it."

Another bird flies from Granny. This one takes a piece of her face and shows an even darker region beneath that.

John Mantooth

"Never mind," she says. "Never mind." Her hand goes to her face, to cover the spot, but then another raven flies from the place where her hand used to be and instead there is a hoof.

"Granny?"

"It's because you won't end it. You have to go. You have to step off. You have to…" Her mouth disappears as two more ravens fly away. The demon goat's mouth is there instead, and how could I be anything except afraid?

The goat granny sees my fear and shrieks at me. Her shriek blows the rest of the birds off her like an explosion. They swarm the loft, dipping and diving, their wings creating blasts of hot wind from the goat.

And that's when the goat lunges toward me, both hooves extended. It's such a surprise, I don't have any time to react. I swing my arms, pinwheeling them for balance, but my balance is gone. I begin to fall until something loops under my neck, catching me with a painful jolt. A rope.

My breath is sucked up into my throat and caught there. My hands fly to the rope, and I try to pull it away from my neck, to create space for the air to flow through, but it's not working. The harder I try, the more I need that air.

The goat smiles and watches me struggle.

It's fully upright goat now, the ravens swirling around it like a windy cloak, its red eyes and black horns exposed for me to look at as I die.

But before I go, before the rope squeezes the life out of me, the bones rattle beneath me again. I peer down into the darkness of the barn and see Granny's dead body—so decayed her skin breaks and falls off as her bones move—stand and try to move forward. The bones collapse in a heap, but she is undeterred and waves one skeleton arm toward the ravens. They break into two packs, one floating down past me toward her bones. The birds attack her skeleton and lift it up, so that it floats just off the ground. I watch, mesmerized, as they fly her out through the mouth of the barn into the storm dark day.

It's storming again. The other bodies are beside me. Or I'm beside them. But I don't want to be. I want to go with Granny. I want to pass from this world into the next on my own terms. I want to escape the demon that stalks us. I want to lift up the dreamstone and throw it at the limits of science, religion, and family, and kill those limits.

But the demon is winning.

As the ravens take Granny's bones past the old tree I loved so much, and ultimately past the horizon, I realize there's more options left to me. I realize Granny promised me I'd be on my own in this dreamwalk.

Alone, except she made sure I brought the dreamstone. It's in my pocket. Instead of fighting with the rope around my neck, I should grab it instead.

It feels heavy in my hand, solid and warm, but the rope is still tight around my neck.

There's not much breath left in me, but with what I have, I use my energy to spin around and stare at the ravens. I'm tempted to command, but Granny said you ask, you speak to them like they aren't so different from us. So, I do. I tell the birds I'm dying.

But these aren't regular birds. These are pieces of the demon, unaffected by empathy or the sacred magic of the Holy Ghost.

I look at the stone in my hand again. And I remember how Granny said she'd put a little of herself inside it. Maybe I could speak to that.

So, I do. I just talk to it like it's a person or a snake or a bird, and when I do, I swear I can feel its smooth surface turning against my palm.

So, I keep talking, I keep asking. The stone rises to the rafters of the barn and the rope that hangs from them comes loose and wraps itself around the stone. The stone then flies me back to the hayloft and sets me down.

The goat glares at me as I take the rope from my neck and let it go. The stone drops to the ground, its work done.

For the second time in the last day and the first time inside of a dreamwalk, understanding dawns on me. I don't know how I know, but damned if I don't.

"I don't have to kill you," I say to it. "I just have to learn to live with you."

The effect these words have on the demon goat are magical. It shrinks back down to a regular goat. One that doesn't even look threatening. It's just a goat, and if it follows me for the rest of my life that's okay, and if sometimes it transforms into something scary again, or maybe I fall into a deep slumber and face it in some dream barn, that's okay too. Because being chased isn't a choice, but maybe being caught is.

17

I DON'T REMEMBER much after that, at least not very much about the barn. I can figure that at some point I really did wake up, and Elijah and Edie were ready to go because we did eventually leave. They took me to the hospital, and we told the necessary lie that when we made it to Granny's the dead bodies were already there.

Things were a little trickier with Edie. Police asked a lot of questions. In the end, we told them the truth. We were worried about her. We believed we had Trudy's consent to take her, that she wanted us to.

Amazingly, Trudy confirmed this. Only problem is Trudy was actually the grandmother, and so couldn't really give that consent. Lucky for us, nobody can find Trudy's daughter, so the court system ended up calling no harm no foul on that one, and damned if that doesn't feel a lot like a miracle.

My new foster parents don't have a barn, which I surprisingly miss, but they do have a decent sized yard with lots of climbing trees. I'm high up in one, thinking about Edie and how she's getting along with her new foster parents on a nice April day when Elijah comes to see me.

John Mantooth

I'm sixteen now. Just got my driver's license, but in no hurry to drive anywhere at all, not when the world is so much more perfect from one of these great climbing trees. These trees are absolutely the best thing about my new home. The foster parents are okay, I guess. They don't abuse me or molest me or even talk to me much, which is fine. I've got three younger "brothers" that take most of their time. But when they brought me here—brought me home—and I saw the trees in the backyard, I knew I could make it work.

I'm in the tallest one—a white oak like the one that used to be on Granny's farm before the lightning—when the backdoor opens and my foster mother leads him out. He looks good, like he's been working out or something. Or maybe it's just the result of eating regular meals. I realize we knew each other in such extreme circumstances that he might be altogether different now, and that makes me a little nervous.

"Well," my foster mother says, "she said she would be in the backyard."

I'm pleased when Elijah immediately scans the trees. He does know me. I shake the branch I'm sitting on. He smiles.

"She's in the tree," he says.

My foster mother—who asked me to call her Mom, something I haven't had the heart to do yet—frowns and stalks across the yard, her head cocked toward the sky, trying to spot me.

"Up here," I shout.

Her eyes find me, and she throws up her arms in exasperation. "Are you serious with this? What if you fall? You should come down. Now."

"But I like it in the trees," I say. "You should try it sometime."

"Forest," she warns. "If you don't come down right now, I'm going to call your father."

"My father is dead," I say. It's petty, but I can't resist.

"Your new father."

"Call him." I lean out of the tree, knowing it will piss her off, and wave at Elijah. "Hey, wanna come up?"

At first, I'm pretty sure he's going to say no. Hell, the old Elijah wouldn't even have considered it. It takes a certain kind of faith in things unseen and in the kindness of the world to climb a tree as an adult. The old Elijah didn't have either of these certain kinds of things. But this new one? He shrugs and grabs the bottom branch, pulling himself up faster than I'd thought possible.

I laugh as my foster mother curses under her breath and heads back inside. Maybe she will call her husband. What do I care? He'll yell at me some, threaten to send me back into the system. I should probably care about that, but I can't bring myself to get too worked up.

I'm pretty chill these days for the most part. The only thing that really bothers me much is, surprisingly enough, what Elijah brings up first thing once he's on the big limb with me, dangling his feet off into the air.

"I've been thinking," he says. "And I realized that in all the commotion that happened afterward, there was something important I never told you."

"Well, I hope you told the police, at least," I say, playfully.

He shakes his head. He has new glasses and a new, more confident smile.

"It's not something the police would care about."

"But I would?"

He nods. "Yeah, I think so."

"Well, lay it on me."

"The baby bird. Remember it?"

"Yeah, of course. I'm assuming it died during the night."

He shakes his head. The sun is behind him, framing his face, and for just a moment, I wish he could be my father. Even if he doesn't believe in the sacred magic, I'm pretty sure it believes in him.

"While you were…" He hesitates. "While you were doing your dream-walk, the barn door swung open, and another bird came in and plucked the bird from the little nest where we'd left it."

My feel my body go warm. I'm glowing inside and it warms my skin. "Its mother?"

"Yeah, I think so."

He reaches out and puts a hand on my shoulder. The limb shifts with our weight.

"I also wanted to thank you."

"For what?"

He laughs and looks a little embarrassed. "For helping me learn to stop thinking of explanations."

I frown a little. What does that mean?

"Hear me out. I'm not sure about a lot of what happened to us, what happened to you. The dreamwalking, the sacred magic, and the Holy Ghost." He swallows. "What I saw on the island and at Ramey Place. Most of all on your grandmother's farm."

HOLY GHOST ROAD

I wait for him to say more, to explain himself, but he's fallen silent.

"And?"

He shakes his head. "That's it. Maybe you didn't hear me. I said I'm not sure about all those things. I mean it."

Realization dawns on me slowly. *Not sure.* That's what has changed. Before, he was sure.

"Being sure is a kind of death," he says. "I was dying because I thought I had everything figured out. It was like..." He sucks in a deep breath. "Like I was making myself a God, and the whole time I knew I wasn't ready for that. Gods are the only things that know everything. I'm not that. I had to learn to be okay with uncertainty. I mean, what I saw at your grandmother's is not the kind of thing anyone can be certain about anyway. And there's plenty of days when I can't quite believe it happened. But I understand that believing it happened is the least important part. Learning from it anyway is what's important. You taught me that, Forest."

"Nah, we learned it together," I say. Still, I'm moved by his words, by the idea I could have this kind of effect on another human being.

And to be quite honest, I'm not exactly sure what happened either. Something did. Sometimes I remember every little detail, but that's mostly in my dreams. In my waking hours, the memories are vague. Something about a goat, a dreamstone, and the beating heart of Ruby Jewel clutched in Nesmith's hand.

What matters is that I survived, that I found out that I could live without Granny even though it's hard. But that wasn't all. I also found out about the difference between vanquishing your demons and learning to live with them.

It gets me thinking. What else has changed for me? As much as I believe I'm a new creation, and as much as I feel confident I finally under-stand—at least in part—what the Holy Ghost is, I'm still me. Still full of doubts and confusion, and yes, sometimes fear.

So, where does that leave me?

I laugh and Elijah glances at me sharply. I haven't been listening, and it's not an appropriate time for me to laugh, but I can't help it. The answer to my question hits me hard, and it feels so right, I can't help but laugh.

Where does it leave me?

It leaves me in the trees, looking down at the world from a different vantage point, where all of it is still confusing enough, sure, but in the trees, I can swing my feet into the void and know the world will never make sense on its own terms. No, it's up to me to make sense of it. Just like I did once on the road to Granny's.

The End

JOHN MANTOOTH is the award winning author of two novels and a short story collection. His first novel, The Year of the Storm, was nominated for a Bram Stoker Award. He has also published three crime novels under the pseudonym Hank Early. Heaven's Crooked Finger (written as Hank Early) was a Next Generation Indie Book award winner and 2017 Foreword Indies Award Finalist. He lives in Alabama with his wife and two children.

CEMETERY DANCE PUBLICATIONS
PAPERBACKS AND EBOOKS!

DEAR DIARY: RUN LIKE HELL
by James A. Moore

Sooner or later even the best prepared hitman is going to run out of bullets. Buddy Fisk has two new jobs, bring back a few stolen books of sorcery, and then stop the unkillable man who wants to see him dead...

"Gripping, horrific, and unique, James Moore continues to be a winner, whatever genre he's writing in. Well worth your time."
—Seanan McGuire, *New York Times* bestselling author of the *InCryptid* and *Toby Daye* series.

SOMETHING STIRS
by Thomas Smith

Ben Chalmers is a successful novelist. His wife, Rachel, is a fledgling artist with a promising career, and their daughter, Stacy, is the joy of their lives. Ben's novels have made enough money for him to provide a dream home for his family. But there is a force at work-a dark, chilling, ruthless force that has become part of the very fabric of their new home...

"Thomas is one of those outstanding Southern writers—seemingly soft, languid, maybe even lazy, when actually what he is, is cotton wrapped about a razor. Half the time you don't even know he's gotten you until it's too late."
—*USA Today* and *NY Times* bestselling author, Charles L. Grant

THE DISMEMBERED
by Jonathan Janz

In the spring of 1912, American writer Arthur Pearce is reeling from the wounds inflicted by a disastrous marriage. But his plans to travel abroad, write a new novel, and forget about his ex-wife are interrupted by a lovely young woman he encounters on a London-bound train. Her name is Sarah Coyle, and the tale she tells him chills his blood...

"One of the best writers in modern horror to come along in the last decade. Janz is one of my new favorites."
—Brian Keene, *Horror Grandmaster*

Purchase these and other fine works of horror
from Cemetery Dance Publications today!
https://www.cemeterydance.com/